This novel is entirely a work of fiction. The names, characters and incidents portrayed in it are the work of the author's imagination. Any resemblance to actual persons, living or dead, events or localities is entirely coincidental.

First published by Colney Books, 2014

Copyright © Christopher Bigsby 20014

Christopher Bigsby asserts the moral right to be identified as the author of this work.

All rights reserved.

BALLYGORAN

A NOVEL BY

CHRISTOPHER BIGSBY

For Bex —
You can have this
one for free!

For Ewan

It is tempting to say that Ballygoran is no different from any other town, tempting but hardly accurate. Places are made by people as much as the other way around and the people of Ballygoran are, shall we say, different even as difference is something they are liable to treat with suspicion convinced, as they are, that the old ways are the best ways even if the old ways involved a degree of suffering and retributive violence. On the subject of retributive violence, it is also a place where education is in the hands of nuns for whom such requires a firm hand or, preferably, some other implement more liable to leave its spiritual and physical mark.

Ballygoran is situated where the land meets the sea on the eastern side of an island divided against itself yet longing to be whole. There are dark days here that winnow the soul but also bright days when the dark days can be remembered and anticipated. And they are talkers, for words are free and free things are always worth having and anyway distract us from the business of living whose logic implies the business of dying. Those that stay are content in their discontent. Those that leave can never quite drive it out of mind for there is something about Ballygoran that makes other places seem stale. After a time, it assumes the shape of a myth, isolated in time and space. But there it is, as real and unreal as any place is once it has entered the memory which itself is as much a maker of stories as a recorder of supposed fact.

I lived there once but do so no more. Is that a matter of regret? At times, the more especially since time itself flows faster than once it did and there is a desire to drop a sea anchor against that tide. But there is more than one way of inhabiting a place. You can visit it in your dreams, not so much the actual place, no doubt, for dreams are not about what is or how would they differ from the day's decline, but increasingly I have a preference for dreams, for memories and the imagined and somehow Ballygoran exists there with a vividness reality could never supply.

***

The rain came in with a rush, as if to get on with the business of ruining everybody's day. The town shrugged and submitted, since there was nothing else to be done. Dry stone walls were dry no more. White sheets, resentfully pegged out, turned grey. Gutters swirled away the previous night's regret. Down in the harbour boats jerked to and fro, their masts so many long fingers waving in reproach. Seagulls cowered in the lee of chimney stacks, feathers fanned. In the tight grey houses that trailed up the hillside children breathed on windows and wrote their names, unfinished jigsaws of the Vatican behind them on tufted carpets stained with Ribena. Dogs lay on cold flagstones, paws ahead, noses flinching, dreaming of their youth. Cats turned and turned about, prickling the flesh of those who imagined themselves their masters.

At the butchers shop half a dozen stood pressed up against the rump steak and white dimpled chickens, umbrellas dripping water into sawdust laid down for blood.

'Would you like some brisket, Mavis. I've a bit to spare.'

'You can keep your brisket, Mr. O'Flaherty. You know I've a passion for kidneys. I'll take a sausage or so, though, or a slice of liver. Do you think it will stop soon?'

It was summer in Ballygoran. It never stopped soon. It was less damp than the winter, though on the watery side as people were prepared to acknowledge. A nicotine-stained spring came off the peat fields and fretted down the gutter, spinning cigarette packets and sweet wrappers, so many limp boats sailing towards the harbour.

'I came without my brolly, more fool me.'

'I could give you a plastic bag.'

'And what would I do wearing a plastic bag on my head? Do you have a little tripe, perhaps? Just the thing for this weather. Add a little milk. Will you be reducing the bacon? There's a lot of fat in it, don't you think?'

'It's how it comes from the pig, Mrs. Gough. Would you have me run it around a little to work it off? Besides, that's where the flavour is.'

A truck drove past, a fan of water spraying the collie dog left outside which accepted it as no more than its due.

'Do you have some dripping? My husband is partial to a little fat.'

The butcher looked at her and held his tongue.

Behind him on silver s-shaped hooks were sides of lamb, red streaked with white, the very lambs that a week since had busied themselves at their mother's belly their whole bodies shaking with the need for milk, the lambs that had leapt in the air for no better reason than that they could, the lambs that brought a quiet smile to all who saw them having a secret others had forgotten.

'Well, I'll have a couple of chops, after all,' said Mrs Gough, wondering whether she had vinegar at home for the mint sauce.

Mr. O'Donnell, the butcher, nodded and picked up his chopper, stained with blood like his once-white apron.

'And I'll have a little kidney while you're at it. And how is Mrs. O'Donnell?'

'Never complains,' he said, bringing the chopper down with a satisfying thud.

'The woman is a saint, Mr. O'Donnell, what with her complaint. I think I'll make it three chops if you don't mind.'

***

Across the road was a draper's shop, its window featuring staid pink underclothes guaranteed to resist assaults. A mannequin, whose plaster nose was broken, leaned forward, a shiny finger extended, insisting that the country might have need of the passing stranger. Inside, Mrs. O'Connell tried on a hat and wondered if it would be fit for a funeral and if for that then for the trip to Dublin she had been thinking of making these twenty years. This was the same Mrs. O'Connell who in her youth had been a bit of a dancer, her heels clicking, legs thrust out, back as straight as a broom handle, staring straight ahead looking for something she would never see.

The shop sold surgical stockings so that for her it had always had reassuring overtones of the medical profession since her husband had fallen off the roof while adjusting the television aerial and the surgeon had respected her request that his life not be unnecessarily prolonged, he being in no condition to join in the ethical discussion. Later, she had tried to get in touch with him at a séance run by the chairwoman of the Women's Institute who when not making jam of a somewhat solid consistency was known to speak to the dead through the medium of an Indian chief who, unaccountably to some, was seemingly on call should anyone from Ballygoran wish a word of two. Mrs. O'Connell wished to be in touch primarily because she had been unable to locate where the departed had hidden his savings book. All she needed, she told Big Chief Running Pony, was a hint or two, as if this were a parlour game and not a serious building of bridges with those who had passed beyond but not sufficiently that they could not to be recalled if there were sufficient need. 'Have you tried the coal scuttle?' suggested the Chief, showing a remarkable insight into the domestic arrangements of a tribe surely remote from his own, 'or if not, the outside lav.' 'We have not used that since my haemorrhoids, as he well knows' said Mrs. Connelly feeling that whether a chief or not this particular Indian was showing less respect than was proper for someone relaying messages from the dead.

'He is dead but not gone,' said the Chief, which was rather the opposite of what she had assumed when he disappeared once for a day, he who had always paid more attention to his pigeons than to her perhaps because they were happy to go back to him.

'Sometimes,' she said to her hostess, as she tried to avoid the strawberry jam held out to her, 'I feel he's been in the house.'

'What makes you feel that?' she asked, wondering whether the mould that had formed on the top was what put people off.

'The toilet seat was up,' she replied.

***

'Sure it's you, Mrs. O'Connell. The very thing. We have it in green but I don't see you in green, do you? It was dreadful sad, though, and her with her growth only just taken out.'

'And her daughter,' said Mrs. O'Faolain, 'going off to England and breaking her mother's heart.'

'It's what mother's hearts are for, so they say.'

'And not even pregnant like her sister.'

'Do you have a little tulle by any chance, or some shot silk. I saw it in a magazine.'

'It's not the fashion, so I've heard,' she replied, who ran a shop whose resistance to fashion was its chief recommendation for the ladies who frequented it. 'Were you happy with the corsetry, Mrs. Burke?'

'Sure I was, though it cut a little.'

'We do alterations, provided it is not too significant. Would it be a significant change you are thinking of?'

'Not significant at all, though perhaps I might have chosen the larger one, to tell the truth. It is some time since I bought any. The one you sold me has served me well enough.'

'That would have been?'

'Before Jamie was born, and he twenty-three last Easter and training for to be a plumber which is steady work and doesn't need the exams. He was never good at the exams.'

'And what did exams ever prove, Mrs. Burke. I've none myself, so you see what I mean. Will you be paying a little off your account do you think?'

'I'll do that certainly, for Jamie has promised me something as soon as he does his first toilet or unblocks the drains. There's a deal of money in that he tells me. And would you have a packet of, you know. I'm a little short and I have it terrible every month. We're a martyr to our bodies, are we not.'

'That we are. Perhaps a little just so I can balance the books.'

'I'll see what I can do. Could you wrap it up for me for I have to go out in the street and there are men out there?'

'I'll do that, though it's raining still so it will go soggy unless you've a waterproof. I might have a plastic bag in the back. I was to the butchers earlier for a couple of hearts. They're something powerful if you stuff them with sage.'

The door opened and a sprung bell nodded up and down but made no noise, its clapper having rusted off.

'Well, Mrs. James. And it's a terrible day.'

'That it is. The worst month for forty years they say.'

'It's the weather I hear. They've been messing around with it. The north pole is melting. I heard it on the radio. What can I be doing for you?'

'Do you have something in blue? I've a second cousin who has taken it in mind to marry and has need of that for her wedding.'

'Is it undergarments you had in mind?'

'Oh, no. She's only a second cousin. No, I had in mind to have a small piece of blue cotton or some such. Or a ribbon. I'm not wanting to be spending much. I've already bought a set of tea spoons.'

'Tea spoons is it. They'd be silver.'

'Silver coloured. Hello, Mrs. O'Connell, I thought I saw you come in. It's better in than out today. And are you thinking of going for the mauve? I used to have a pair of shoes that colour but I was very young of course.

'Good day to you, Mrs. James. Would that be the second cousin I heard tell of?'

'That would depend on what you heard.'

'Sure it was nothing at all. The wedding will be here, I suppose.'

'Not decided yet.'

'And you looking for blue.'

'Did I hear you had your old trouble again, Mrs. O'Connell. You're a martyr to your feet.'

'My feet are just fine, thank you. She would be the second cousin who left a year or two back. Disappeared so fast.'

'There was an opening.'

'Opening?'

'She was after getting a job and there are none around here.'

'I have just the thing. A length of ribbon. And I could let you have it for … very little.'

'It looks a mite faded.'

'It's the light does that. It's blue, though. There's no denying that.'

'Well, I'll be off, Mrs. Burke.'

'Would you not stay and take a cup of tea. You'll not want to go out and catch your death.'

'I've left the fire banked up but it'll be out soon unless I get back.'

'And this summer. It's the melting icebergs.'

'They said we'd be growing grapes in a year or two. We'd be like the Mediterranean.'

'I couldn't take the olives. I've never liked them. And they'd be lying on the beach without their tops like the foreigners do and we know what that leads to.'

'It's the icebergs.'

'I thought it was supposed to warm up.'

'I'm not against that. It could do with warming up.'

'That would be your feet.'

'My feet are fine.'

'Does the rain not make them act up? I'll take the ribbon if there's nothing else. And do you have a pair of nice thick stockings. The cold gets up my skirt this kind of weather.'

'Do you have meat in that bag, Mrs. Connell.'

'I do.'

'I ask because there's a trail of blood over my floor.'

'A trail of blood. My heavens you're right. He must have given me an imperfect bag. You'd think with prices what they are he would have better bags.'

'Would you like one of mine? Best not put the meat in with clothes, though. Each thing to its bag, I say. Shall I wrap the hat Mrs. James?'

'Are you sure the colour is quite right? Maybe I should try it in green.'

'Green's a fine colour, I always think.'

'Except that sometimes under a light it can make the face seem a little sinister.'

'Green is the colour of Ireland. What can be wrong with that? I think you should go with the green.'

'On the other hand if it makes me look ... peculiar. Perhaps I'll stick with the mauve.'

'Purple, we call it. The colour of royalty.'

'Is that so?'

'And there's a little bit of black lace at the front.'

'What would that be for?'

'In case you want to convert and become a Muslim. Only joking, of course. It's a decoration. Makes it look more formal. Shall I wrap it up?'

'I think you should or I'll be here all day and I've things to do.'

'You're welcome to a cup of tea.'

'No, I'll be on my way. Where did I put my brolly?'

'Your bag's bleeding again. People will think you have a head in there.'

'Then people will need their own heads examining,' she replied, considering whether she should get in touch with Big Chief Running Pony again since she had still not found the savings book and fancied there might be a deal of money in it, wondering all the time if her husband, now either rotting in the grave or available for long-distance calls, would know that she had exchanged the pigeons for a joint of beef at the butchers, pigeons that had been stupid enough not to fly away when she first threatened them.

***

The Shamrock had just opened its door, but even this early there were two men sitting on the bench outside staring ahead until the bolts were thrown. They sat in the rain with a single umbrella between them, and that lacking a spoke or two.

'Sure you took your time, and us getting soaked with this feckin rain.'

'It's the hour on the dot.'

'Ay, but you could have let us in, at least.'

'We're open now. Are you staying out there all morning? The rain's coming in and I've a barrel to see to.'

So do we, they were thinking, but the thing was to be out of the rain. Inside was the satisfying smell of stale beer and the place dark enough to hide all sins.

'I'll be having a half, if you please Michael.'

'And I will, too,' added Jamie Synge, holding his yellow jumper out ahead of him seeming to believe it would dry in a moment, the smell of damp wool being added to the general mix.

'Big spenders,' replied the barman, lifting part of the counter and stepping round the open trap door down which his predecessor had fallen, breaking his collar bone.

'If our money's not good enough…' It was an empty threat, the only other pub having burnt down in circumstances the local police had called 'mysterious,' which is to say they had no idea why it should have done so and suspected the worst while having no evidence at all.

As the half pint was pulled, with a head that would take a minute or two to settle, Jamie pulled a packet of cigarettes from his pocket.

'Do you have a match?'

'Shall I add it to the price of the drink?'

'You're thinking of charging for a man to have a smoke. You're a terrible profiteer.' Wearily the barman slid a half empty box towards him. It came to a halt in a puddle of beer. He picked it up and rattled it by his ear. 'That beer doesn't look right.'

'Neither do you, but I'm not complaining.'

A match flared and a cloud of blue smoke drifted up towards a ceiling stained mahogany brown.

'They say they're going to ban smoking.'

'Smoking, is it? That never did anyone any harm.'

'They say it kills you.'

'Well, that aside of course.'

'Could we not have a light on? I can't see to kill myself.'

'Have you got a spare ciggy,' asked his companion, known to all as Slick, though for reasons none could recall for it was not a name any would give him today.

'I'm down to my last.'

'You said that yesterday.'

'I was down to my last then, too. Here's to you then,' he said, raising his glass, clear now with a colour like amber, though with no creature trapped inside for a million years.'

'To the old days.'

'May they never return.'

'The old days were old when we lived them the first time. And what is that you have in your cigarette for it smells like something's been dead a week or more.'

'It's not the cigarettes for they came out of a machine. It's this place. It's never been the same since they laid out Patrick McGee after he'd been missing a week.'

'Fine looking man was Patrick.'

'Not after a week in the river he wasn't. They should have closed the coffin but for his sister who insisted everyone was to see him, blaming us as she did for the fact he had been out so late and had a glass or two to drink.'

'The wake was a fine thing, though.'

'That it was for I cannot remember it at all which in my experience is the guarantee. I was sad to lose Patrick who would sit up later than any I knew and could drink for his country if required.'

'There's a funny taste to this, I am thinking.'

'I'd not drink it then if I were you.'

'It's drinkable, right enough. But you've a right to expect the best.' He spat a penny piece of gob on a handkerchief that hung from a top pocket and was a kind of linen petri dish in which he was perhaps seeking to develop a new antibiotic.

So they sat alongside each other and looked across at the mottled mirror above a row of bottles -- red, orange, green, blue -- a rainbow without a pot of gold. And in the mirror what did they see but their own blank stares and a trickle of blue smoke. Above it was a clock, its hands immobile, always stuck at twenty-five past twelve, that being the time the landlord's mother had been struck down as she poured a Jameson's, that being her favourite restorative, from which few in the Shamrock would have dissented, brave souls themselves ready to risk their lives to sustain a national industry.

The barman disappeared into the cellar, cold and with the smell of yeast. The barrels stood on wooden cradles, plastic pipes looping up like the arteries of a man laid open in an autopsy. He picked up a spanner and stood for a moment, listening to the throb of a fan, encrusted with dirt, that flickered on the far wall beside the chute.

'You'll not be long, Michael,' came a voice from above that could never be mistaken for that of the Almighty.'

'Hold your water. Am I not changing the barrel.'

'I've a terrible thirst.'

'Your terrible thirst will have to wait for I've work to be doing. And if I know you two you'll be holding onto the drink you've got rather than paying for another.'

'Do you have pickled eggs?'

'Would you bide your time? Did you have no breakfast? What do you think this is?

'A fine businessman, you.'

He made no reply, for there was none to be made. It was not a job he had ever wanted but there was little enough to be done in Ballygoran and there were times of an evening when it satisfied his needs, or some of them. He allowed himself a drink or two when it was nine or so and the police were not over zealous about closing time, not least because one or more liked to drop by for a taste when there were no strangers there, and sometimes when there were. Then one would put his head inside and say, 'Is it not time, Michael?' He would close up and then re-open when the strangers had chosen to take themselves away. Not that there were many strangers for what is a bar when you know nobody?

Up above, his customers had begun to settle themselves, as people do when they come home in the evening and take off their daytime faces along with their working clothes, except that this was not evening time. They would nurse their half pints for an hour or more before ordering another. Then others would begin to drift in and they would retreat to a table and stare a little more for they had known one another for more than fifty years and had long ago run out of things to say.

'Take your time,' Michael said, as his head emerged above the counter rubbed smooth by elbows and with indentations where coins had been impatiently rapped. It was said with irony but taken as wise words since those with little to spend had best spend slowly. But it was something more than that for nursing a half pint was like falling in love, Jamie had once observed, having himself never had more than a half at a time except when he found a deal of money down the back of the settee when he was trying to reach a piece of cheese he had left in his place when going to the lav. 'Did you wash your hands?' he heard his mother say whenever he moved his bowels, though she had been dead these many years who had polished her front steps every day so they shone bright and smelled of lavender should you have felt inclined to bend down and give them a sniff. 'Take your shoes off,' she would call when he was all sticky from playing in the park, drawn back by hunger and the smell of the stew she had surely kept on the boil since she was first married, throwing in whatever came to hand, including, once, a sock, and pouring a bottle of stout into it every now and then which, young though he was, he had known for a terrible waste. 'Did you wash your hands?' and the coins were there like buried treasure as though it were meant that he should be able to sink a few while thinking of his mother and her print apron with daisies on it and thinking too, God forgive him, of her pink under things that would hang on the line when the neighbours were not around, blowing in the wind, to his embarrassment, and heavily armoured, hidden from view by an elder tree that had gradually taken over half of the Garden and from whose fruit he had once tried to make wine one summer succeeding in doing no more than kill a few hundred wasps that found it to their taste. And what a summer that was, he thought, staring up at the ceiling, glazed shit brown from those who had smoked their lives away in the public bar, though why they called it that he could not say for certainly there was no other, the gentle folk never coming here, preferring to drink in their own homes and not Guinness either but good strong whisky in crystal glasses. What a summer when there was no rain, miracle of miracles, and the grass was crisp and brown, though not shit brown more a yellow brown, and his mother's geraniums died in a horticultural holocaust as the water company banned hosepipes and you could only flush the lav when you'd done number twos and she had been in despair that someone would come by and ask to use it only to see it pea green or pee green, and her so proud of her geraniums and her lav and her front step who had no man to love, his da having left to sail the seas or explore the jungles, for she never told the truth of that. And if he asked, as he did once or twice, she would scrub harder at his underpants believing, perhaps, that nothing could remove a stain from her life until she stood at the polished front step of Paradise. 'Why is it not Mrs. Synge,' would say St. Peter, 'and did you not keep your front step shining to the glory of God and were your geraniums not something to behold, except for the once and that was not your fault, nor the lav either for did God himself not decide you had had enough rain for a while, though all good deeds have consequences, as does He not know better than most.' And her eying St. Peter's step and thinking it not quite up to her standard.

***

The wind here rises from the Atlantic, its edge honed by so many miles of metal grey sea. There are trees bent almost double, so many old women holding their arms out for departed sons. This is a no place that is a place, except to those who cling to it without knowing why beyond submission to necessity which can seem like a purpose after a time. But this is what we think of the places others choose to live. How could they survive there? How live beside the railway, with its thundering trains shaking the ornaments on the mantelpiece, or in the countryside where the silence would drive one to drink? We all belong somewhere, we think, finding nothing strange in our choices, if choices they truly are. 'Sure habit is a great thing. How could people live in Dublin, which is all kerfuffle and the like and shops selling things that must bruise their souls?' asked Mrs. James, who had ventured to Dublin just the same and trod in some dog's dirt she couldn't get off and that was still there on the corrugated souls of her shoes when she knelt in church for all to see, and smell.

An American had thought to establish a sanatorium to cure tuberculosis in Ballygoran, having purchased a tourist guide published in the closing years of Queen Victoria's reign and still sold to unwary visitors by those who ran the post office and who had an irrational yearning for the days of empire. This referred to the complete absence of malarial fog, something to which many could attest, and the invigorating ozone which was a consequence of the waves pounding on the foreshore, ozone being derived from the Greek verb 'to smell,' as well it might since what the American smelt was rotting seaweed, ozone also, had he thought to enquire, causing respiratory problems, being known to destroy lung tissue and even explode.

He was an admirer of the Irish American playwright Eugene O'Neill who had entered just such a sanatorium in 1912, the year of the Titanic, manufactured in the Protestant North and hence doomed from the beginning, and had O'Neill not been cured and gone on to write many miserable plays of the kind the Irish were inclined to like, in one of which everyone was in a drunken stupor throughout? The people of Ballygoran, however, were not inclined to see foreigners with illnesses arrive on their shores. Sending money to lepers was one thing. Having people coughing up phlegm on the doorstep was one doorstep too far. As a result, he was discouraged, not least after spending a summer in Ballygoran and glimpsing the health-giving sun only on rare occasions.

On a bright summer's day, though, Ballygoran could feature well on the advertisements in glossy magazines selling hope mixed with nostalgia with its green and blue and brown springing from the soil or falling from the sky. Its tumble of cottages and grey staid houses seem to tell a story of times past, rising up the hillside on narrow roads that turn this way and that seemingly having a choice as to which way to go. Some have bright flowers in hanging baskets; others keep curtains drawn against intrusion. Some doors are brightly coloured: red, green, blue. Others are a sombre black or grey. Even though it is summer there are some who have chosen to light their fires and smoke trails in the wind as if they are steaming across an ocean or rushing down a railway track instead of anchored here decade after decade, century after century.

There are two round-arched bridges at either end of the town spanning a river that sparkles in the sun and invites bare feet to go paddling or a worm or two on a hook. There are even two schools, beyond the one for the Protestants, in a nearby town, that does not count, one for the youngest and the other for those who know more than they should. They are Catholic, of course, but the others have only to go a few miles where they can be heathens in peace. And if there are cars to be seen so there are carts and the odd horse or two for they are cheaper to run unless you have the red diesel from a man who would sell you anything and ask only your soul.

This is a place where the bewildered are left to themselves, for who is to say where wisdom lies and who is to know the power of the strange. Mad Peg may be mad for reasons best left unknown and is suspected of powers it is preferable not to test. So no one hears her rude words or pays mind to her blasphemies, content she should pass on her way, be-whiskered and dishevelled as God perhaps intended. 'The sane are strange enough, God knows,' opined Mrs. Kendall who had married a Ballygoran man who had upped and died and left her there when her real home was across the water in Liverpool. Why had she not returned, when there was a ferry could take her there? She stayed because going was no different than staying but required rather more in the way of energy. And besides, something had happened there that she would not even tell the priest for who knows with priests that have been known to have terrible sins of their own.

The old one, Father Boyle, had lived with his housekeeper and fathered a son. He was an intemperate preacher, and admired as such, his white hair ablaze with indignation, his hands describing wild circles in the air as he conjured up images of hell. He was to be seen occasionally on the television, when it was possible to see anything at all, reception varying from poor to non-existent, discussing mortal sin with intense young men who were perhaps hankering for it. The son, though, knew nothing of his heritage, any more than did his parishioners, until his priest father dropped dead one day coming back from the pub having a liking for un-consecrated wine. Then, though, the whole thing came out.

So why, Mrs. Kendall thought, would you entrust your own secrets to men such as he, though his replacement was a deal younger and his housekeeper such as would repel any man whether wearing priests clothes or not. You would not, she told herself. Confession, anyway, as was known to all here, was not an invitation to tell everything, merely those things it was convenient to whisper through the lattice of the confessional. 'It's terrible hard,' remarked Anthony Almansi, or Toni Cornetto as he was known locally on account of his trade, 'to keep coming up with sins to justify confession. I've admitted to things I never did. What's a few Hail Marys if it keeps him happy.' Since Catania had been the heart of the mafia, however, and ice cream making, as everyone knew, a convenient cover for other ventures, it was hard to believe he had exhausted his list of infractions and to be sure he was not the only one who parcelled out truths like jelly at children's parties: 'Would you like a red one. It tastes of strawberry. Or would you prefer blackcurrant with a scoop of vanilla?'

What do priests represent if not certainty? It is all very well for Protestant ministers to have their doubts about miracles, saints and indeed God himself. They are liberal people of two minds about everything and therefore with no mind to tell anyone anything except they are doomed. The Catholics require absolutes but reserve the right to pay no attention if it makes no sense. Father Carrol, who replaced Father Boyle and who had to clean the lavatory before he would use it and scrape the fat from above the gas ring where his predecessor had cooked chips, felt he should have been a Protestant for did he not doubt so many of the things he was bound to tell his parishioners. 'Don't marry a Protestant for no good can come of it.' 'Do you promise to raise any children as Catholics,' knowing of course that they lied their souls away if love was too strong to resist. And then there were the contraceptives, which he knew in truth he would use himself if only he had the chance, longing, as he did, for the touch of a woman, any woman it seemed at times.

Was it because the Holy Father was against sex, as surely he was since he refused the balm to his priests and left them to find what comforts they might, discovering them, too often, in sweaty embraces that would embarrass a brothel owner, of which, incidentally, there was one in the town, though it had so little trade it was compelled to rent videos out as well. Did they not carry the Pope on some sort of chair, held high so the cardinals could have a glimpse of his genitals, a woman having once made it to the

Papacy? Or at least so he had discovered when sailing on the high seas of the internet in search of enlightenment or stimulation. Not that the internet was easy to receive when it would take half an hour to make a connection and downloading a sinful picture would take the best part of an afternoon.

And what was he to say to homosexuals, like Martin Beck, who confessed so often and with so many tears that he was hard pressed to think of a penance to match the crime, the more especially since he was none too sure it was a crime, whatever it said in the Bible. For it all came down, as far as he could see, to where one chose to put a part of oneself and even then, he had heard, it was perhaps permissible for a man and a woman to do what was denied to two men, though in truth he had never found occasion to enquire of the Monsignor, not being on terms sufficient to blurt out such enquiries. Besides which, he had his doubts about a man who had squeezed his thigh when he was taking instruction. Had he not spent a long retreat trying not to catch his eye?

As for himself, in his own confession he kept back such doubts as were sent to test him as he was sure did those who knelt on the other side of the confessional and sang their sad songs of imperfection. At least he could restore people to themselves, though. 'Go and sin no more.' 'Yes, father,' And say ten Hail Marys.' 'Yes, father.' 'You'll not do it again, will you Margaret' 'And if I should, I'll come straight back father, for he is such a darling man and I don't want to be losing him.' The swish of a curtain, the bang of the great door. What was he, after all, but the lubricating oil of the machinery of the community? Else it would be metal on metal and the tearing of flesh.

***

At the end of the town there is a small statue of Our Lady, chipped a little where the Protestants had fired at her as a reminder that they had direct access to God with no need for intermediaries. She wore pastel blue and held her hand high blessing all who should pass by, excepting Protestants with guns one presumes, not least because a finger was missing where a bullet had exploded it, a bullet fired by a gun smuggled across the border by those who had stolen the six counties. Her halo had first turned green, being made of copper, and then been stolen for scrap, being made of copper. There was a bunch of flowers in a jam jar at her feet, the jar having proved a convenient place for frogs to enter if not leave so that they formed a kind of green coagulate of amphibian though since the flowers were plastic no harm was done.

Once a year there was a procession in which the statue was placed on a pallet and carried through the town by strong men while the jam jar was discretely emptied of its liquid frogs and the plastic flowers given a quick rinsing in disinfectant which for a while gave the shrine an air of purity which owed less to God than a pharmaceutical company which promised it could purge 99 percent of all germs if not sins. Since the strong men had often partaken of strong drink before they set out, however, the Virgin looked on occasion like a rodeo rider desperately trying to stay on the saddle for the requisite amount of time.

The Virgin would be garlanded with flowers – not plastic – and the day ended with the young people throwing tomatoes at one another, a ceremony stolen from another country as a result of the cheap air travel that had enabled even the people of Ballygoran to see how the heathen lived, except that there the tomatoes had been red and not green, sweet and not bitter and soft rather than hard.

The ceremony itself had been prompted by a priest's holiday in a place where a much larger Virgin had been carried. He had also seen where men rode horses through the streets and still another where bulls were set loose to kill people at will but he had regretfully decided that such events could probably not be staged in Ballygoran where the horses mainly pulled carts or stood disconsolately in fields flinching as horse flies earned their name, performing barrel rolls to indicate their victory over noble creatures who never did anyone any harm, except when one had rolled on top of a couple lying in the grass which was a just desert for their brazenness. As to letting bulls loose, appealing though it was, this seemed even less likely, not least because it would distract them from their primary function which was servicing cows as vacuum cleaner engineers are required to check under the conditions of the guarantee.

The paraded Virgin passed the town's only Jew, Emmanuel Goldstein, who lived in the ghetto, that is to say he lived in a cottage set back from the road, a Christ killer tolerated for his skill with needle and thread.

'They have a different calendar, you know,' said Mrs. James as she walked alongside the swaying Virgin.

'What do they call Tuesday, then?'

'I think it's the years. They have more of them or less.'

'Is it like dog years, do you think? So instead of being 49 they are 7.'

'He's good with the alterations, though.'

'Mrs. Connerty had him put the elastic back in her drawers.'

'You don't surprise me at all.'

At Passover -- which commemorated God's grace in defending his people against the slaughter of the first born, which worked the first time with a Pharaoh but not the second when Herod, a plagiarist as well as a baby killer, it seemed, tried the same -- he would open his door for Elijah the Prophet who, somewhat curiously it seemed to Emmanuel, was presumed to have what was surely an unhealthy interest in circumcision. As tradition dictated, he left a glass of wine in case Elijah should have need of it, as well he might since he would be heralding the arrival, at last, of the Messiah. It was the fifth glass he had poured, though, he being Jewish but also Irish, and having, therefore, consumed the other four. As he prepared for this, Ballygoran's Jew called down wrath on his persecutors and oppressors as tradition dictated, though since the baggy knickers of one of them was even now on his table, ready to be expanded, he was inclined to exempt his fellow citizens. For years, Elijah had failed to put in an appearance but once when he opened the door there was indeed someone standing there. It was a besuited Mormon who wished to ask him if he had Christ in his heart.

***

The school was called St. Cronan of Roscrera and was named for a man who had gone blind and once, on receiving guests for whom he had no liquor, had prayed for beer. The miracle occurred and his guests became blind drunk. This was not a story told to the girls when they gathered each morning for prayers and to hear Sister Hilda's battle with the piano forte. There were rumours it was Mozart she was trying to play and certainly she used several of the notes he had used before her, though not quite in the same way and certainly not to the same effect. No one told them, either, that they were twinned with St. Meadhbh's in County Wexford, whose name literally means 'she who intoxicates.' With all the many Irish saints on offer – and there are enough, had they all been alive together, to have fielded the entire Irish rugby team ten times over – it was strange that these had been selected from the canon. A portrait of St. Meadhbh, incidentally, was on show in The Shamrock and after a drink or two several of its customers could pronounce her name.

'Let us give Sister Hilda a round of applause,' said the Mother Superior, to whom suffering was second nature and much to be encouraged. 'There's nothing like beginning the day with a go at the classics.' Sister Hilda beamed, being blessed if not with anything approaching musical skills then with ignorance of her own shortcomings which were, in truth, not limited to her daily contest with the piano.

She taught poetry, having convinced herself she had committed an entire anthology of such to memory. That memory, however, was less secure than she assumed. So it was that she would stand in front of the class, hands clasped, brow furrowed, and declare that she wandered lonely as a clown, subsequently explaining to her pupils the sadness felt by those obliged to amuse others while suffering in their hearts. 'If,' she assured them, 'they could keep their hats while all about them others were losing theirs,' it would be the making of them, recommending they use hair clips to keep their own in place on windy days. Even Shakespeare did not escape her. One day, in looping white letters, she wrote across the blackboard, 'Mercy droppeth as the gentile Jew from heaven' which had the virtue of being ecumenical if not necessarily correct.

Even when memory proved reliable poetry could, she discovered, prove dangerous, especially when she had distributed copies to her pupils without recalling anything more than the first lines.

'In Xanadu did Kubla Khan a mighty pleasure dome decree. Yes, Bridget Riley.'

'Sister, what's a pleasure dome?'

For some reason that question had never occurred to Sister Hilda who suddenly thought that it sounded like the kind of place good catholic girls were best kept away from.

'Better ask where is Xanadu, Bridget Riley.'

'Where is Xanadu, Sister?'

'A place far away from this sacred island.'

'That would be because of the pleasure dome, would it, Sister? And, Sister, what is a demon lover and why is she wearing thick pants?'

'Thick pants?'

'It says so, Sister. It says she was breathing in fast thick pants. And why would they be fast?'

The Sister thought it best to change direction. 'Have you each brought in your own favourite poem as I asked?'

'I have, Sister.'

'Could we not hear from someone else, Bridget Riley, for you are not the only one in the class.'

'But it's Keats, Sister.'

'Keats, is it,' said Sister Hilda, reassured, feeling that perhaps she had misjudged the child. 'And what is it called?'

'It's his Ode to a Grecian Urn.'

'Very suitable, for there is great beauty in such things. And can you recall the first line, Bridget Riley? For committing poetry to memory is a fine thing.'

'I can, Sister.'

'Very well. Attention class. Bridget.'

'Thou still unravish'd bride.'

'Bridget Riley, you will see me after class for the Devil is in you today.'

***.

This morning's assembly was an occasion for more than a musical interlude.

'Who has brought in today's object?' asked the Mother Superior.

'I have,' said Bridget O'Neill, the anti-matter of Bridget Riley, having learned ingratiation at her mother's breast.

'Very well, Bridget O'Neill, and may it not be like yesterday's which was not entirely suitable if of use to an old lady with that particular affliction.'

Bridget O'Neill made her way with difficulty to the dais, being kicked a good deal about the ankles as she stepped between her fellow pupils who were sitting on the polished floor with their skirts pulled tight around them having been taught the danger of reflections.

The Mother Superior stepped aside as Bridget faced her tormentors, biting her lip.

'And what have you brought, child?'

'I have brought my mother's veil from when she was married.'

'Isn't that nice. The Holy Sacrament of marriage. When would this have occurred?'

'Fifteen years ago today.'

'Is that so, Bridget O'Neill?' said the Mother Superior, her lips no more than a pencil line since unlike the sixteen year-old Bridget, and being something of a gambling woman used to working out the odds, she was entirely competent at mathematics. 'It is certainly beautiful. You may now return to your seat.'

'Can we ask questions?' asked Bridget O'Reilly, who was herself able to subtract one number from another.

'No time for questions,' replied the Mother Superior in a voice that could have cut through toughened steel. 'Because of the rain there will be no nature walk today. Sister Benedicta will teach you the virtues of chastity in room six.

'We had chastity yesterday,' said Bridget Reilly.

'You can never have enough chastity child,' observed the Mother Superior, nodding to Sister Hilda who immediately began her assault on Beethoven who might have been grateful for his deafness had the Sister been alive when he was.

Sister Benedicta taught needlework and chastity, the former with more success than the latter, and was a dab hand with the tortoiseshell hair brush she kept in her desk and with which she would enforce discipline. She would beat her charges for insolence if they spoke and beat them for dumb insolence if they did not. 'What is the capital of Peru Bridget O'Reilly?' she once asked, being required, on occasion, to teach other things than the need to keep at least three feet between themselves and any boys they might encounter.'

"'P',' replied Bridget, receiving by way of reward two strikes with the brush, a forehand and a backhand that might have won her fame had she thought to substitute a tennis racket.

For Sister Benedicta life consisted of pain, and she was there to deliver it. The only brightness came when the priest visited whereupon she seemed to turn into a giggling girl herself, offering him cups of tea and even, it was rumoured, hard liquor. 'Give yourselves to Christ,' he urged the girls who sat bolt-upright in their desks as they had been taught to do, and who had indeed been thinking of giving themselves but not in that direction. 'There is no higher calling than to become a nun,' she added, the priest standing beside her, 'unless it be the priesthood itself.'

'And why can women not be priests, father?' asked Bridget O'Reilly, who plainly appreciated pain more than a young girl should.'

'What is your name, dear?' asked the priest, reaching for his glasses, for in truth he could see very little.

'Bridget O'Reilly, Father.'

'And is your father not at this moment in the police station, Bridget O'Reilly, for challenging authority?'

'He punched the constable,' she replied. 'who was discourteous to my mother, father.'

'Was she not drunk?' Bridget O'Reilly.

'My mother does not drink, father. Save to dull the pain.'

'The pain.'

'From the abortion, father.'

***

So it was that Bridget would secure entry to a state school a few miles away where boys were plentiful and needlework not in much demand. Nor chastity either, it was believed. The others stood in awe of her. Had she not accepted eternal damnation? On the other hand, eternity stood a long way off and in the mean time she would be free of the hair brush and invitations to graze her knees by edging forward across gravel in imitation of the stations of the cross. The original being far away they had had to settle for the driveway down which the Monsignor was liable to appear in his Morris Minor, plastic dog nodding in the back, and more often than not with a young boy beside him who was training to be an altar boy. Suppress the thought. It is not worthy to doubt those who have sacrificed so much and who are required to take tea with women dressed all in black and with teeth which stick out at different angles, like rotting signposts indicating distant places. Much is to be forgiven of those who have suffered much.

'Hello, girls,' he called, winding down the window and waving to the kneeling pupils. 'Mortify the flesh!' he said brightly, his left hand patting the white knee of his putative altar boy, a knee not required to scrape over stones in search of redemption and hence deprived of the pleasure that comes with the picking of scabs.

***

Ten miles inland is a lough, deep black and with no bottom, it is said, left where a thick finger of ice had pointed for thousands of years before withdrawing, leaving boulders like some prehistoric creature dropping its shit along the edge of the dark water. There are marks on the hillside, as a carpenter cuts a groove with his router, layers of time laid out to see, one of crushed sea creatures, another of burnt land, then one offering perfect fossils. Today's layer will no doubt contain pot noodles, a contraceptive or two and a syringe, for even here there are those who search for something and look for it where it can never be found.

There are scientists who come to count the variety of fish and test to see what chemicals man has added to purity in his ignorance. And there are those who chase them off for fear they will report on the illegal fishing they do having been forced to leave the sea for this pale imitation as foreigners with boats like warehouses vacuumed up everything that moved and much that did not including, occasionally, the body of a passing cruise ship passenger preserved by the multiple tequilas that had led to a plunge into the unforgiving sea. There are stories aplenty about the lough and the caves nearby where ancient peoples lived and which today young men and women visit for no good purpose. There are stories, too, about the wild hills and the rivers, and about houses where such and such happened as would hardly be believed.

The lough has another reputation, however, and another history. It is a place where people die, where they choose to die. Just below the ruffled surface is a layer of water cold enough to stop the heart. Some who have walked miles across scarred hillsides to reach it, sweating with the effort and bewitched by the sight of blue green water, strip off and plunge in, swimming out with a few brisk strokes, the coolness so refreshing. It is only then that they feel a tightness in the chest, a sudden blow, and spin around to fight their way back to safety. Many make it; a few do not. For centuries others have come, on a suspect pilgrimage. They do not arrive red faced and glistening. They make their way deliberately, mocked by the purple flowers that lie close to the ground and the birds circling above. They walk slowly, carrying an invisible burden from whose weight they seek deliverance. They are gathered in by men in a rowing boat. Rather than being hauled on board, and risking capsize, they are tied alongside like marlin or Minke whales and brought back to land.

In the height of summer, birds of prey ride the thermals, turning in slow circles as they rise high, looking down on this place where men have lived many thousands of years never in all that time working out why. Then down will swoop one of them, kissing the waters of the lough and daintily picking a silver fish, bowing this way and that in firm talons, dropping crystal beads of water. A fish swimming in the air. Can we imagine it happy?

***

'Penny for your thoughts.'

And Jamie was back in the bar with that smell of tobacco and regret.

'Sure, they are not worth the half of that.'

'Michael Flaherty. There was a man.'

'Michael, is it?'

'Who lived with the widow Baynes.'

'The one with the leg.'

'That would be her.'

'He could drink more than any man I knew and still walk a straight line.'

'Except when he was sober, as a result of walking beside her with her leg being what it was. He could sing any song you chose to name.

'Within reason, no doubt.'

'Certainly within reason.

'And what became of him?'

'Secure accommodation, for he was crazy as they come.'

'The bin then.'

'It was, indeed, though we can't call it such any more.'

'You can call nothing what it is or they say you're down on other people because they're black or on the short side.'

'Or with a leg.'

'With a leg, indeed.'

'Do you remember O'Reilly?'

'Which O'Reilly would that be? It seems there are O'Reillys wherever you look.'

'Is that not the truth. I am thinking of Michael.'

'Another Michael is it? No, I have no memory of such. Who was he?'

'Who was he? Has your brain retired? Have you given up entirely?'

'When was this?'

'Twenty years ago.'

'That would be it, then.'

'What would?'

'I remember nothing from that time, I'm glad to say. Drank from sun up to sun down. Those were great days if only I could remember them.'

'Michael O'Reilly was a diviner.'

'A priest was he?'

'A priest? Not unless they were given to walking around with a bit of a twig looking for water.'

'Why would he need to do that? Have we not enough water and to spare?'

'There's a need from time to time, if you are digging a well.'

'Certainly it would not be good to dig down and find nothing at all. Well, what of him?'

'Nothing. He just came across my mind. He was very generous, though, in buying drinks for others.'

'Is that right. Would that perhaps be why he is in the bin today?'

'That was Flaherty. Are you listening to nothing I say?'

They fell silent a while as the blue-flamed fire burned down, the coals shifting from time to time, a scatter of sparks flying up the chimney.

'Where was your grandfather when mine was fighting for freedom at the General Post office?'

'He only went in for a stamp.'

'You say that because yours was on the outside with his Lee Enfield ready to snuff out freedom.'

'So it was a freedom fighter he was, was it? A postage stamp and a postal order. I had it from your grandmother, God bless her soul, who was mad that he had lost the money and her wanting to place a bet for she was a gambling woman as I recall.'

'The best died.'

'Judging by your grandfather that would be true for on a scale of not bad to awful he was useless.'

'Have you no respect for the dead.'

'I'd be wasting it on the dead since they're not around to appreciate it.'

'A heathen to boot.'

'A heathen, is it, you old rascal, and you a terrible teller of lies. Did you not promise two women you would marry them?'

'That I did, and I would have done had I not met a third.'

'And her seeing straight through you and marrying a didicoy.'

'He put the evil eye on me.'

'That would account for your never doing a day's work.'

'Sure I have worked from time to time when my back has allowed.'

'You back is it? It doesn't stop you coming here to the pub as I've noticed.'

'It's the alcohol dulls the pain. After a few glasses I'm fine but who would employ me with liquor on my breath, even if it is medicinal?'

'Do you remember Fogherty?'

'Who would not remember Fogherty. Who was he, for I have forgotten?'

'The man with the unfortunate dog.'

'Unfortunate, was he?'

'Losing one leg was bad enough but losing two showed he had the wrong disposition.'

'I do, indeed, remember him for when he tried to lift his leg to pee he had forgotten that he was trying to rest on the one that was not there.'

'Used to fall down.'

'That he did, and his pee going up in the air like a fountain and falling back on him. Stank through the town he did.'

'And him once a teacher.'

'You are speaking of Fogherty.'

'I am not speaking of his dog, though he could hardly have done worse.'

'The unfortunate incident.'

'The very one, not that anyone would have known if he'd only thought to draw the curtains. I remember my father saying to me, always be careful to draw the curtains.'

'Good advice for anyone. Certainly for him and her only sixteen.'

'How did the dog lose his legs, for I have forgotten?'

'The IRA.'

'The IRA?'

'They put semtex in a bin thinking the constable passed that way and he …'

'Peed on it'.

'They found his left leg up a tree.'

'But he lost the two.'

'That was Fogherty himself. Did he not forget his key and thought to push the dog through a small window.'

'What was the dog to do? Open the door?'

'He thought there was no reason for both of them to be out in the rain so he pushed him through out of the kindness of his heart, having taken a drink or two on account of the shame, and didn't the dog fall on the television and break its other leg, though Fogherty said the reception was better after that, so it's an ill wind.'

'Oh, it's an ill wind right enough.

'Remember the Atlantic Breeze?'

'Who does not remember that since there was wood enough to build a house if you'd a mind. Great piles of it.'

'Five dead, though.'

'Foreigners to a man, and did I not build a fence from it that would keep out a regiment.'

'And you with your back.'

'I did not have my back then.'

'Is it another drink for you?' asked the barman.

'Are you offering, Michael?'

'I'm closing, unless you are thinking of sleeping here.'

'We only just arrived.'

'That was an hour or so since. Do you have no sense of time?'

'It's infinite, I'm told, or relative, so how would I know how long I've been?'

'So is it another drink?'

'Let's see. Have I had an inheritance? Has the government paid me back my taxes? No, I think not, Michael, so I will have to give your kind offer a miss, though I would have thought that for such regular customers as us you might be willing to offer us one for the road.'

'The road is right outside the door and I dare say you'll be coming through it tonight.'

'We will have to see about that. For the moment I have not quite finished what I have. How about a Jameson's, for I know you have a generous heart?'

Then a miracle occurred for the barman let out a deep sigh, reached behind him for a bottle and set two glasses before them. The men watched as though an angel had descended from above as the glasses were slowly filled to the brim leaving them only with the dilemma of how to drink from them without spilling even a drop.

***

Today, it is a rare summer that a yellow helicopter does not come fluttering over the headland, the rapid thud of its blades tapping the eardrums, to pluck some innocent from the base of the cliff or sometimes halfway up for there is something about holiday makers that makes them reckless. Not that there are many such here for Ballygoran has little to offer besides shrimping nets and whirligigs on sticks to be bought from the post office along with beach balls you can blow up, if you've the puff to do it. They are put outside the door every July and taken in come September and rare is the year that more than half a dozen are sold and one or two of those to people passing through in search of real beaches and cliffs less likely to kill you or a town less likely to fold in on itself when the rain comes down and the streets are bare of everything but mad Peg who, incidentally, is another reason for being on their way.

The reception of television has never been good. Ghostly figures will flit across screens or emerge for a moment from a flurry of electronic snow, so that it depends on the temperature, the wind, leaves on the trees, whether it is possible to see anything at all, though there are days when the sudden clarity will shock those more accustomed to divining images from a speckled mist. 'Did you see his Holiness last night? For it was himself that was bending down and kissing the ground. Do you suppose he has to do that for it is not something I can see myself doing?' 'His Holiness was it? Our Mary thought it was some singer she likes. It is the oak tree that stops us seeing things clear.' But what is television to a place such as this? Is there not a world of nature to admire for those with a mind to turn aside from far away places?

***

Pride of place in the town was the undertakers: Murphy and Murphy. To some it had the sound of a firm of solicitors – and there was one of those to be sure, pin-striped, earnest and, like a certain young lady, charging by the hour – but the Murphys had been burying people as long as anyone could remember. The shop front was on a corner, its plate glass window giving a sight of nothing but a tasteful urn and bunch of plastic flowers. The business, so to speak, was all behind. There was a double door at the rear with a notice on it, screws rusting and bleeding a trickle of brown: 'KEEP CLEAR. TWENTY-FOUR HOUR A DAY FUNERALS.' To strangers it must seem that the dead were queuing up, refusing to wait until day break, so many vampires fearing the dawn. The truth was that there were sometimes families who wanted death removed as fast as possible. More often, though, a trestle would be set up in the front parlour, curtains drawn, and the coffin placed across it, which was good for the trade for all could see the coffin and work out how much it must have cost and how much, therefore, the dead person had been loved.

'Is it an open coffin you would be wanting, Mrs. Sligo? I could clean him up remarkable. You need have no worry for the flowers will mask anything. Would you like a smile on him or would you want him serious? There are those who like a smile. It lightens the mood. If you close it up there are those who will put their beer glasses on it. Then he will go to his rest with terrible stains. Is it the mahogany? It's a matter of taste, really, but it takes a nice shine. Just a day, though, I think, since he had been lying in the field for two.'

At the back, behind the reception area and through what was called 'the place of rest,' where they had copies of magazines like the dentist's surgery, and just as old, was the show room, with coffins leaning against the wall, white silk against dark wood, or crimson catching the light of artificial candles. Here prices would be mumbled discretely and, like sellers of second hand cars, one Murphy or another, for they came by the handful, would judge which price range might be the more appropriate.

Further back was the workroom that would take its regular deliveries like any other store, though here there was no sale or return. The young Mr. Murphy, now eighty or more, the old Mr. Murphy having passed away some time ago – white lacquered with deep blue lining since you ask – wore a suit every day, except when there were funerals. Then he would go to a cupboard and unhook a dress suit of his father's, along with a top hat with black ribbons. There was no joking in the back room. 'I'll have no larking,' he would tell those who came to work for him, some leaving quickly enough when getting a lungful of a deceased. 'And no drinking or smoking either. Would you want that and your own mother lying there? And I want no probing or poking and no parts taken away,' once having to account for a lost finger that someone had thought would be a good joke to play on someone when giving change.

The funeral business was serious and not to be confused with other trades. He had noticed that a rival company in a nearby town had posted an advertisement through people's letter boxes offering two for one in the case of children. 'It was terrible to hear about little Jamie, but I hear his brother is none too well.' In another town someone had started a woodland burial site, hoping to raise the value of his land above the agricultural rate. Such a scattering would not do in Ballygoran where people wanted the blessing of a nearby church rather than the possibility of a Shell garage or a bypass coming along to disturb the rest of the departed.

So, in would come the waxen bodies of the dead, slack-jawed, cold, no longer opinionated, no longer affiliated with mankind, and out would go figures who seemed about to pronounce on the evils of the world or complain about their bunions or the state of the streets. In other words his job, as he understood it, was to make the departed seem less departed, the passed over to pass back at least long enough for a final glance or even, if you held your breath and had no objection to formaldehyde, a final kiss. Then it was off up the hill to the cemetery, the fifteen year old Bentley in first gear, the radiator boiling gently, and Mr. Murphy the younger walking steadily in front of it as the Irish Guards are trained to do the slow march. Then at the cemetery there was the coffin to be slid out and lifted up so the pall bearers, like some graceless centipede, could shuffle forward and into the church where a junior Murphy had been stewarding people to right or left as if this were a wedding and not the end of a man's life.

When the hymns had been sung and the tears run down the faces of those who had steeled themselves not to betray what they felt, it was out to the graveyard and its mound of earth and the sudden awareness that it was to be piled on top of a man who would have to wait for the Second Coming before making his way back up again. Mr. Murphy always carried two packs of tissues, three if he thought the family cared about the dead, and a hip flask in case of necessity. If necessity had not occurred, and once the Bentley was parked and wiped down with a leather cloth, he would drink it down himself, priest-like, seemingly obliged to do such to end the ceremony. There were busy days, however, when there were three funerals and he had some difficulty with the third, but such days were rare for Ballygoran was not large and people had a way of hanging on beyond the point when reason would suggest they should be on their way. Nonetheless, when the underwear business slacked off, and even the butcher had to put much of his stock back into the freezer, against health regulations, the dead obliged him with a steady living and the town with a service on which it could rely.

Mrs Murphy, an over-large woman, judged by the standards of a country in which potatoes have played a major role, had developed a skill at detecting potential customers, though in truth there were none who did not fall into that category. She could sense the cold that would turn to pneumonia, the breathlessness that was the sign of a heart attack in the making. So assiduous was she in what struck many as her scouting expeditions that people would cross the street or cross themselves if they saw her approaching.

In truth, she was not on the best of terms with her husband. The bargain he had supposed to have been struck when she succumbed to him the evening of their engagement, an engagement precipitated by her calculated submission, had not been fulfilled, showing as she did a greater fondness for lemon meringue pie and suet pudding than other satisfactions of the flesh. For his part, he would disappear to Dublin from time to time to 'investigate new stock' and spend a little of the money earned from dead flesh on flesh which showed a more gratifying degree of animation.

'That's a powerful after shave you're wearing, Mr. Murphy,' said Slack Brenda, as she turned back a freshly laundered sheet, she never having smelled embalming fluid before being more used to distinguishing Jameson's from Paddy's. 'Sure, I could grow to like it in time.'

So life and death have ever conducted their conversation, for did Joe Darling in the garage not depend on Murphy and Sons, servicing their Bentley? Did the flower shop not sell floral tributes fertilised by those who themselves once wore a rose as they walked down the aisle where one day they would be carried to their rest? And what would Slack Brenda have done but for regulars such as Mr. Murphy who she could show photos of Kathleen to, the Kathleen who had left one day with a salesman who had creases in his trousers and a bow tie such as should have been a warning in itself. 'Top of the day,' he would say, another warning it seemed to Brenda, and him with two other wives it turned out when at last he was brought to court. 'But I loved them all,' he had told the judge.' 'That you did,' the judge had replied, 'and that is why you will be spending a year or two in prison where the scope for your mischief will not be quite the same.'

***

It was May in Ballygoran and spring was late again, as it had been as long as anyone could remember so that it was difficult to say when it should have arrived. The sheep shivered sullenly in the green folds of fields randomly punctuated with rocks, waiting to be worried by dogs, except what dog would venture so far from the hearth on a day such as this. 'There's nothing more stupid than sheep,' said Eamon O'Brien. 'What can they say but baa. There's nothing like a spring lamb, though with a little mint sauce, don't you think. So I can bear a little stupidity.' Somewhere in the hills is buried a young man shot by republicans except that that was many years since and no one now can recall where he lies or would care to do so if they could. There are a parcel of bodies, after all, scattered over this island chosen by God, more Catholic than the Italians, more Catholic than the Pope, they proudly boasted. And what is faith if it doesn't require a little blood.

There is a tangle of motives in human affairs, Eamon might have thought, when nobody knows his own let alone those of others. Passions rise and passions subside but the facts stand out plain as a tree in a field not felled for fear it contains magic. 'Is anyone without sin?' the Father had asked, staring straight at him, as it seemed, so that he looked down at his feet, his best brown shoes now splattered with mud, or something worse. But are all sins equal, even the taking of a life whatever the cause? The passage of time, though, deadens all. How else do we survive the death of parents? How else does a woman forget the pain of birth? And there you had it. On the one hand we remember century's old slights; on the other we forget what is torture to remember, or so he might have thought if his mind was not primarily upon sheep.

***

Ballygoran boasted little in the way of shops. Besides the butchers, with its bleeding carcasses, and the drapers, with its heavy-duty underwear, there was a co-op, a post office, a fishmongers, greengrocers and a garage which is as much as anyone could require as its citizens assured themselves, though a betting shop might have been a useful addition. The co-op was managed by a round-faced man, on the short-side, at least when compared to his capacious wife. He wore a white shirt with braces and looked like the man in western stores who crouches underneath the counter when the gunmen come to town. In the back store he still had salad cream that dated back to the last days of the war. The concept of a sell-by date had yet to penetrate into this part of rural Ireland. If it was on the shelves it was available for sale even if it should bring back memories of the Relief of Mafeking.

Payments were placed into small leather receptacles attached to looping wires and fired across the interior at the pull of what looked like a lavatory chain. At the other end, in a small compartment set high above a sawdust-scattered floor, his wife removed the money with a twist of the wrist perfected in strangling chickens sold in competition with the butchers.

There were people who knew their co-op numbers better than their wife's birthday, though forgetting either could have serious effects. There was nothing self-service about this shop. Indeed, there was barely anything one might reasonably call service. For the most part the owners ran it for themselves, opening when it caught their fancy. Nor was the word co-operative entirely justified. Once they employed Jamie O'Neill, an altar boy of angelic appearance if diabolic habits. They installed a padlock on the refrigerator to mark his arrival, though he discovered that while it locked the handle it had no effect on the door that could be pulled open with no difficulty. Inside, however, was nothing but a large pair of women's knickers and a tub of double cream. It was an image that stained his mind for many years to come and might account for his decision to go to India in search of himself or, more likely, thought some, to lose himself entirely.

There was a certain hostility between husband or wife, or so it seemed from the vigour with which they would send the leather containers flying across the shop like guided weapons. There were those, though, who read this in a different way, judging by the darting glances they addressed to one another, that this was a way of expressing their passion.

For those who regarded the cost of jars of jam as fixing the universe in place, shopping in the co-op could be metaphysically disturbing. There were no sticky labels, nor bar codes, no indication of any kind as to the cost of a tin of beans or the evaporated milk to be poured over peach halves in sugar syrup for Sunday tea. Instead, prices would be announced by the husband or wife with the finality of a death sentence. Nor was it any use telling friends if a tin of ham had been offered cheaply, for ten minutes later it might cost double. Once they offered bottles of wine cheaply on the grounds that they were old. There were some, though, who took a perverse pleasure in this, seemingly confirming their sense of the world's inconstancy.

The post office was another matter. Here was a place to stand and talk. It was run by a couple from India, or some such place, for no one ever ventured to ask for fear of offence. They spoke in sing song voices that many could not understand but of the intricacies of the postal service they were masters. They understood arcane regulations, knew about weights and sizes, returned forms incorrectly completed with a shake of the head. Behind the counter was a photograph of a street, with a cow amidst a bustle of traffic and a house set back. It had been coloured in by hand. One day, for want of anything to say, Mrs. Oliver-Smyth, one of the Protestants who lived in a large square house on the Dublin Road, asked what place it might be. 'Oh, that is my family home. Do you see the tree outside it?' 'Yes,' replied Mrs. Oliver-Smyth. 'The English hanged my grandfather from that tree.' For her part Mrs. Oliver-Smyth believed herself essentially English, though her family had lived in Ballygoran for several hundred years, devoting themselves with an admirable consistency to displacing their Catholic neighbours and tenants. She therefore received this news as a personal accusation. She was, however, raised to be polite. 'I'm terribly sorry.' 'Oh, no. It is things like this that bring us together.' Mrs. Oliver-Smyth left without the stamps she needed, confused as to what she might have said next.

The garage, meanwhile, was less a garage than a place where various pieces of machinery were randomly arranged around a lean-to workplace. Every now and then a vehicle would enter and occasionally the same vehicle would leave repaired. But that admirable logic was not always respected. Nonetheless, there were an agreeable number of empty oil drums while Michael James and his son, Sam, were to be seen on a fairly regular basis. It was never clear, though, whether this was their business or whether they had some other line of work for which this was a convenient front. Red diesel, it was said, could be bought from them, though not at their garage. Certainly few in the town used their services. It was more those passing motorists whose clutches gave out in the surrounding hills or who never realised the necessity for oil and water, never having lifted the bonnets of their vehicles.

***

It is not that every shop in Ballygoran was staffed by those supplied by Central Casting. The greengrocer was a haven of peace and normality. There is, perhaps, something about cabbages and carrots that discourages the eccentric, though potatoes, of course, are a different matter being charged with a politics that can make them seem incendiary, but radishes and lettuces, tomatoes and plums are blameless. Of course Mr. Beven, the transplanted Welshman who owned the shop, was adept at the usual tricks of the trade, picking the best of the apples and polishing them with a little – well, best not say – and placing them at the front while casually serving the windfalls and spectacularly blemished from the rear, but we all put our best face forward so who is to worry about a little spit.

Mr. Bevan is married to a German woman who had punched his ticket on a train to Heidelberg, a place whose castle museum had once begged Mark Twain to donate his German, it being of a kind never previously encountered. Despite not sharing a language and the fact that he had got a little bored while waiting for the verb, they had fallen in love before the train arrived at its destination, precisely on time, he noted, with a twinge of alarm his father having harboured a hatred for a country with a fixation on trains and invading Belgium. Indeed he had been raised with stories of the war as others would learn of Winnie the Pooh. He remembered being told that after the defeat of Dunkirk, and with invasion imminent, the only plan the British had was to turn the sign posts round the wrong way. The idea was that the Germans would invade, follow the signs, and find themselves back in France. He was not the only one who suspected that the British, metaphorically, had never turned them the right way round again but then the British thrive on defeat and retreats. He remembered his father giving him a history of Britain in which the first chapter was entitled, 'THE RETREAT OF THE ICE AGE.'

His German vocabulary had originally been restricted to the words for 'two beers, please,' 'the same again,' 'and another,' along with 'Bratwurst mit kartoffel salad,' which had led to him having a somewhat restricted diet for the best part of a month before his wife-to-be retired from punching tickets, though she would, from time to time, give him a punch perhaps celebrating the old times. For her part, she was fluent in the English for a whole range of vegetables though still surprised at how short English words are, hardly seeming adequate to an existence requiring that language should fill the gap between hope and disillusionment, a gap not always as wide as one might have hoped.

People gathered in their shop much as they did in the butchers or fish shop, though buying was plainly only an incidental activity. Once a group of women were in a lively conversation by the brussel sprouts while showing no signs of wishing to order.

'You are getting on well,' Evan remarked, he hoped with a slight air of irritation.

'Yes, we've got a lot in common,' one of them remarked.

'Oh,' he said, 'what would that be?'

'We've all got cystitis.'

Somehow conversations seemed to adjust to the setting so that amidst the cabbages and spring onions, the leeks and Swedes, there was an earthy quality as they discussed the elemental and the elements. In the fish shop, with its crushed ice and white marble, death would be a natural topic of conversation but for the sizzling of hot fat, the smell of vinegar and the scattered grit of salt which hinted at illicit pleasures.

'If there's one thing you can say for Brion it is that he makes the best batter,' remarked Mrs. Coyle, who had developed a taste for rock salmon while never quite being sure what it might be.

'It's the beer he puts in it.

'He puts beer in batter?' said her son who had clear ideas where beer belonged and it was assuredly not soaked up in flour and tossed into boiling oil.

'The alcohol all boils off,' added his mother, knowing her son's predilections.

'And what would be the use of that?'

'What would that be?' asked Mrs Coyle, partly to distract him but partly because she could make nothing of what she saw.

'That would be squid,' said Brion who was trying to broaden the tastes of his customers having been on a package holiday to the Costa del Sol where most of the beach front restaurants specialised in the' FULL ENGLISH BREAKFAST' and

'FISH AND CHIPS LIKE MOTHER MADE,' though his own mother had never cooked any such thing being a Protestant for whom fish had Papist overtones.

'Squid, is it?' And what would I do with that?'

'They're big in Spain,' Brion replied, though why he thought that might be a recommendation was hard to say given that being Spanish was no advantage in the eyes of Mrs. Coyle who had a dislike of the European Union which let foreigners flood into the country and take good Irish jobs, though she herself had yet to see any, Ballygoran not being on the lips of many asylum seekers or fellow Europeans come to that.

'Crabs are coming into season,' Brion observed, realising he would have to reduce the price of squid.

For Mrs. Coyle, however, the phrase had overtones of licentiousness so that she did not deign to make a reply, instead saying, 'I'll have a mackerel, without the bones. There's a fly on your salmon.'

'It's how it was caught,' he replied knowing that wit was wasted in the wet fish section.

'Do you remember how we all had to have fish on Friday,' interjected Aileen McBride who it was rumoured had once been young and who had never understood why God would have something against meat that was alright to eat on Easter Sunday.

Brion had a special reason for regretting the end of the tradition, though there were still those who ordered fish on Friday like children bracing themselves for medicine and covering themselves in case the new theologians had maybe got things wrong.

'Can you filet my mackerel,' said Mrs Coyle , 'I got a bone in my throat the other week and had to get it out with a knitting needle. I dropped my stitches as a result.'

This was not the kind of information best shared in a fish shop, though Brion picked up his knife, worn down through slicing through so many of God's creatures, and seemed to contemplate for a moment which had the greater need of filleting.

'Is this fresh,' Mrs. Coyle added, thus further endangering herself.

'They're fresh off the boat,' he replied except that the boat had been Spanish and had delivered its illegal catch in a home port so that the fish had not swum across the sea but spent some time packed in ice in a ship's hold before being off-loaded in Dublin and transported from there in a van that delivered before daybreak in Ballygoran whose own fleet of three fishing boats was doing nothing more than bob up and down beside a quay long since abandoned by the cats that used to wait impatiently for some strange fish to be tossed their way -- no fish being strange to cats – so they could start their day with a fight.

Aileen McBride had never liked the fish shop which had so many dead eyes staring up at her.

'Would you like the head on or off?' Brion asked, as Henry VIII's executioner might have enquired.

Aileen edged towards the door. 'Leave it, for it adds to the flavour.'

Shopping was a principal activity in Ballygoran there otherwise being relatively little to do. It did not necessarily involve buying for a person was not likely to need meat more than once a week and fish rather less often not least because it leaves a smell not always to everyone's taste. The post office was a meeting point for youths who lacked anywhere else to gather, the bolder, for whom death held no terrors, smoking cigarettes as a sign they were no longer young. Every now and then one of them would pass his test and acquire a suspect car from the suspect garage and they would all cram inside and disappear into the countryside. What did they do once they were there beyond throw a few stones and smoking a few more cigarettes? They returned to the post office drawn there, it seemed, by destiny, should destiny have a strange idea of venues.

***

The Almanses had been making ice cream in Ballygoran for thirty years. Their daughter had married a Ballygoran man she had met when he was on a school trip to Catania with the Christian Brothers, whose efforts to keep their pupils from the opposite sex, or even sex of any kind, had for once proved inadequate. Thereafter had followed five years of passionate letters and photographs until at last he was settled as a salesman of ladies underwear which no doubt brought him to the necessity of seeing her once again. He had even sent her a sample of his company's latest model, all under-wired and up-thrusting and separating, words which entered his soul as daffodils had inexplicably entered Wordsworth's. She replied by return, sending him a photograph of herself wearing such. He was on the next boat and train and taxi and so they were engaged and the marriage fixed for St. Ignatius Church, with its effigies of the Son of God in torment, blood pouring down from gaping wounds.

'Who gives this woman?'

'Is me,' said her father.

Her family came over and never left. They were not idle, though. Having been known for their ice cream in Catania, where the heat made ice cream a necessity, so they were quickly in Ballygoran and beyond, where the rain had never stopped anyone from pursuing their desires. Their tutti frutti van would drive up and down the streets playing extracts from Italian opera. 'Your tiny hand is frozen' rang out, drawing children to them, clutching money in clammy hands.

'Gelati,' she would cry. 'You lika the sprinkle? Is made from cows.'

The priest who presided over their ceremony was a confused man. There were moments when young boys seemed to shine with life, soft and desirable, but there were others when his secret desires took another direction entirely, the church having thrown his compass entirely out. His magnetic north seemed to shift with each full moon. He would sit each night listening to *La Bohème*, unsure whether it was Mimi or Musetta he loved, before remembering it could be neither. He dabbed at his tears with tissues he ordered in bulk for not a night went by without him crying over the death of a young woman who was no better than she ought to be but quite good enough for him had he not made certain promises. Love of God, he had been told, had replaced love of women, that being a sacrifice required of those who would devote themselves to a life of service. Which woman would go to a doctor, he had been asked, if she assumed he was a man as other men and hence not to be trusted? And yet at the university, where he had taken a course, had the medics not been a by-word for lasciviousness and had God really given men feelings only for them to denied? Besides, who could martial defences against such music, even when he heard it chiming out from an ice cream van with a chocolate flake sticking up?

He had confessed to doubts and was sent to a man who was on-call for doubters, with a beeper clipped to his soutane. Doubt, he was told, is the essence of faith for without doubt how could faith have a definition. The Jesuits, he thought, had earned their reputation. He had, though, studied with the Christian Brothers, and had the bruises to prove it. Stray an inch and they would shove you back into line. Doubt to them was like an invitation to do battle. 'You're having doubts, are you? You see this ruler? It is twelve inches long and made of beech wood. A hard wood, beech. You see where the edge is made of lead. A heavy metal, lead. If you're having doubts it would be best for you to hold your hand out, for do I not have the ultimate cure for that?'

But you heard things about them that made you doubt. Nonetheless, he was required to be obedient, to ask young couples if they were using contraception. Who in their right mind would ask anyone such a question? Would you go to a cocktail party, he enquired of himself, as the music soared in his soul, and who himself had never been to such, and introduce yourself to someone by asking what his view of johnnies might be? 'Ah, father, I'm glad you asked me that question, for I was just thinking of having a sly one and had forgotten for the moment the teachings of the church. Do you have one about you by any chance, for I've used up the gross I bought in a godless England?'

Then a duet would sweep him away. Did he suppose that Mimi or Musetta would use such? Well, he admitted, perhaps they would seeing who they were, but did love not conquer all? Was that not what Ovid said? He had learned his Latin for something, after all, the Church having abandoned it under the illusion that people would rather understand what was being said. For himself, he thought it would be rather better if they did not. What were they looking for but mystery? What was he looking for but love? And yet he had to bless young couples knowing that they would be off on their honeymoon and everybody knew what that meant. 'I hope you don't have your johnnies with you?' he felt tempted to shout after the departing car, tin cans jumping up and down behind it reminding them of the true metal of their love.

'Tell me the nature of your doubt,' asked the man with the beeper, which had already gone off twice since they began their conversation. 'Do you doubt the existence of God?' 'No, I do not.' 'There, then,' he replied, 'you see you have no doubts after all.' 'It is the teachings of the Church,' he replied. 'Oh that,' said the man, checking his watch. 'Sure, you can take a view of that.' 'And what about infallibility?' 'Infallibility, is it? Well there's infallible and then there's infallible, is that not so?' 'Surely infallible is infallible.' He now noticed a certain irritation in his mentor, even as the beeper announced another doubter whose doubt was the evidence for faith. 'Have you tried speaking to your bishop?' 'They've not appointed the new one,' he replied, 'the other is still on trial.'

***

There is, did I say, a deal of rain hereabouts. Why else would the country clothe itself in green moss and rich grass? Why else would the crops lay close to the ground, turning black at last? And what else would lubricate the sign above the Shamrock pub, for certainly no lubricant approved by mechanics had ever been applied to its screeching sign? 'Rain is God's tears,' the children were told, 'for the sinners who challenge God's laws.' 'There must be many of those here, then, father,' said Mickey Rourke, fourteen years old and already lost to the church, his parents having promised him to it in return for good fortune when first he was born, and look what they got. 'There are, indeed,' said the priest, hitting him neatly with his missal, sharp-edged with electro plated nickel silver. It had been given to him by his predecessor and its uses explained.

There are those who are mystified by the love some nuns and priests have for well regulated violence when really it is no more than an extension of their faith. Were we not given feelings so they might be conquered? Were we not required to discipline the wayward? 'Come here, Margaret Ellen. Was that a note I saw you passing?' 'It was, Sister.' 'And had I not told you there was to be none such in my class.' 'You did, Sister Mary.' 'And what did this note say, Margaret Ellen.' 'It was about someone, sister.' 'And would that someone be a boy?' 'It would, Sister,' 'And would you be kind enough to fetch the cane.' 'Yes, sister.' 'Is that the cane I would be wanting.' 'No, Sister,' 'No, it would not. It is the other one I would be wanting, as you well know Margaret Ellen. Would you fetch the other and then hold out your hand.' And so she did, in front of the class. She held it out as she did at the mass and was to believe that a similar grace would result from doing so. For what is a stinging hand and livid bruise beside salvation? And is the bruise not a reminder of the darkness of her ways? 'Thank you Sister Mary.' 'Return to your seat Margaret Ellen and fetch me the note for I have need to pass it to the Father who will have a deal to say to the person you name in it.' 'I swallowed it, Sister.' 'You swallowed it child?' 'It was only small Sister.' 'It will be the other hand, will it not?' 'It will Sister.' 'And you will confess your willfulness and lies at confession, will you not?' 'That I will Sister. Should I mention the cane do you think?'

At least the rain, it was said, kept the girls from the fields, where the first warm thrust of the sun into dark earth would stir up passions and send them out beyond the town's edge -- skirts too short and a look in their eyes -- to lie in the long grass, with bees bouncing up and down on invisible threads, and damsel flies mating turquoise in mid-air, as though all they were doing was awaiting the call, as in truth, they were, as all do for why else are we born but to mate and die.

***

Some are born into an ordered life, in which parents exist to guide and direct, praise and comfort. At least so the nuns had suggested. But the nuns were liable to believe that legs could be restored if you could only hop as far as Lourdes and that young girls longed for nothing so much as running up and down in winter with hockey sticks, white shirts tucked neatly in navy blue knickers that would not have inflamed the lust of a man released from a desert island after twenty years of contemplating ice cold stout and young women with a desire only to divest themselves. 'Knickers, girls,' Sister Marie would call into the cold air, her breath a cloud of lavender mist from the lozenges she sucked, her tongue an ominous purple, 'knickers,' for sometimes elastic slackened from having been washed a few times too many and scandal threatened.

Bridget O'Reilly's parents were of a different breed. They paid her no mind, almost surprised to discover her in their home as they waged battles with one another that would have been the envy of military tacticians. They would ambush one another, jump out with a saucepan or even half a brick. They would plot whole campaigns and then negotiate a truce as they took themselves to the bar, returning later to disgust their daughter with their cries of ecstasy or pain. The next day battle would recommence, an echo, perhaps, of the hundred years war that had once swept across a continent. So she brought herself up and learned to stand on her own feet, unlike the lepers of whom she used to dream

Her father had only one hand (hence, perhaps, her dream), which gave her mother an advantage and made him feel his assaults were not without their fairness, his injury having levelled the playing field as it were. He had lost it in the cause being a dedicated IRA man if also an inept one. The explosion had destroyed the kitchen units that had only just been installed, along with a bedpan bequeathed to his wife by a forebear before he left for America when the potatoes failed. Living on a battlefield, however, had bred in their daughter an independent mind along with the kind of reflexes necessary to avoid domestic appliances flying across the room. As a result she was older than her years not least because her parents were more like children than was she.

***

Mrs. Connell was not the only one to attend the O'Connors' séances. In one sense it did not quite accord with the Catholicism that had been spliced into their DNA but it was a religion that had a certain fascination with the dead and life everlasting so who was to say that a quick chat or two might not be welcome to those on the other side for, as Maureen McDowd, twice-widowed without being enriched, remarked, 'everlasting life must seem a little on the long side.' Did the Church itself not believe in exorcism and spirits? Indeed, in living memory there had been an exorcism when a spirit had possessed a pig, 'the spirit leaving by its back end,' observed its owner, 'for certainly something did.'

'Would you like a little raspberry jam on your scone?' asked Mrs. O'Connor, ever hopeful, before commanding 'Cyril, the drapes.'

Cyril O'Connor rarely spoke. He had married a young woman who had seemed obliging but swiftly obliged him to be disabused of this conviction.

'Sit around the table, ladies,' she said before, at the word 'Cyril,' he leapt forward to re-arrange the chairs.

'You must understand that the departed are not always within earshot when we call and there are times when the Chief is in communion with others.'

'Communion,' thought Mary Fallon, who in truth thought the worst of everyone.

'We will lower the lights,' we being Cyril.

'Lower?' thought Mary, doubting it could be much darker what with the new light bulbs that saved energy at the expense of anything approaching illumination, and velvet curtains reminiscent of theatre.

They sat for a while, Maureen McDowell covering the sound of a fart by coughing before being shushed by Mrs O'Connor who placed her hands to her head and frowned. The air smelled fecund.

'Are you there, Chief?' she called in a low voice, though a whisper hardly seemed right, as it appeared to Mary, if you were summoning someone across the void.

'I am here,' replied the Chief in a markedly Irish accent of a kind that might possibly have been common on the Great Plains but probably not, Mary was thinking, among the Arapahos, and not with a suspicious falsetto. 'What do you require?'

What was required, it turned out, was a coin or two – 'Not too much, not too little – Mrs. O'Connor directed, for the moment freed by the Chief to conduct the necessary financial arrangements in her own voice.

Cecil sneezed and Mrs. O'Connor threw a shoe at him. 'We must be careful of infection,' she observed, not unreasonably given that the Plains Indians had come close to being wiped out by the small pox with which the white man had thoughtfully seeded the blankets given to them, but rather less reasonably when it came to the fact that this Indian was not likely to succumb to the common cold as an immaterial being deploying the larynx of a woman whose breath smelt faintly of sherry laced with mouthwash.

'Does anyone have a question to ask the Chief?' she asked, aware that people need a return on their investment.

'On the matter of my husband's savings book,' began Mrs. Connell.

'He cannot help with that. He has said there is a mist when he tries to enter your house. Did something happen there that is blocking his vision?'

'The septic tank leaks.'

'Of a spiritual kind. An argument, perhaps? A disturbance in the ether?

'Just the septic tank. Get the Chief to have a word with him, for I've looked everywhere.'

Mary McDowell kept her peace, knowing precisely where it was, having cashed it with him on his visit to the farmer's fair in County Claire where they had shared not only his savings but his bed, country fairs being notorious for stirring the senses. The Big Chief must have been looking the other way, however, for he did no more than say 'something good is coming your way,' then, perhaps realising he was turning into a gypsy, added, 'I am summoned.'

'Could he stay until half past for I'm not being picked up until then. And I was wanting to ask him what it was like on the other side. Do they still have their bodies and do they wear clothes at all?'

A certain renewed interest was evident as they leaned forward. Even Cecil seemed to stir. Mrs O'Connor paused unsure of the propriety of asking questions of this kind or perhaps of formulating an answer that would satisfy. Finally, the Chief replied, 'all is as you would expect. We are not here for long. After a while we are summoned. There is no funny stuff.'

'Funny stuff,' thought Mary, 'now that's not a phrase you would expect from a man who had been waiting to be summoned for a hundred and fifty years and hunted for buffalo.'

'Cecil, the lights,' she said, first in the voice of the Big Chief and then in her own. 'He has had to go but promises to return. We are not the only ones who look for the dead through the smoke.'

'Too true,' thought Mary McDowell, who had seen more than one go to their graves in Murphy's hearse amidst a cloud of smoke generated from the agricultural diesel.

***

Above the town, in a field shaped by irregular stone walls interleaved with sprouting tufts of grass and purple wallflowers, is an orchard, if it any longer deserves the name for no one tends the trees or collects the fruit. Half a dozen brown-tinged and arthritic branches, scattered with leaves that curl in on themselves, reach out towards a sky so broken with cloud that it seems incomplete. Most years it bears little but what seem like aborted and cancerous oak apples that rot as they grow, turning wattled brown then speckled black, never reaching full size. This year, though, the branches are heavy with fruit, a scarlet abundance, memory, perhaps, having jolted them into life. None, however, come to harvest them for why should they who had been disappointed for so long. Broken promises breed distrust and this is a country of broken promises.

So, one by one, they unsnap themselves and fall onto the unkempt grass or the slurry of other apples reduced to pulp by wasps that tunnel in and out and lie replete. There is a smell in the air of fermentation though nothing but these wasps gain the benefit or pay the price.

What to make of the un-milked cow, the uncut wheat, blackberries too ensnared by their brambles for a reaching hand. What to make of the ocean never breached by the hull of a boat, never open to a trailing finger? Where is meaning born and what to make, one day, when the last of us have gone, victims of hubris or neglect, of a planet bereft of those who once turned mere fact into coherence? There are, surely, a billion creatures that swim eyeless in the deeps and others that crawl and mate and die in unvisited forests, never seen by man. What is their purpose if they exist only in God's eye, or is that the answer? Never a sparrow falls. Yet what if there is none? On a clear night the sky is a smear of stars and, beyond what is visible, a billion others and on and on with a gathering speed. No human eye nor any other but God's has seen them nor ever will. But what if God be dead? What if his hand cannot reach the blackberry or gather the apple or gift us the meaning we crave? What purpose then to these creatures where no light reaches and there is no sound to be heard, nor has been since the beginning of time.

There is in truth a reason for the neglect of the orchard that goes beyond simple disappointment, an explanation in the eyes of some for the blight that descended more years than not. It was a hundred and fifty years and more since a body was found hanging there, one shoe off, swinging in the wind as regular as a pendulum on a clock. He had betrayed thrice over: a girl, a faith and an idea. Perhaps two and he would have lived with denial but three was clearly more than he could bear. A pregnant girl was one thing, not uncommon and a sin of the flesh. Abandoning the church was what others had done seeing that it could do so little when there was need, but the third was not to be tolerated for he had turned informer for his own protection discovering it was no protection at all. When they found him there were none would offer to cut him down until the priest himself did it in dead of night, his horse picking its way up over the flat stones and seared grass, with the clouds blotting out the moon, returning with the dead weight of a man who had gone astray.

He could not be buried in the churchyard, though many were being buried at that time of starvation. Nor did the priest ever tell where he was laid for fear there would be those who would dig him up as a warning, should more warning be required than him swinging in the wind, one eye pecked out. Nor were they more gentle with the girl he wronged thinking she must have had a hand in what he did. She was shown the road, with nowhere to go except to another man should she find such along a path where all were in despair or dying or moving on.

It was a full crop of apples that year but no one reached out for their sharp sweetness or stooped down to the ground, and though time would pass and memories fade there are still plenty who will never take the path the priest had taken, for were not apples the cause of sin, nice though they are, sharp on the tongue. And is there not a curse on a place where a man had chosen to die, a sin against God following sins against man?

It was many decades later that his poetry was found and published under a different name in a volume bound in green cloth, but you could smell the death beneath the words, the sorrow in the celebration. And the last were of a girl who was more than a girl being the spirit of all he embraced. Yet there was sadness, too, and a desperation sunk beneath the words, filling the white spaces, fracturing the rhythm. Those who knew nothing of his supposed treachery could feel the disturbance without understanding what its cause might be. Yet it was this gave his poetry its disturbing power, its mystery.

Who would gather his poems up and think to offer them anew, who would wish to see them rescued from something more than obscurity, than a woman abandoned by death, a woman once loved, a woman widowed who was never married and had then been no more than a child? For the young girl who had been set on a road to nowhere had arrived somewhere and built a life, drawn back, finally, when age wrinkled her skin and gifted her the past anew even as the present passed her by. She had visited the orchard visited by none others.

Her child, though, had died, in a village not so far away, mourned only by the one who bore him. It was the name of that child that was inscribed on the white page of the book with a green cloth cover and that came to be treated with some reverence as time passed, not least because nothing was known of the man who had written such poems beyond the fact that a woman had discovered them and refused to speak of her own past or his. She is buried now in the cemetery with a line of his verse cut deep in the grey stone of her grave: 'Listen for me in the wind, for the wind is all there is of me.' The grass is long and seldom cut. There is no fruit in the cemetery, only a holly tree that every Christmas is covered with berries like the splatter of blood.

**

'Old stories are the best,' said Sarah, who knew no new ones.

'They're not,' replied O'Shaunghessy, his eyes red-rimmed from a Guinness or two too many, though that was not a concept he could acknowledge. 'They're just worn thin with the telling. You can see straight through them.'

They looked out at the rain, now streaming down the barroom window like the tears of saints dropped from the canon.

'Shall we have another?'

'That would be a swell idea, except that I spent my last coins putting them on a dead man's eyes.'

'You who are known for taking them off?' she replied, dipping into her bag.

It would take an age, he knew, for her to find anything in there who kept all she owned, as far as he could see, in that great leather stomach of a thing, cut, he assumed, from the living body of her long-dead daughter's favourite cat for it was covered with a kind of mildewed fur. He watched. There was time enough, what with the rain and there being nothing at all to do for one such as he with no one to support him but a wife who believed in sacrifice.

'Ah, she cried,' like someone spotting a shipwreck and calculating what might be had. It was not money she had found, however, but an old photograph of a man she had once loved and who had committed suicide, as a result, O'Shaunghessy presumed, having been told the story a time or two.

'You would not know who this is,' she said with an assurance.

'Indeed I would. It is a picture of a poor man who might have been saved if he had the price of a pint. And if there is no money to be found we had better nurse what we have or Murphy will be throwing us out.'

'Him?' Sarah replied. 'I am the equal of two of him,' as, indeed, she was for had O'Shaunghessy not witnessed her lay him out from behind with a half-full bottle of imported lager. But since it was from behind, Murphy the barman, first cousin to the undertaker, never knew who had sent him to the Hospital of the Two Miracles in hope of a third.

'I have it,' she cried, and to his surprise flourished a note. 'I had had it in mind to buy some flowers for my sister's grave. But now I come to think of it she suffered terrible from hay fever and never liked living things, her husband especially. So we should drink her health.'

'Her health?' queried O'Shaunghnessy, in truth ready to drink to anything at any time but still a little puzzled about drinking to the health of the dead. 'Mine's the usual,' he added, in case she felt obliged to enter into a metaphysical discussion.

'Murphy,' she cried. 'We are in need of drink.'

'You're in need of a kick up the arse,' he replied, so that it occurred to her that perhaps he had seen her reflected in the bar room mirror when she felt obliged to take exception to his remarks.

'I've only enough for the drink,' she cackled, the jokes she liked best being her own.

To the surprise of all, the rain had passed, but it had achieved what it set out to do.

'I would venture out,' she said, 'but you never know when it will begin again.'

And there, O'Shaunghessy felt, was his own philosophy. If it doesn't get you this time it will the next.

The door swung open and in stepped a woman of a certain age, holding herself erect with careful dignity. She held an umbrella that had blown inside out and was plainly perplexed at how she should be holding such a strange object. After a moment or two she dropped it by the door and walked a shade unevenly to the bar, perching her not inconsiderable backside on the peeling crimson plastic of the stool. Water traced down from her black-slicked hair, dropping from her nose as one suffering from a winter cold. 'Ah, and that's a relief,' she said to the world at large. 'My corns are killing me. It's the rain.' She looked across at the two companions and smiled amiably, if also somewhat crookedly. 'Sarah,' she said, nodding like the plastic dog in the back of the Monsignor's Morris Minor.

'Theresa,' replied her friend, carefully sliding her change from the table and into her bag lest she be required to stand treat.

'Is there such a thing in this town as a summer? Is that drinking you are?'

'No, we were wondering if you might be closing the door for there is a draft that's freezing the bones of me.'

'It'll blow closed on its own,' she replied, who was entirely familiar with a place that was more like home than her home, which was comfortable enough but lacked the company of those who might buy her a drink. The door obliged, shaking the bottles on the shelves.

'It's days like this when I miss my Seamus,' she offered to those for whom sympathy was not normally on the agenda.

'Him that was a prize fighter in the circus?'

'It was not a circus entirely, more of an entertainment. Did they not have an exhibition of the Saviour's nail clippings in one tent and a two-headed baby in another. That's not something you see every day. It was educational,' evidently an expansive term to one such as herself who had never been to school beyond the age of ten.

'He was hurt was he not,' said Shaughnessy, who in truth was not interested but thought that attention might be rewarded with a round.

'More like dead, despite the Holy relics being so close by. Are we drinking?'

Rhetorical questions of that kind were familiar in the Shamrock and treated as such.

'Did I not see some coins on the counter when I came in?' she asked, though plainly again the question anticipated no answer.

'Were you left something when he died on you?'

'There was no insurance since his job was to be hit about every day and he left nothing but his boxing shorts. The gloves were not even his own.'

'How would they have got the toe nail clippings do you suppose?'

'Sure there are parts of Him scattered across most of the world.'

'Was it the disciples maybe wanting a little bit of him?'

'And what happened at the Resurrection? Do you suppose he was entire or was he missing parts here and there?' asked Sarah.

'I'll have a half pint of Guinness if you please,' Theresa announced, reaching under a coat that had seen better times no matter how bad the present might be judged to be.

Theresa squinted at her one-time friend, trying to imagine her as she had been when they were at school. How short a time ago that was, she thought as she tilted her head and allowed the cold blackness to flow down her throat, how short a time since the two of them had smoked cigarettes and bicycled with two boys into the nearby wood, separating then, only to return and compare notes. 'He didn't.' 'He did.' 'You're lying.' 'May I hope to die.' 'If he did you will.' What was it happened to time? Back then everything was waiting, waiting to become something else, the tadpole a frog, the chrysalis a butterfly. 'When you're grown up, young lady.' Ah, but when would that be? So much promised. So long to wait. Then it was done and it was as though the world tipped on end and everything began to speed up as you slid towards the grave. Meanwhile here they both were, in a familiar bar, and the years had collapsed on themselves like a horse at the knacker's yard hit with a sledge hammer, and did she look as bad as Sarah? In the mirror each day she hardly seemed to change. The same crooked smile, the same twinkle Daniel Michaels had told her she had that day by the lake when she had gone further than she should but not as far as she did the next day.

'And what do you think, O'Shaunghessy, am I still what I was?'

Not having been inside her mind and hence following her thoughts these many minutes he was a little thrown at first except that, knowing women as he did, he felt safe in saying 'as beautiful as ever,' watching the while to see if there was change enough for another half pint.

Even so, a tear began to work its way down the channels carved deep in her face by disappointment and its opposite, until she wiped it away with the back of a hand that smelt of fish, she having secured some cod in the pocket of her coat where it would still be in three day's time. 'To hell with it,' she said, staring not at him but her own regretted past.

'To hell with it,' he replied, thinking it a toast perhaps. Certainly he raised his nearly empty glass and attempted a smile who had forgotten how that was done these many years. But had he not been young once and chased butterflies, throwing his cap on them, wondering at the golden dust that shone on his hand as he released them to jerk fitfully in the sun? Where now the butterflies and where the sun that had bathed his youth?

***

The girls, scrubbed clean and resentful, were the subject of continual exhortation. They were told of the infinite pleasures of being immured inside a closed order, or lending a hand in leper colonies, hands, as they gathered, being in short supply there. They were urged to shun the world, the very one they were most concerned to join. Be-whiskered women, whose breathe smelled of rotting flesh which, it was said, could remove stubborn stains, would warn them against boys who wished to get close to them as assuredly they would not wish to come down wind of the nuns who offered the advice. Boys had only one thing on their minds, they were told, though what that thing was they would discuss in the toilets while smoking cigarettes stolen by Mary Magdalene Fitzgerald O'Keefe who would undertake, for a price, to obtain whatever they might have it in mind to have. She had even secured a contraceptive, though none could guess how it worked, this being a product that was not merely sinful and forbidden but scarce on an island committed to denying reality. They all stared at it for some time, unsure what it might be or how to activate it, thinking, perhaps, it required batteries that had not been supplied. 'It stops babies,' Mary Magdalene pronounced, seemingly declaring a fundamental law of physics. 'Doing what?' asked Bridget Riley.

***

Colleen Mc Bride had what others might call an independent spirit but which the Sisters regarded as a stubborn will that needed to be broken for the good of her own soul. Their fear was that she might form an alliance with Bridget Riley for then the army of the ungodly might assume awesome size. Colleen, after all, had once been caught with a boy when she should have been at netball practice, a game which was surely specifically designed to use up energy that might otherwise be recklessly deployed. Nor was that the only sin of which Colleen was guilty. For she was discovered wearing knickers of a terrible brevity, having found them at Chez Moi, in nearby Abbey Glen, a store whose underwear was never pink or of industrial strength. It dealt in wispy nothings, usually sold to travelling salesmen who imagined that movement alone would absolve them of their sins. 'What size would the young lady be,' enquired Eileen Evans, of mixed Irish and Welsh stock who had managed to combine the worst aspects of each nation being dangerously passionate and irritatingly insinuating. And they, in their forties, would blush and buy as soon as possible, found out, as they assumed, in their lechery.

The school rules were very clear about the garments pupils could wear. 'Modesty,' observed the Mother Superior, is next to godliness.' 'I thought that was cleanliness,' observed Tracy, daughter of a convert and hence bearing a name that no saint had as yet assumed. 'And cleanliness,' added the Mother Superior. You are to be brides of Christ.' To young women dressed in grey gymslips, a pale blue shirt and dark blue tie, it seemed unlikely they would be brides of anyone let alone someone who had already been dead for two thousand years.

Nor, in truth, had Colleen just bought the one garment. Her mother, who was occasionally, and somewhat mysteriously, in funds, would give her a banknote from time to time, with a flourish of her wrist seemingly inviting her to indulge her every whim, and

Colleen did. But what was the purpose of possessing such clothes if she never wore them so that she took special pleasure in slipping them on under her navy blue knickers or beneath the pale blue shirt? Except that one day she had forgotten that just beneath a prosaic surface she was flaunting sin and undressed ready for gym.

'And what is this, Colleen McBride.'

'It is my underclothes, sister.'

'That I can see for myself. But what are these?'

She hooked the supple willow cane in the top of an irreproachably voluminous and elasticated pair of knickers and pulled down, and there, with a label sticking up bearing the words, 'Nuits de Paris,' she exposed the black shiny silk of the panties Colleen had brought from the nearby Sodom.

'And what is the explanation for this?

'I liked them, sister.'

'Liked? And how much would they cost?

Colleen made no reply.

'Do you know how many lepers they would heal?'

At this, Colleen genuinely felt baffled. Quite how her panties could cure the sick was beyond her. Did the church, perhaps, ship container loads out to Africa to grateful sufferers who would put them on and regain their limbs.'

'Such garments are designed to enflame.'

'Enflame, sister? I think they've been treated.'

The Sister tried another tack. 'They'll have been made by some children in China who will have had no breakfast and have to sew labels on all day long so they go blind.'

'Do they do it by touch, then, Sister?'

'Touch?'

'Being blind. And besides, it says they are made in France.'

'France? France? Say no more, child. The French are...' She searched for a word that could be used in front of a child, even one so easily corrupted. 'Different.'

'Is that not where Lourdes is, Sister?'

'I'm thinking the Devil is in you, Colleen McBride. Lourdes is where the sick are cured and there are more of those in France than here.'

***

Ah, but he was a brave lad, Miss Heaney said to herself, stooping to put another shovel of coal on the fire. 'Mostly dust,' she muttered angrily. 'Villains.' She settled herself with a shawl about her though it was May and the mists had not yet come down. 'Him standing there,' she said, speaking aloud, for she had long since ceased to know the difference between what was in her head and what was said, living alone these many years with no one to talk to but herself and God and since He had not had the courtesy to reply she had not spoken to Him these many years. She did not go to church. 'I will not go,' she told the young priest, his bright smile not yet collapsed from the burden of sin, his own and that of others. He knew nothing of her past and felt it his duty, no doubt, to reel her in like a fish picked from the depths to lie gasping on the ship's deck of redemption. Besides, what would people make of her turning her back on the church? Such defections can be catching. Give him his due, he tried again only to have the door slammed so hard that brick dust sifted down anointing him.

'What will we do today,' she asked herself, knowing the answer for what did she ever do but make herself fresh tea every hour and write notes to herself in coloured pencils. NO MILK she wrote in blue capitals, for had the milkman not left a pint she did not need that had gone sour and she would not be paying for that she told him. Take it away. Then another: 'CAT,' it said, and then below, 'KILL MOUSE.' She put it down where her cat could read it when it woke at last, for it never seemed to do anything but sleep and sick up hair. And every hour the clock in the hallway struck and she went out to look at it suspecting it might be leading her astray. WIND, she wrote, then paused for she could no longer remember if winding a clock was written in the same way as the wind that blows. Language was a snare and delusion, which was why she wrote her words so large as if she was shouting out, while expecting no reply.

It is time, she thought, lifting the curtain to see if it was raining, and in the fold she detected a touch of yellow and black for a wasp had decided it was time to sleep the winter away and had failed to respond to its inner alarm. She reached up and took the fold in both hands, pressing them together so that there was a popping sound. When she released the pressure the creature hung for a moment, retained by its own ooze, then it dropped and she kicked it under the chair for she had to be leaving now. Out she went in her sensible shoes, in truth having no other kind, and made her way up the hill, looking down afraid, perhaps, she might be required to greet another on her pilgrimage.

It was harder work than it had been when she started out. 'Twenty years,' she said, stopping for a moment for her breath to catch up with her. Then she was off again, clutching a shawl across her throat, no longer smooth as milk on satin, withered now but swan graceful. And then at last she was at the gate where weddings and funerals took place, each oblivious of the irony. She lifted the latch, avoiding the puddle that had been there longer than anyone could remember, before closing the gate behind her.

Her eyesight was going but she could have made her way there if her eyes had been cloudy white for she followed more than a path. She was drawn by feelings that began to flare again the closer she came to where he lay. Then she was beside him and kneeling down to trace his name with her fingers, thick at the joints and twisted now but once so subtle on the piano, gliding back and forth, speaking poetry as they did. The letters were cut in sharp and the wind and rain had yet to do their work, those and the lichen that blossomed rust red and stippled green on other stones. It was his name she traced first and then the year of his death, which was the year of hers, though she lived on for no reason They were twenty-one together, having been no more than two days separated when they came into the world. And she had seen him broken from the accident, his neck awry and his eye out, though two days later at the wake he seemed as perfect as he had ever been.

There were no tears left for she had spent her inheritance of those, but she whispered so that only he could have heard. Then she rose and turned where she could glimpse the sea, grey with remorse for had it not smashed him on the rocks who was only out for the day before coming back to her arms so they could lie together whatever the world might say. It was to be forever, except that forever was gone. It was not until the shadows lengthened and the first prickle of a star appeared in the eastern sky that she rose at last and made her way back down the hill and into her room where the cat still lay asleep with the note beside it. The fire was burned down and she lit it again before writing her last note of the day. She chose a red crayon and a piece of paper as white as the spring moon. 'COME BACK,' she wrote, and then stared at the words until she could see no more and the ashes faded to black.

***

Mothers wish for their daughters to become nuns and their sons priests, human sacrifices having always proved popular with the faithful. It was thus with an excess of pride, surely not a deadly sin, that she could never stop talking of her Mary who was, she declared in the butcher's shop even as he pushed some corrugated tripe into her bag, 'gone to save the heathen.'

'That would be the English,' observed Mrs. Connelly who had been there once and was still recovering from the shock. 'They have advertisements there,' she had explained in a hushed voice, 'that show men and women in their underwear,' not unreasonably you might think given that this was what they were selling.

'Not at all, for she is in Africa with the pigmies.'

'The little people?' queried Mrs. Connelly whose mind was straying in the direction of leprechauns.

'Certainly, though she had a terrible time finding them at first what with them tending to be on the short side, though they have bones in their noses I believe.'

'Bones, is it?' replied Mrs. Connelly, remembering that she had meant to ask the butcher if he had any for her dog.

'She had the calling. God spoke to her.'

'And did he say find yourself some people on the short side for we've got enough of the other kind.'

Mrs. O'Shaughnessy looked at her, suspecting she was being mocked perhaps. 'They live in the jungle. I don't think they have much light. That would be why they are short. It is the same as trees. God makes all kinds,'

'He does, indeed,' Mrs. Connelly was tempted to say but Mrs O'Shaughnessy was in her bridge club and usually brought the cakes. 'Stop me if I'm wrong but was not Mary on the short side herself and a little on the chubby side?'

'It was the glands.'

'Glands, had she? Still I prefer nuns with something on them. The thin ones can be vicious in my experience.'

'You are thinking of Sister Bernadette.'

'Her and the other one, for they would hunt in pairs those two.'

'Mary is a gentle one. She never said a word while she was having her tonsils out.'

Mrs. Connolly looked at her a little strangely before asking, 'Do they have black nuns, do you suppose? Surely it would be difficult to see them in poor light.'

'She had to have injections. Every coloured fever you ever heard of, and stuff to kill the mosquitoes.'

'And alligators.'

'Alligators?'

'Wild animals and such, though they probably couldn't see the black ones.'

'She never liked snakes.'

'Sure we have none of them here. Haven't we St. Patrick to thank for that?'

'She never liked them on principle. I think the Garden of Eden did it for her.'

***

As the dawn approached so the stars faded. A shimmer of pink light and they closed their eyes on a sky swiftly turning the colour of an abalone shell. The ground seemed liquid, flowing in an onshore breeze, undulating gently. Colleen McBride stood entranced, not understanding at first what she saw, only that something was happening she could not understand. But, then, Colleen McBride was in love and therefore likely to see the world at a tilt. And was he worthy of her? Yes, he was but never realised such. He was the son of the organist at St. Brides, and hence the butt of too many jokes to make his young life comfortable. Nonetheless, he survived their laughter for his heart was full of music and left no room for their crude assaults.

Before the first breath of light had appeared she had lain back in the damp grass and stared up at the smother of stars, feeling her soul sucked up by time. 'Millions and millions and millions and millions,' she had whispered to herself imagining it, perhaps, a secret to be shared by none. 'And no end to it all.' At that she felt a shudder of wonder, she being alone on a hillside on no more than a speck of dust. 'And is there God up there?' she asked herself, afraid even to ask the question for did it not imply doubt and was doubt not a sin. And if He is, and created all this, then why would He think of her and not those living on the countless worlds circling countless suns. She was scaring herself to see if she would be scared and was so now, the hollow call of an owl echoing around her and the whisper of wings as a shadow blotted out a handful of stars. There is no contemplating the night sky, it seems, without wonder rimed around with terror. She closed her eyes.

What was she doing so early in the day? She had risen to tend two cows, stirring in the barn, warm and needy as she was cold and feeling bereft, though of what she could not have said.

It was then that She appeared. One moment Colleen was alone on a hillside, with the first opalescent glow of dawn, the next she was watching as a figure seemed to distil out of the air, enfolded in a simple robe if also in mystery.

She scrambled to her feet, heart racing. Who would be here at such a time? For even if it was a woman, who she could make out as even now a cuticle of sun cut the distant horizon, where had she sprung from with such suddenness? Perhaps she had lost her way and sought no more than directions, but the Holy Virgin would have no need of that, she thought, understanding in the instant who it was who stood with such stillness, Her face in darkness even as Her robes flared with light, the ground beneath her feet flowing and shining like a multitude of diamonds crushed and blown on the morning breeze.

How long she stood thus she could not say either then or later. No words were spoken and yet meaning seemed to spill into the soul of Colleen McBride who before had thought of boys and the dance that was planned and the poetry of things. When she had first appeared the Virgin might have been no more than a trick of the night, a shadow recast into familiar form. Had she not been in fear of the shadows she saw at night and of sounds from the cellar where nothing was kept except coal and an old tin bath? Now, though, with the stars faded and a first hint of blue, there could be no doubting who she saw no more than a dozen paces from her, smiling and casting a shadow. Spirits did not cast shadows, she knew, or was that Beelzebub himself? Two gulls shrieked above her, riding the wind.

Did She speak? It seemed that She did, for surely She was aware of a gentle necessity. Then, recalling why she was herself here at such an hour, Colleen McBride glanced down towards the barn and its waiting animals. When she turned back the figure had disappeared and it was as though She had never been. Or was that Her, amidst a maze of gnats stirred up by a breeze, their wings drying in the new-risen sun? Colleen sank to the grass, feeling dizzy, but then she had had nothing to eat or drink and her mother had warned against that. Now she could see that the liquid ground, that had seemed to move in gentle waves, was no more than a thousand cobwebs and the rainbow glow that of the sun fracturing on dew. There was a reason for all things, it seemed and miracles perhaps no more than reality seen at an angle. Yet even now she could not believe she had seen a mere phantom. Had she not been singled out? Had she not in that instant become a messenger?

Yet, when minutes later her face was pressed against the warm flank of a cow that smelled of hay, she had already begun to doubt what before had seemed so clear. But surely she had seen the Virgin and was required to make this place holy, and was there not a significance in her being in a stable, now.

***

She kept the secret for a while, not least for fear of ridicule, not least because of the clip round her ear she expected from the nuns were she to speak such blasphemy aloud.

'So, Colleen McBride. The Holy Mother appears to you but not to the Mother Superior? She reveals herself on a hillside in the middle of the night when respectable people are abed. The

Blessed Virgin, searching around for someone to speak to, can think of no-one better than Colleen McBride, whose shoes are seldom clean and who can never remember the order of the commandments. Adultery, child, adultery before covetousness. Ask Father James. He will tell you.'

So she kept the truth from others as in some moods she kept it from herself for the longer the time since her morning on the hillside, with a rising tower of gnats, the less she was inclined to believe. Yet who can keep such secrets so that the moment came when she told her very best friend, Veronica, who in turn told her best friend, who told her mother, who told Sister Ignatia who fell to her knees in St. Anthony's chapel knowing, as she had all her life, that she was to be a witness to a miracle. Something, something had happened in a place where nothing happened with such regularity that it seemed in itself part of God's providence. 'Holy Mother,' she whispered. 'Here. In Ballygoran. Praise be.'

'What might be the cause of you excitement, Sister?' asked Sister Theresa, she who would smoke a Woodbine behind the bike shed, cigarettes sold in packets of five for those who wished to indicate that theirs was a passing fancy and not addiction at all.

'There has been a miracle.'

'Has Liverpool beaten Manchester City, then?'

Sister Theresa was one for the football, and the racing, it has to be admitted, chancing a little if she had word of a good thing.

'Liverpool has not, sister. It is something more miraculous than that.'

'Manchester United? Or is it Rangers v Celtic you are speaking of?'

'What I am speaking of is a miracle that will make this a place of pilgrimage. The Holy Mother has appeared.'

'She's not at all. She went into Dublin to buy a lottery ticket. I saw her board the bus myself.'

'Not the Mother Superior. The Holy Mother. Mary, Mother of God,'

'Mother of God!' shouted Sister Theresa. 'Are you losing your mind, woman?'

'She has appeared to Colleen McBride.'

'Colleen McBride? The one with the scabby knees and a squint.'

'No, sister. You are thinking of Sarah McReedy, the daughter of Sam McReedy who beat those horses and is serving his time. No, Colleen McBride. Black haired. Once wore glasses. The one whose skirts have been getting higher. The one with French knickers.'

'Ah, right you are. And she has been having visitations, has she. Has she started the curse?'

And so a miracle might have been talked into invisibility were it not for the fact that Sister Ignatia, though limited in intellect, was generously endowed with faith by way of compensation so that little by little word began to get around until Colleen McBride was summoned before the Mother Superior, whose temper that day was somewhat short since, despite her hopes of divine intervention, she had once more failed to win the lottery.

'Colleen McBride, you are a dreadful liar.'

'I am not, either.'

'Did I not have occasion to chastise you for the smoking?'

'You did Sister.'

'And for standing around with that boy who was after tempting you to sin.'

'We were talking of geometry, sister.'

'You were not either, Colleen McBride. You are a stranger to the truth. God sees right through you.'

This struck Colleen as a disturbing idea.

'The exam was coming and I was helping him somewhat, he not being good with numbers.'

'You will shut your mouth, Colleen McBride, for nothing but lies have come streaming out of you to the shame of God. Do you think yourself a fit person for the Mother of God to appear to? Why you're tenth in your class at history and the worst at cross-country running. Is that the kind of person she would choose for a revelation?'

'I did see her, sister.'

'See who?'

'The Virgin Mary.'

'Is that so? And when I caught you smoking did you admit to the truth of it? You did not. And am I to believe a word that you say? You are close to blasphemy as it seems to me. You had best write me a hundred lines: 'I will not tell lies to the Mother Superior,' in case you have forgotten who I might be.'

'It will make no difference. She said that I was to tell everyone. and that the glory of the Lord would shine all around.'

She was embroidering now, for in truth she could not remember if She had spoken at all. It was merely what she had felt. Standing outside she had determined that it was perhaps all a dream but being spoken to in the way she was she set herself to brazen it out.

'And she said that people should come and do reverence.'

'Reverence, was it.'

'Some such. It was difficult since she spoke so quiet and I couldn't tell her to speak up for that would surely have been impolite.'

'Impolite? Sure it would. Who are you talking of here but the Mother of God? The lightning will strike you down and you go on this way. I want to hear no more of this or you'll be attending the godless state school next term and what will you think of that?'

Such was the imperfection in the chain of command that the Mother Superior was unaware that the same threat had been made before, indeed was made on a regular basis. It was anyway unlikely to prove much of a disincentive since the state school was co-educational, the thought thus being far from unappealing to those required to exchange religious discipline for the very wanton debauchery they had been promised the state offered its pupils on a regular basis.

'And what were you doing so early on the hillside who should have been abed or at her prayers.'

'I was milking the cows, sister.'

'Cows, was it. And that was where She would appear, among the cow pats. Imagine if She should have put her foot awry. How would you have felt about that Colleen McBride?

'She was ethereal,' Colleen replied, having learned the word in a poetry class and loving it, along with 'transitory' and 'lubricious,' though it seemed the last was of a doubtful kind.

***

There was, Sister Hilda announced at the school assembly, to be an excursion. Bridget Riley thought she had said 'execution' and was scarcely surprised. It seemed a natural enough extension of their ideas of education. 'We are going to the shrine of the blessed Margaret,' she added with a beatific smile, gathering her black clothes around her like a giant bat considering tangling itself in someone's hair. 'There will be a charabanc.'

It was not a word with which any of them were familiar but it was doubtless some religious ceremony that would require them to polish their shoes and remove grips from their hair. 'You may each make a request of the blessed Margaret. So stare into your heart and decide what it will be.'

'A chocolate cake would be nice,' a young Mary Malone thought.

'You may wish for the hungry to be fed.'

'Exactly,' thought Mary. Charabancs clearly were not so bad, after all.

It is true to say that the charabanc was a disappointment. It carried advertisements for products that had long since disappeared and emitted a degree of blue smoke. There was to be singing, they were told, of a religious kind. So, as the dyspeptic bus swung from side to side, Sister Hilda endeavoured to conduct with a Mars bar oblivious to the alternative lyrics Bridget O'Reilly was improvising with such skill. Sister Hilda had once had hopes she might have sung professionally before she had seen the light. It was one of many illusions she treasured. In truth, it would have been a rare venue that would have chosen someone whose singing regularly set the local dogs to howling. Not only was she tone deaf but she was deaf to the fact that she was tone deaf and there is nothing more irritating than the beatific smile of someone as confident of their performance as they are self-evidently incompetent. So the bus continued on its way, setting dogs to howling as they passed by singing to God's glory. The driver wore headphones. 'Sure I'm learning French,' he had explained though it was not what was printed on the hand-made label on the cassette even if 'French' was certainly one of the words. 'And what if you do not hear the horn sounded by another vehicle?' 'I have a sixth sense,' as indeed he did. He could detect alcohol even if it had been placed on the top shelf of a back bedroom against some medical emergency.

Their destination was an old abbey Cromwell's troops had taken evident pleasure in despoiling. There were the remnants of statues, their faces chipped away by swords or their heads removed with blunt force, an experience the Protector General himself would later suffer albeit when he was already dead, being disinterred for the purpose and his body liberally distributed. The girls of St.Cronen of Roscrera were not thrilled. Besides the ruins and a small kiosk – closed – which sold – when open – religious items and ice creams, there was no sign of anything or anybody.

'It's the off-season,' said Sister Hilda, detecting their disappointment, though for their part her pupils found it hard to imagine that there might be an on-season.

'Collect your sandwiches,' Sister Hilda announced once they had pulled into the car park. 'There are no toilets but we will be back in school in no more than three hours.'

'Please, Sister, I had no chance to go before we left. The toilet was bunged up, and there was blood. Loads of it.'

'Hold your tongue Theresa Collins. This is sacred ground.'

'But I won't be able to last.'

'There are saints, Theresa Collins, who were shot to death with arrows and others eaten by lions or tortured for their faith.'

'Would that be the Inquisition?' asked Bridget Reilly.

'It was not. That was a testing of the faithful. There were saints who suffered all manner of things and you are telling me, Theresa Collins, that you cannot wait an hour or so.'

'I might manage an hour, sister.'

'Mortify the flesh for is that not the avenue to salvation.'

'And does not going to the toilet count as that, sister,' asked Bridget Reilly, 'for I can sometimes go the whole morning if I try.'

'Enough of this silliness. Sister Frances will give you a guided tour when you've finished your sandwiches.'

'Sister.'

'Bloater paste, Catherine Anne O'Rourke. Is it not Friday and is Friday not bloater paste?'

'I'm allergic to bloater paste, Sister. It brings me out in spots.'

'It is not the bloater paste that does that. It is over indulgence in caramels. Did I not find a packet of those in your desk last Thursday. Bloater paste is full of goodness. During the war it was bloater paste and cod liver oil that pulled us through. You do not know what it was like in those days. We were grateful for what we could get while you are treated to semolina and jam and other suchlike luxuries. I never saw a banana until I was ten and then didn't know what to do with it. Father, is that not so?'

Father James made no reply suffering, as he did, from motion sickness and finding this talk of bloater paste, olive oil and semolina a deal disturbing.

'Father, are you thinking of being sick?'

He was indeed, and had been thinking of little else for the last half hour even as he was urged to sing 'rise up, rise up for Jesus.'

'It would be better in the charabanc, Father, for it is holy ground we will all be treading on.'

He waved a hand, perhaps to indicate that the choice was not entirely his to make.

'There is lemonade that Sister Frances made, though any of you with fillings had best give it a miss. This time it is made with real lemons. Theresa Collins, why is your hand up?'

'Would it not be better, sister, not to take anything to drink if there are no toilets.'

'Would it not be better, Theresa Collins, if you got your mind off such and gave your attention to the brave souls who perished here for their faith?'

'Did they not have toilets either, sister?'

'Of course they had toilets, child.'

'And why are there none now?

'Did not that devil Cromwell destroy them all.'

'The toilets?'

'He was a man whose wickedness knew no bounds. Now, will you all get off the bus, though let the father go first for he is not looking too well. Perhaps a bloater sandwich will settle your stomach, father. Catherine Houlihan!'

'Yes, sister.'

'Fetch the paper towels. The rest of you step around it for I will not have any of you walking on sacred ground with sick on your shoes. Sure, it doesn't matter, Father. God works in mysterious ways.'

As it happens, Father John was thinking much the same as he was sick again.

So, they were led forth, sandwiches in their hands, to see the scatter of broken walls and damaged statues that was all there was to see.

'And were they nuns or priests lived here?'

'It was nuns when Cromwell came by.'

'And why did they live here miles from anywhere?'

'They were not miles from God.'

'But God is everywhere, Sister. You told us that last week, so they could have lived somewhere more convenient. It took us more than an hour to get here.'

'I don't think they had much thought for your convenience, Anne McKechnie. They were a closed order, and silent, too.'

'Silent, sister. Did they talk in sign language?'

'Sign language?'

'I mean, what did they do if they wanted to say, I'd use the toilets if I were you for Cromwell is on the way?'

'They were as one. They understood one another perfectly.'

'Or if they wanted to say it's bloater paste again. I'd rather give it a pass.'

'This is not the place for frivolity. Do you know what the fate of the nuns was?'

'No sister.'

'Things were done to them before they died.'

'Things, sister?'

'It was men did these things and let you learn a lesson from this. Men were put on earth to lead women astray.'

'I thought men were here first, sister. Wasn't Adam here before Eve and was she not the one who ate the apple and told him to go on and have a go?'

'Does anyone here have any sensible questions about the abbey and its martyrs?'

'Why is the kiosk closed, sister. I was thinking of buying a small statue of the ravished nun.'

'Veronica Pearce, wherever did you hear such a word?'

'It is written on a notice by the gateway. It said this was where the nuns were ravished and please not to drop sweet papers.'

'Did it mention toilets?' asked Maureen O'Grady, suddenly attentive.

'It is closed until the summer season when visitors come from many miles around. There is a pilgrimage and if you complete it you get a certificate, though you have to have travelled the last miles on your knees, and it would do you no harm to do that one day.'

'I'm not allowed to scab my knees, sister. I have a note.'

It began to rain.

'Can we get back on the charabanc, Sister?'

'It has not been cleaned yet. What is wrong with a little rain?'

It rained harder.

'Sister, it is raining harder.'

'I am aware of the rain. Think of Noah.'

Quite what thinking of Noah was likely to do was hardly clear.

'Or of Jonah?' Sister Francis added, having herself realised that building an ark was not immediately practical though why invoking a whale was any better was as lost on her charges as it swiftly was on her. She had a tendency, she acknowledged, to speak before her brain was fully operational.

'What did they do here, Sister, for there is nothing for miles?'

'They prayed.'

'All day?'

'I expect they exercised a little. What's good for the body is good for the soul.'

A number of the older girls had been wondering about something similar of late.

'Perhaps they played hockey. We do not know.'

'Hockey, Sister.'

'Or perhaps running.'

'So they could run away from Cromwell. They'd have had a head start.'

'They would have submitted to God's will.'

'What about the ravishing, Sister.'

'Perhaps the charabanc is smelling better now, girls.'

The rain was falling harder and a stream had begun to rush down the hillside towards them, making Noah not such an unlikely figure to invoke. The sound of running water, however, was not making things better for Theresa Collins who would willingly have traded salvation for a functioning toilet that Cromwell had somehow missed.

The journey back saw most of the girls slumped in their seats. On the way out they had had the energy of expectation. Now there was nothing but distended bladders to keep them focussed. Sister Hilda tried to interest them in singing but gave up after a time and suggested instead a game of 'I Spy.' 'I spy, with my little eye, something beginning with R.'

'Rain, Sister.'

'Right Anne McKechnie. Now your turn.'

'I spy with my little eye something beginning with T.'

'You cannot have toilet, Anne McKechnie, for it has to be something we can see.'

'I'll have C then,' she replied sullenly.

'Charabanc,' said Denise Riley who had been wondering whether to squeeze a spot on her chin.'

'Is that right, Anne McKechnie?'

'It is Sister.'

'Then it is your turn, Denise Riley,' with some trepidation.

'I spy with my little eye something beginning with M.'

This time there was no reply until at last Sister Joan called a halt. 'What would it be for we have run out of guesses. What does M stand for?'

'More rain,' said Denise.

The moment was saved by the fact that they were now pulling onto the school grounds.

'There's one bloater paste sandwich left,' Sister Joan announced triumphantly. 'Does anyone want it before the bread starts curling?' Then, after a few seconds, she called out, 'Cathleen Houlihan, fetch the paper towels and girls, when you get off don't go treading the sick into school. Are you better now, Father?'

He waved a hand and then bent forward, head between his knees.

'Please sister.'

'What is it Cathleen Quinlan? We are nearly there.'

'Please sister, Theresa has wet herself. Can I change places, please?'

***

High above Ballygoran is a great house, built full square out of grey stones. Its blank windows flare at the end of the day as the sun melts on the horizon. It is where the Alberys live, where they have lived for a century or so, though it has been burned more than once by those who resented its position looking down on the doings of lesser folk. At the time of the latest burning he had been a Protestant and she a Catholic so you could take your choice as to who had the rags and the paraffin. It was a deal ago now but there were a few who remembered a woman flying out of the door, all ablaze, determined, perhaps, to light the world with her pain. She did not die, not then, but lived on after a fashion, the skin of her face drawn back so you could see the sinews, a living picture for medical students. Now, such things are forgotten in so far as anything here is ever forgotten, but they keep themselves to themselves, knowing, perhaps, how cheap the price of paraffin and how ready the supply of rags. Once a year they open their house and have a kind of fair in the Gardens, the proceeds to go to the orphanage which is still to be found at the end of the town, though there are few still sequestered there by their fate if not the law. Tables are set out on the lawn, if it is fine, and the family sit together, lifting cups of tea to their thin lips, pinky fingers raised doubtless in some Masonic signal. They judge the fruit and vegetables and he speaks over the public address, still sounding English for all the years he has been perched in the Irish hills. His voice echoes back from the resentment of those who accept his hospitality. Memory here is not a matter of the brain.

When it rains, which is more often than not, people are allowed inside though there is nothing to see except a few family pictures and some books on a shelf, uniformly bound. They are generous enough, if you have a fondness for cucumber sandwiches and strong tea. In the study he offers Jameson's to the men who light up cigarettes while he watches them as a scientist might observe some strange tribe recently discovered. When, along with the rain, it is cold, as it can be in any month, and the wind cuts in from the sea, he would have a huge fire lit in a grate wide enough to take small trees. He would stand with his back to the flames, hands behind him, and stare ahead challenging anyone to penetrate his privacies, for though he was always courteous he shared nothing of his thoughts with anyone. No one spoke.

Over the fireplace is the portrait of a boy, with the same sharp nose, the same coiled hair. But everyone knows better than to ask about him who had been found in the lough one September when the mist snared on a million spiders' webs so that the ground seemed to flow like an inward sea, as it did for Colleen McBride, with a thousand fractured rainbows but no gold at their end, only the slumped body of a child pumped up with the gas of his own decay. No one ever knew if it was an accident, a suicide, or whether those who had sought to purge the land with blood decided that not enough had yet been shed.

They chose not to bury him in the cemetery, not even the Protestant one. The father himself dug a hole by a solitary beech tree and laid him there. Nor was there a headstone, only a black rock with his name upon it. So when he stood with his back to the fire and stared ahead perhaps he believed that someone might materialise in front of him, and who could that be but the son long ago brought to his door on the back of a mare, it being impossible for any vehicle to make its way there. Not that anyone cared over much either way. He was not anyone people knew, or cared to know. And when ill fortune comes, well, there is maybe a reason for it. For those who muddle along beside one another for year on year, it is amazing, nonetheless, how little it takes for the shedding of blood and always in the name of a glorious cause no matter the squalor of the action it requires.

There is a path leads up from the nearby road. It is full of holes so that more than one delivery man has found his tyres punctured. They do not encourage strangers and for the most part seem to wish that the whole world should come within that designation, except on those annual occasions when, for a reason none can understand, they lower the drawbridge, fill in the moat, and extend a cold hand to their fellow citizens. There is a flag pole at the main entrance but no one has ever seen a flag fly from it. Perhaps he is waiting for the moment he can hoist one half way up to announce the death of hope. Would it, some wondered, be the flag of Ireland or that of its oppressors.

Along the wire that marks the outer limit of the estate are strung a score or more of moles, in various stages of decay, a warning to their kind which, since they are blind, seems a mite optimistic. For the most part, though, it is stone walls that mark them off from those below, that and history which is more substantial here and less easily dismantled. None knew of their true loyalties, except that his connections were good. From time to time he would be driven through the town to Dublin by his chauffeur who himself seldom mixed with townspeople, living on the estate.

What his profession was nobody knew. Perhaps he needed none. As for his wife, she seemed abstracted. On the day of the fair she would appear, dressed apparently for Ascot, and drift over the lawns light enough to be blown by the wind. She would talk to people, to be sure, but never in such a way as to suggest that she knew them or even that she was focussed on what she said. There were rumours about her and the chauffeur or, to be true, about her and any man who was to be seen for when there is no knowledge there is a deal of speculation and a sea-going vessel of gossip. Certainly, she was never to be seen in the town, except once when she had sat in the café and ordered a piece of Battenberg, slicing it in four with a small knife she took from a reticule. She had drunk her tea, little finger akimbo, paid the waitress, leaving no tip, and stepped back into the car.

It was a house that had no purpose being there, as they were intruders no matter how long they had lived on that levelled plot among the hills. If you went out in a boat though, and looked back at the shore as the sun set behind you, it was possible to see the eyes of the house light up, the devil himself, perhaps, having awoken to claim the night as his own. And there were those who suspected this might be so.

***

It has to be admitted that the choice of Colleen by the Virgin Mary was an unlikely one, she having never taken her Catholicism seriously and being given to a quick ciggy and an occasional visit to the gorse bushes. Her mother had a fondness for the bottle, and for anyone who might be willing to supply her with one, and hence was not the most dutiful of parents, though she was the only one Colleen had. Her father, after all, had been struck by lightning, something of a joke to her fellow pupils, children being the Devil's spawn, and certainly not much of an indication of the Almighty's aim for her father had been kind and tolerant and sober while his wife failed to qualify under any of the above. It followed that Colleen was not so much raised as grew up, as any other creature would. Having nobody on whom to model herself, except the nuns for whom she had developed a fierce antagonism having somewhat to do with the bruises she carried, she was her own invention, much as Jay Gatsby had been and there were those who thought she might have a similar end.

Once, she had slipped away from school and spent the afternoon in the small cinema, heated by wall-mounted gas fires that had to be turned on and off by means of a long pole with a hook at the end to pull down on the chains that hung beneath her. She found herself along with twenty or so silver-haired pensioners who kept complaining that they couldn't hear a thing when in truth the whole place reverberated with Dolby or surround sound or whatever it was that made film going so painful for the majority. A man moved to sit beside her and laid a hand on her knee. 'Get your hand off my knee,' she suggested, in a voice of such clarity that for a moment it sounded out louder than the simulated passion on the silver screen. It was an 18 certificate but the woman who sold the tickets never paid attention to such things, having to keep her mind on selling Maltesers and ice-creams that had to be fetched from the fridge in the manager's office where it was not wise to venture if he should be around. The film had featured much nakedness and behaviour such as would have stirred memories in the pensioners if very little else. All would have been well if Father John had not been there as well, not to watch the writhing on the screen, of course, but to report that the film must be placed on the list of those to be shunned by the faithful who might be stirred to unthinkable deeds with inappropriate people.

That Sunday, he preached against it and mentioned that he had seen one of St. Cronan of Roscrera's young pupils there but that he was not going to mention the name and hence bring shame on the family – not likely, of course, given that one was seldom sober enough to notice while the other had been singed to his bones. He would leave it, he said, for the school to administer the necessary correctives, much, mused Michael Collins, the butcher's assistant, as the Wehrmacht preferred the SS to do their business for them, but then he had seen the film and hence was irremediably damned, along, it must be assumed, with those few in the congregation who had themselves seen the film and in one case more than once: 'I went back for my glasses,' explained Martin McGuiness at the box office to a woman whose Cornettos were melting onto her shoes.

***

At the end of the town, where the grandly named Dublin Street ran beside the sea, was Ballygoran's only hotel, in fact a guest house with pretensions. Anglers would stay there, along with commercial travellers and in summer a number of misdirected families on holiday, bright with expectation for a day at the beach, having yet to discover the absence of such. From time to time there were also those running away or towards.

There were six rooms, each with a wash basin. All other facilities were shared, which came as a shock to many visitors but not to the hotel's sole resident, a woman of substantial age though not of substantial means for otherwise why would she stay there. She had a room that looked out over the sea whose shifting colours she could watch from a rocking chair she had installed for herself. The owner occupied the other room which looked seaward. The other guests had to be content with the green hills that rose up behind on which a few desolate cows were to be seen from time to time.

Miss Prynne had been a resident, the only resident, for some twenty years since her husband disappeared in Africa – 'Aaf-ri-caa,' she would say, like Meryl Streep in *Out of Africa*. They had gone on holiday together, hoping to mend a broken marriage, brought together, as they imagined, in the face of danger. In truth there had turned out to be little of that. The only lion they saw was asleep, rolling on its back inviting someone to tickle its stomach. Her husband departed early one morning leaving a note propped up against an industrial strength bottle of Imodium. 'It's no good old girl. I wasn't meant for marriage. I've gone off with Mary Stewart. She's a good sport and has promised to sort me out. When you get home look in the bread bin. There's a loaded pistol there. Best unload it and toss it in the sea. Goodbye old girl.' As evidence of his finely-honed sensitivity it was signed, 'Yours Faithfully.'

To her surprise, she felt nothing but relief and made her own way to Egypt where she had an affair with a camel driver whose only English words were 'very cheap.'' She thought of taking him home with her like a trophy but even she could see he wouldn't fit in. He took her to see the pyramids by moonlight, his camel farting with such vigour that she felt she might shoot forward like a jet plane.

'Goodbye,' she said to him at the shipside.

'Very cheap,' he replied with a smile. Even at the distance of a hundred yards or so she could hear his camel fart. She wanted to cry. It was as if she were Celia Johnson in a film. She touched his hand. He brought her hand to his lips. Then she strode up the gangplank where a group of local musicians were playing what was vaguely recognisable as Colonel Bogey. She was glad her husband had gone. She could still not remember why she married him in the first place. He was Irish but had the manner and accent of one who had gone straight from Eton to the Guards. At first 'old girl' had seemed affectionate. Later it had seemed an accusation.

On the way back she danced the foxtrot with an Albanian, or perhaps an Australian. She had been drunk when they were introduced. She took to wearing sunglasses every day to hide her eyes. She lay down on a reclining chair and read a novel about an heiress who falls in love with a ski instructor who has a bronzed body, blue eyes, and speaks with what was described as a Swiss accent, though she was none too sure what that was. From time to time the ship's siren sounded but this reminded her of her lover's camel and she retreated to the bar, asking for a Tom Collins, suddenly wondering if that was named for an IRA leader.

A Turkish professor with a scarlet cummerbund asked her if he could lead her into dinner. She assented, but only because she was fascinated by the way his jowls shook whenever he laughed, which he did despite the fact that she never spoke to him, choosing instead to smile and nod as one who was deaf and dumb as, in part, she was for something had closed down in her.

When she returned to her house she found the gun and a note which read 'sorry old thing' and said he would do it in the bath to save on cleaning. She did not throw it in the sea but tucked it in the pocket of a suitcase. Deciding she could no longer live there she moved out though not before discovering the box of money, not, admittedly, much money, to which he had thoughtfully directed her in a separate note in case the first was required by the police or tax authorities. Why he had not killed himself but gone off in the night in a far away country was beyond her but she had never understood him, certainly not his habit of slapping her on the backside as if she were a horse. So she set sail for Ireland where no one would know of her past and that seemed, to her, to be less of a country than an idea.

She presented herself at Mrs. McCann's for had her husband not also disappeared, one night having picked a fight with an IRA man over the relative virtues of Rangers and Celtic.

'I'll give you the room with the sea view.'

'That would be very civil.'

'And what would you have tied up there?'

'That's a camel blanket.'

'It has a particular smell.'

'There's a reason for that,' she said, lifting a case in one hand and the blanket in the other.'

'Your bath night will be Thursday.'

'I will be the judge of when I bathe,' she replied, making her way up the worn carpet of Faraway Hotel.

'You'll not be going out after ten,' Mrs McCann called after her, 'for there are funny people around at night.'

Mrs McNaughty, who was now calling herself Miss Prynne, stopped where the narrow staircase turned to the left.

'There are funny people the world around,' she said, 'and on both sides of locked doors.'

A moment later she was in her room, locking her door, aware suddenly of how her life had shrunk. She walked to the window and pulled a yellowing lace curtain aside. A gentle silt of dust and a dead fly or two fell to the floor. Outside, though, the sun was shining crimson on a beetle-black sea, a beacon or a warning, she could not be sure which.

Twenty years passed. The same sea, dark with age, stretched out to the horizon while the same sun shed its deceptive light. Outside the door came Mrs. McNulty's voice.

'It's Wednesday,' she called, 'Your night's Thursday.'

Miss Prynne sighed. From somewhere she heard a familiar voice whisper 'Very Cheap.' In recognition she let out the quietest and most subtle of farts.

***

There is a quality to the light that says something for those who live in Ballygoran. In Mediterranean towns the sky has a lucidity that resists ambiguity. Things are defined. The eye of the artist seeks out bright surfaces and sharp shadows. Blue skies are bleached, buildings a smudged ochre or sullen white. The light is shattered by its own relentlessness so that men and women are driven in doors to sleep away reality. In Ballygoran, the green of the fields reflects from the grey underside of clouds creating an undersea sheen. The mist that rolls in from the sea diffuses a light less concerned to illuminate than console, for there are many in need of consolation.

There are bright days, to be sure, when the damp fields breathe out and the sun offers the grace of forgetfulness, days of primary colours with flickers where indecisive cabbage whites tremble about the land. On such days, crystal water shivers, shocked by its own purity, and breezes gather up perfume from royal heather and the heavy waft of poppies. On such days doors are left open and carpets beaten for their insolence. Time is in suspension and the night is resisted with simplicity.

More often, though, the air is viscous, with a deep dullness that speaks of things not uttered, while on certain days thunder clouds pile up above the town. The sea and the mountains carve out a territory that is particular while those who look up do so less in expectation than in confirmation that a hand is pressing them down against the truth of their lives.

On such days, people will stay in doors, watching the blue flicker of a flame in fires that are lit in sequence, a conductor seemingly inviting them in turn to join the mournful tune. To be kept within doors is to have one's mood changed, to be driven within in more ways than one. Memories are stirred, like dust by an impatient housewife, for with doors and windows closed there is nowhere for them to go, unless, perhaps, up the chimneys where the oily smoke of burning peat rises, occasionally to be pulsed back by a passing gust of wind so that rooms fill with the smell of the distant past.

It is thirty years now since one storm transformed the stream into a thrusting river, its course straightened by an eagerness to reach the sea. It bit into two houses and carried a car bobbing past the butcher's and the post office nodding to them as acquaintances. The houses stood exposed, their privacies revealed. No one died, though the car disappeared to join the remnants of the armada. It was sufficient, though, for people to stand warned.

Does the weather shape people, then? Why would it not. We are part of nature, ourselves made of water and star dust. No wonder the moon beckons some as it does the sea, pulling it in and out as a man will reach for the counterpane in his sleep only for it to drift back again. We answer, perhaps, to something more than our own fragilities and a storm will recall this resisted truth. Centuries since, thunder was heard as the voice of a god whose language was untranslatable but whose anger was not. There is a memory of such days built into us or passed down perhaps with nothing more articulate than a narrowing of the eyes. More than one person endures storms sitting in a cupboard under the stairs, convinced the time has come for a tap on the shoulder from a vengeful god, and sometimes it comes. Once a tree was split in two by lightning, along with the young boy who sheltered under it. Not everyone was ready to grant it an accident, not least because the tree under which he sheltered was that from which a man had once hung himself long before. And what was he doing there in a place visited by few?

The broken houses were repaired but a jagged line is still visible, a flaw in something more than stone blocks, for that night there were those with expectation of a summons. There is a deal of apprehension in Ballygoran and loss sufficient to justify it, loss and unexamined guilt. These Catholics should be Calvinists for spiritually they would recognise one another's delight in submission to a fate in which they wish they did not believe.

There are clear nights, though, when a glow surrounds the moon and everywhere seems silver, redemption perhaps streaming down. Every now and then the northern lights perform a symphony, folds of colour, fading, strengthening, rising, a living dance across the winter sky God, in the best of spirits, having taken it into His mind to dance a jig or two. This, too, is surely a sign for in the end all things are.

***

Not everyone who lives in Ballygoran, or the folded hills that stretch away from it toward the west, was born here. Some chose it for the very reasons others fled. They selected it for its isolation, for the mists that rise up from the dank ground or the clouds that press down on their privacies. It is a place that is forgotten and a place some go to forget. They hold their lives to their chests as a priest does the Bible when he looks at the sinners who face him dull with labour and bright with illusion. They have their stories and are not anxious to share them with others.

Away from the town are houses and cottages perched unaccountably in sullen fields or wedged into narrow gullies. Most have the electricity but other services are not to be looked for or, if looked for, not to be found. These are places for those confident of their abilities or in retreat. A town or a city can do little to cure broken spirits that the countryside may yet restore. Those who once served on the front line of reality may here withdraw with honour finding consolation in invisibility.

There are those to whom we owe much but who shrink from a recognition that can only stir dark thoughts, open up a world they had thought they might close. It is always a wonder that people live where the roads melt in summer and crack open in winter. Some choose to live in hive-like tenements or wander the desert, their eyes gritted with sand, so it is not so strange that others travel to this spot where defrocked priests and loveless women, poets and poisoners, highborn and lowborn, hopeful and hopeless, live side by side. Could it be that in truth there is nowhere else they would rather be?

***

'Millions of years. Just think of that. Millions of years.' Brion O'Grady had once been a solicitor but had retired early overcome by the pettiness of human nature and the lies he was required to tell. He still wore a suit, though, even when he was cutting turf in neat rectangles, taking pleasure in the downward slide of the spade. 'To think that God had it in mind that trees would grow and die so that we might be kept warm in the winter these many years later.'

'It stretches the mind,' observed Seamus Reynolds, leaning on his spade as his friend laboured. 'Stretches the mind.'

'It is history we are cutting here. Time by the spadeful.'

'Spadeful.'

'And to think this would burn when it looks like mud.'

'Like mud, indeed. It is a wonder. Are we through yet, do you think?' said Seamus, an undertaker's assistant by profession but a drinker by inclination and feeling the need for a little something to eat and drink, though he would have settled for the latter over the former.

'Time is such a thing, is it not?'

'Such a thing. Indeed. And so much of it. Should we be going, do you think? It feels a mite like rain.'

O'Grady stopped digging, staring up at the sky that was indeed beginning to look sickly.

'Is there truly such a thing as infinity? Sure it makes no sense.'

'No sense at all,' replied Seamus, who had rather lost the thread.

'Yet we look at our watches needing to know to the second what the time might be, even though you have only to travel for the time to change.'

'To change,' echoed Seamus, who had a habit of repeating what he heard determined to confirm it before attempting a reply. 'I lost my watch to a tinker once.'

'To a tinker,' replied O'Grady, Seamus's habit proving catching. 'And how did you do that?'

'He made me a bet.'

'And what was the bet?'

'He bet me I could not run round three square field in under ten minutes.'

'Well surely that's not so difficult. What was the bet?'

'Whatever I had in my pocket.'

'And was that much?'

'Had I not just been paid for cleaning a septic tank.'

'Surely it was not worth the effort.'

'Except he was such a boastful figure and I had done that run many a time before. This was before my leg. I knew I could do it in not much more than five.'

'So how did you lose your watch?'

'Well he said he would have to time me but he had no watch. So I lent him mine.'

'And he was gone when you came back.'

'He was gone before I was half way round. I could see him running down the hill.'

'It destroys your faith in human nature.'

'That is does. And I did it in under five minutes.'

'Did you never see it again?'

'Why else would I be wearing a Mickey Mouse watch to this day? The one I lost was my father's who had it from a traveller.'

'He gave it to him.'

'In a sense, he did. He was dead and it was on his wrist. It is understood among undertakers that this means it is offered as a tip by the relatives. I was working at Murphy's at the time.'

'Do you think he was maybe a relative of the one that ran off with yours and who may not have understood the power of tradition in undertakers?'

'To tell the truth that has never occurred to me until this moment. But why would he wish to have a tip returned?'

Leaning on spades has a tendency to lead to philosophy, even if the reverse is not quite so assured, so that within a minute they were both relaxing as they smoked cigarettes rolled on a machine that Seamus retrieved from an inside pocket of a waterproof jacket that had long since forgotten its principle quality. His cigarettes had a tendency to flare into flame, there being rather more paper than tobacco about them, and they did so now, but since both were used to this they merely held them a little away from their faces to save their eyebrows, before sucking in the smoke.

'A cigarette is a thing, indeed.'

'It is, it is. And all the better for not being in those packets that tell you you are going to die.'

'That should not be allowed.'

'Not allowed. Who are they to say things such as that? Sure it cannot be right to mess with a man's pleasure. There is many a man who has lived to be a hundred and smoked each day.'

'Sure, if I lose a year or two I am thinking it worthwhile for what would a man do who could not smoke a little?'

'They've packets with pictures on. There's one saying 'SMOKING KILLS' and another says 'SMOKING MAKES YOU IMPOTENT.'

'I'd have the ones that kill.'

'Kathleen Hoolihan used to say she would not kiss me if I did not give them up.'

'Would that be the Kathleen Hoolihan who married a Protestant?'

'The very same. And him a smoker, too. It was a different brand, though, so perhaps it was the tobacco she took against.'

''Just think, if she was going out with a Protestant at that time and you had kissed her you would have been kissing a Protestant at one remove.'

'Remove. Hardly bears thinking of. I kissed a Protestant once for a dare. I couldn't have been more than ten. I spent a week on my knees, and them all scabbed from the football.

'And what did you do when Kathleen Hoolihan made such an unreasonable demand?'

'I gave up for a week. It was more than I could bear. I asked for a kiss but she said it must be a month or nothing at all, though she hinted that there might be more than a kiss at stake if my breath didn't stink of rat's urine. That's what she said.'

'Not the basis for romance, language of that kind.'

'Oh, she was a terrible one for language was Kathleen. You should have heard her have a go at her father who was not her father, after all, being married to her mother after her first husband had run off with the fishmonger's daughter. They never got on and she would tear away at the poor man who had done nothing wrong except step into another man's bed when it was still warm. She would never eat fish again, though she was loyal to nothing else.'

A wind had got up and their cigarettes were blown out. They huddled together, cupping their hands as they did at mass, and relit them.

'Marriage is all very well,' said O'Grady, 'but it is a terrible killer of passion. Once the children are born all they want is a cup of tea and a washing machine.'

'It's a sacrament. It's in the Bible.'

'In truth there is a lot in the Bible that is best forgot. People begetting like rabbits for a start, and people turning into table salt and cutting out their eyes.'

'It's best read as poetry, I have heard tell.'

'It's a strange poetry that talks of eyes in that way. A tooth for a tooth I can understand. There's many a Saturday night I've seen that one obeyed.'

'Still, all in all, where would we be without religion?'

'England.'

'Ah, that's the truth. They're a terrible heathen lot over there. I went there once, to London. They're most of them Arabs as far as I could tell. And the noise. A man couldn't hear himself think. No, there's a lot to be said for peace and quiet.'

'We've a lot of that here.'

'That's true enough, Seamus.'

'Would you think I was going too far if I said there was too much?'

'No, I would not. There are times for a little noise. Christmas is one.'

'Do you recall Dr. Riley last Christmas?'

'Would I not? I have never seen a man so taken with drink.'

'And him having to deliver a baby between the turkey and the Christmas pudding.'

'It's a wonder it survived, but it was a terrible inconvenient time for a woman to give birth. You would have thought she'd have some consideration. I had a mind to become a doctor myself, once.'

'A doctor, then. And why did you not?'

'The handwriting. You could read every word I wrote. And I think you needed Latin. Do you know, for years at the school sports day I kept wondering who Victor Ludorum might be since he seemed to win every time. I think they speak Latin amongst themselves so as not to let ordinary folk know what they are planning.'

***

It was colder than when they had first climbed the road to Michael's field, named after a Michael so long ago that nobody knew who he had been. The clouds were now swinging by at such a speed that they seemed to be on board a ship and not standing muddied to the knees beside a pile of shiny-sided peat as if life was not too precious to be dribbled away in conversation.

'I heard that the weather is changing because of cows farting,' Brion said, looking across the valley to where a number of cows were gathered doubtless planning together to end life on earth.

'Have cows not been farting this many years?'

'And has the weather not been changing. Look at it now.' He looked across at the cows, suspiciously.

'There were cows in Noah's ark.'

'And was there not a flood?'

'There were only two of them. They must have been mighty farters.'

'Today there are millions of them. They go into those hamburgers they sell.'

'And now we're all going to go under water just because of them. Could they not bung them up'

'And if farting is a problem then someone had better tell my cousin Flynn who could fart for Ireland if it were an Olympic sport.'

'Now there would be a sport worth watching on the television, though no doubt the Americans would win that as they win everything else. Sure, to them winning is all and if they heard that farting was to have a gold medal attached to it they would be searching out the drugs that could put them in first place. They are terrible committed to winning are Americans.'

'Beans.'

'Beans?'

'Beans. They work for Flynn. Have you never met him?

'No.'

'I would advise against. At least in enclosed spaces.'

How long this would have continued is difficult to tell for in truth both regarded time as something to be passed or killed rather than inhabited, but at this moment something caught the eye of Brion O'Grady. Jutting out of the smooth side of the peat was what suddenly struck him as a bony finger which shone as the sun broke through the clouds and sent a shaft of light downwards as in a painting he had once seen in a Dublin museum when he went in to avoid the rain.

'Do you see what I see?'

'That would rather depend.'

'There, before your eyes. It's a finger.'

Seamus's eyesight was not what it had once been when he could have read a road sign at a hundred yards, had there been any in Ballygoran besides the one that had been bent sideways and down when hit by a lorry trying to overtake a tractor towing a tank of slurry. It was not a day that many forgot. Indeed, it was several weeks that not many forgot having to adjust to having their tea spoiled by the smell of the liquid projectile sprayed out of the back of Eleanor Sturges's cows.

'What would a finger be doing there? They don't just drop off.'

'They do if you're a leper,' lepers having been a fixed point in the education of generations of Ballygoran men and women instructed by priests and nuns in the misfortunes of those in distant lands who has a tendency to mislay parts of themselves.

'That must be terrible inconvenient?'

'Do you think maybe it's attached to something?'

'To something? My bet would be a hand.'

O'Grady looked at him. There were moments when he had his doubts about Seamus.

'It will maybe be a grave. It's terrible bad luck to disturb a grave.'

'Maybe it's a bog body.'

'What would a toilet be doing in the middle of a field?'

'No. One of those bodies tens of thousands of years old. Some stone age person shot with an arrow for stealing another man's…'

'Stone?'

'Wife, maybe. Struck by an arrow and falls in a bog.'

'Why would he do that? There must have been plenty of other places to fall back then. And did they have arrows?'

'Certainly they had arrows. They used to kill mammoths.'

'Those great woolly things.'

'Certainly.'

'What would they do with it?'

'The mammoth?'

'The mammoth. If we had killed an elephant what we do with it? I've only got a small fridge that mostly has Guinness in it. And they didn't have that.'

'Guinness?'

'Fridges.'

'They had the ice age.'

'So it was cold.'

'Certainly it was cold. Ice a mile deep. And salt.'

'Salt?'

'To preserve it.'

'That's an awful lot of salt, to preserve a mammoth.'

'Why are we talking about salt?'

'Because of that fellow who went off with somebody's wife and then jumped in a bog with his finger sticking up.'

They both stopped speaking. Something about the conversation had brought them to a cliff's edge. The sun had dipped down and a cold breeze sprung up. Down below, yellow lights had come on one by one. Above, the sky was a mist of stars. For a few minutes they stood still, their minds apparently switched off.

'It's a drink, then,' said Seamus, reanimating.

'That it is.'

'And the fellow over there with the finger?'

'I don't think they drank. It was mostly mammoth milk.'

'Jees, I wouldn't like to have been the milk maid.'

***

Now there was a miracle, even if Colleen McBride had been the unlikely witness. He knew a thing or two about Colleen, though not, of course, from the confessional when her voice was low and sincere. In truth, he was not sure what to make of miracles.

He had been to Lourdes and seen faith in the eyes of those carried there, or who limped along sure of an answer when an answer, he felt, would only come if they changed the question, and all because a young girl said that she saw something many years ago. Yet if you could believe in God why would you not believe in everything that went along with it. Faith is a wonderful thing, he had been told, yet did he not remember that it was the last thing taken out of Pandora's box, or was that hope, put there because of its power to tantalise, for the ache it caused. Had not faith for centuries kept the peasant in his hovel and the slave under the owner's lash? Was faith not a substitute for action and understanding? Were there not those who had been hoped to death?

He remembered being told the story of the man falling from the top of the Empire State Building. 'How's it going,' he is asked as he passes an open window, 'All right so far,' comes the reply. And imagine if a woman had been falling beside him, and a priest perhaps. They might have married if the building had been tall enough. He might have been offered a job as he fell past the 2000th window and hoped to be promoted by the 1000th. Then, with the ground approaching fast, the priest turns to him and says, that is not the earth. The moment you reach it the ground will open up and you will be on the other side where your wife can join you. Hope, you see. Without it, there is nothing. With it, there is nothing but irony. 'How's it going?' 'All right so far.' He had found himself saying that to his parishioners. 'How's it going, father.' 'All right so far,' and them looking strangely as they walked on by.

These were the kind of thoughts he had so that a miracle seemed something he might hold on to. He had had enough of irony for a while and anyway it would deflect him from his other worries that sometimes took him to one of the town's two intellectuals, he being the editor of the local newsletter with headlines such as 'Yoghurt Farmer Fined for Dung-Splashed Walls,' along with classifieds that noted the price of still-born lambs and offered second hand beds such as Shakespeare himself had left to his wife, whose affections had clearly wandered far from Stratford Upon Avon. He had read philosophy at the university and hence was disqualified from doing anything of any real value.

Was there not another priest, in another place, who had embraced a miracle and persuaded Rome of such, and was there not a runway there now, that could take jet aircraft and that had its own gift shop. Surely to God, he thought, something had to wake this place up and what if it was the slip of a girl whose morals he could not attest to. Faith, it seemed to him, was leeching into the soil, being spilled in every bar, laid aside for pornography on the web when the wife was abed or, worse still, when she was not. And could there be harm in summoning back the faithful? At present his church was half full, except at Christmas when there was a smell of alcohol that had nothing to do with the host. At the very least he should visit the hillside where what he was already beginning to think of as the miracle had occurred, though there was nowhere nearby that was flat enough for a runway so that they might have to settle for a bus service instead. And who knows, perhaps his own faith might be restored. Then he was struck by a sudden thought. What if the Virgin Mary really had appeared? Well that would be better than winning the lottery. But would She speak to him, knowing that he was soft on contraception?

***

Seamus and O'Grady retired to consider their position.

'A pint or two of Guinness has a way of clearing the mind,' said Brion who in truth had always found rather the opposite.

'A truer word. Shall we sit by the fire for I'm cold right through.'

'You're cold on midsummer's day,' Brion observed, which was true enough for midsummer's day in Ballygoran had been known to start with a frost.

They settled down and watched the low blue flame that flickered along the peat.

'Who was the fella, then?'

'The fella?'

'In the ..'

'The bog.'

'Should I recognise him maybe, and him no more than bones and us seeing little enough of them.'

'Who do you think he was back then?'

'When would then be do you think?'

'Who can say?'

'And didn't I see just his finger?

'Fingers can tell you something.'

'They can?'

'Fingers Finnerty.'

'It was him in the bog?'

'Do you not remember Fingers Finnerty?'

'Did I know him?'

'Fingers Finnerty?'

'Ah, Fingers. Can't say I do.'

'Could take the second hand off your watch while you were looking at the other one.'

'Why would he do that?'

'Figure of speech.'

'What would that be come Tuesday?'

'Are you so tired you are turning stupid?'

'I was wondering. Should we go to the police do you think?'

'Why would we do that?'

'He was maybe murdered.'

'By the Vikings, or Cromwell. I doubt the case is still open.'

'It's a skeleton.'

'That it is and skeletons are best left alone. Who knows who put him there, if you know what I mean?'

'Should we cover him up or people will think we did it?'

'If we keep our mouths shut no one will know anything at all.'

'But we were digging there. They'll know it was us.'

'You've a point there right enough. Maybe we should dig him up. Or perhaps just his finger.'

'What would we do with a finger?'

'Shall we have another Guinness for my head is beginning to pain.'

***

In the hills above the town academics from Dublin had arrived in their foreign cars and set to with spades and trowels, sieves and brushes, to burrow down through time, layered like Mrs. Gilpin's Battenberg cake. On the ground there was nothing to attract attention, except that here and there the grass was a different colour and there were bumps and gullies like the holes of over-sized moles that had been holding a convocation. From the air, though, the professors and their eager students had made out what seemed to them regular features, the past seemingly waving at them through the earth. Mr. Dromgoogle, the local historian and natural born liar, had sworn they were signs of Saxons who had ventured over and slit the throats of the natives, ignorance, as ever perhaps, being burnished with prejudice. This was not, though, what the pipe-smoking, tweed-jacketed, suede-shoe-wearing professors and cagoule-wearing, track-shoe admiring students sought. They were in search of Norsemen. The Vikings were known to have sailed up and down the coast, raping and looting at will in a way that made it difficult to relate them to their modern-day descendants with a fondness for open sandwiches and herring. Indeed, the very name of Dublin was their gift to the world being settled by people like Kirk Douglas who had also played Spartacus. 'I'm Spartacus.' 'No, I'm Spartacus.'

The excavations, however, provided a useful subject for conversations in a certain public house.

'Why would they want to come here?'

'To do the digging.'

'Not them. The others. The Vikings.'

'How would you like to live on herring? I was to there for a weekend's drinking once and they have entire menus with herrings. You expect them to slap their hands together and make noises until you throw them some.'

'But all that raping and such. You reach fifteen and they say 'happy birthday, son. Time you were raping''

'It's their culture.'

'But why come here.'

'Cheaper than Dublin.'

'Not then. Everyone lived in caves drawing pictures of their hands.'

'That was earlier. They had the wheel and everything.'

'They were great sailors, though, the Vikings. They had long boats.'

'Better than short ones. And axes.'

'No women, though.'

'No women?'

'Why else the raping?'

'There were rules against doing it there, I expect.'

'Why come here, though. Women, yes, but no herring.'

***

For a country that so many had left, for reasons good and bad, and which had scattered its seed in distant places, the one who returns provokes the most mixed of feelings. There is a famous photograph of an immigrant arriving in America that is in fact a picture of one leaving. We mistake it because the woman pictured there, shawl drawn tight around her at the ship's rail, is moving against history, against logic, against myth. For if she could find nothing in such a land of plenty, where landlords did not rule, soldiers did not kill and crops did not fail, then what can she have been looking for? Was it shame, perhaps, that made her draw the shawl tight, half covering her face? Leaving one country is pain enough, leaving a second something worse for surely then hope has been snuffed out like a candle and how could she find her way in the dark of her despair? Weeks in steerage meant more suffering except that this time freedom's beacon had been extinguished.

Mary O'Donnell left Ballygoran when she was a bare twenty-three. It is true there was a young man who abandoned her, but that is a fate common enough even for one as beautiful as she. It was a sense of insufficiency she felt. There was little work to be had where she was born and Dublin seemed not far enough away to open up new worlds. England was not to be thought of and hence was not and though her mother cried and her father reproved her, she took a small inheritance from her grandmother and bought herself a ticket. A distant cousin was contacted and agreed to board her while she sought out a place to work. Within a fortnight she had gone. Her bedroom was empty, though her bed remained made and her slippers beneath her chair for what parent can ever finally say goodbye, no matter how many summers have passed, how many winters endured.

Five years later she was back and would offer no reason why that should be so. She took a job in Dublin, working in a shop, but returned every weekend to stay with her parents where she stored paint brushes, an easel and a large pad of white paper. She would then spend her time capturing the town in watercolours, seating herself on a small folding chair by the harbour and painting the fishing boats at rest or sit above the cliffs and create canvases of wide skies above a wide sea. She had no training but had an eye and a steady hand and an imagination that lifted the real into another realm. 'Why you've caught it perfectly, Mary,' they would say, 'it is the very thing itself,' except that it was not for there was something about her art that passed beyond the moment and the place. There was a quality to it that no one could quite explain. Could it be that she was nostalgic for what was directly in front of her eyes, for there was a melancholy to her art, a sense of something lost though the very thing was undeniably present? It was as though she had never returned in actuality but was still there in a distant place remembering fondly what she had left behind. She would take her work with her to Dublin and, it was said, had a following there.

She had had plenty of young men around her when she was younger but nobody quite knew what to say to her now. She had not explained her return beyond saying to her parents that she had decided to come home. She hardly kept herself aloof and was happy to pass the time of day. One or two had even spied her in Dublin, offering to spray perfume on the wrists of passing women in a store with lights so bright they almost hurt the eye. She wore such make-up and clothes as might have suited the models that filled the windows where people scurried by in a race with their own lives. In Ballygoran, though, the makeup was wiped away and she let the wind blow her hair.

Then, one day, a man, with a young girl of some four years, arrived in a hire car and asked after her. He was an American and therefore exotic enough for word to spread faster than any hire car could be driven. Did anyone perhaps know where Mary O'Donnell might be? They directed him to her parent's house, for it was a week day and she was off spraying people who no doubt had need of such. They must have telephoned, though, for she climbed down from the bus earlier than usual, even as the street lights turned on and the white beam of the searchlight swept the ocean clean.

Several reported later that they had seen them together, with the child running alongside. The following day she was gone, and the car besides. When friends of her parents enquired they were greeted with tight smiles and nothing more. Here were the pieces of a story and it was for the readers of that story to work out what its true meaning might be. One day she had been there, the next she was not. Her paintings, though, remained and in time her parents had them framed and hung on the walls of their house. One sketch, however, remained unframed and unseen for at the back of a small pad of paper, in which she had tried out her ideas, was a charcoal portrait of a baby, one hand reaching out to the viewer. She had begun to colour it in but left it unfinished and abandoned evidently not satisfied with what she had wrought. It is the way with artists, perhaps, that seeking perfection they will settle for nothing less.

***

A mile inland a small golf course had been created. It was a mere nine holes and some of those not quite what would have been regarded as acceptable in many other places, but, then, this had a restricted clientele. It was for the exclusive use of the retired priests who lived in a large gothic house donated by a rich sinner, rich in money that is and not the splendour of his sins. Those who lived there had served their time in scattered parishes around the world, the Irish priesthood having seemingly negotiated a near monopoly.

Now they divided their time between fishing and whisky, golf and whisky and the occasional visit to a similar establishment where the fishing and golf were rather better, even if the whisky was a constant.

'I had this fellow once had three wives, and he confessed as much. So I told him he had need to relieve himself of two as the Bible was particular as to numbers. And he said, 'surely, father, divorce is a sin, is it not?' And I said, 'you were never married to two of them,' And he said, 'do I get to choose the one I keep?' And I said, 'the true wife was the first one' and he said, 'but it was because I didn't like the first that I had the second. If I am to lose two of them surely it's no sin to keep the best.' And I said, 'You've made promises to God and they have to be kept.' And he said how the first one had promised him things she would not deliver once the reception was over so that she had broken her promise to him and had she also not promised to obey. And I said, 'You have made your bed and have to lie in it.' And didn't he say he was happy to do so but thought that he might have the choice as to who he shared it with. And I said, 'in the eyes of God you only have one wife' and he said how God's eyesight must be fading since he counted three of them, each happy in her way for his first wife didn't like the sex, preferring mackerel for tea each day, which didn't fit well with sex anyway and it was all very well but that she kept the fishmonger happier than her own husband so wasn't he within his rights to choose another?' And did he have to marry her? I asked.

'Father, I am surprised,' he said, 'are you suggesting we should have lived in sin?'

'But you were living in sin,' I said, and he said, 'how could that be when I have married not just once but a second time.'

'And what of the third?' I asked.

'Sure that was a mistake.'

'Ah' I said, 'so you do have a sense of shame.'

'Shame, indeed, father, for the shame is that I preferred her sister but she had an eye for one of the young men who works at Murphy's, though to me he smelt too much of the chemicals.'

'Then why didn't you marry her sister?'

'Well, father, I had already proposed so it was a matter of honour.'

'Honour,' said I,' 'how could it be honour when you'd married two others already?'

'I'm surprised at you, father,' he said, 'did you not finish telling me we should keep our promises?'

'But you had already promised two other women,' I said.

'You are right, father, and there's the truth of it. If you are available for confession I confess that I am given to promising too much. It is a fault and I know it.'

'To hell with promises,' says I, 'that is your sin. Three times you've walked down the aisle.'

'Excuse me, father,' says he, 'that would be the bride. I just stood there waiting for her.'

'Three times,' I echoed, 'three times you got married who should only marry the once. Did no one leap up when the priest asked if anyone knew of any reason you should not be married?'

'And why would they do that, father? Did my best man not have two wives of his own? If you ever fancy a fish supper of a Friday,' he said, 'just let me know. The fishmonger always has a little on the side.'

***

John McIlroy was a killer, though mostly of moles, rats and anything that scuttled where it should not. His best customer was Maeve Binchy who was afraid of anything that moved of an animal kind. She wore a hair net having once seen a bat eying her with intent. She had heard that rats sometimes come up through the toilet, but could think of no way of protecting herself other than dwelling on it for as short a time as possible while keeping a rolled up copy of *The Tablet* to hand. She distrusted squirrels which she was sure were no more than rats in disguise looking to see how they could get into the toilet. As to ravens, one of which for a while took up residence in her Garden, they had the evil eye, though not for long as it turned out since John McIlroy blew it apart with his shot gun at her request. Never more. She once saw a snake in her Garden and beat it to death in a frenzy with her long-dead husband's hurling stick, only to discover that the snake was a length of plastic clothes line. You can, though, she told herself, never be too careful. Yet for all that, she kept a dog, albeit a miniature creature whose stunted legs moved so fast it was more like a millipede. John McIlroy would have willingly shot it for free.

He was much in demand at the golf course where moles had conspired to destroy one of the only simple pleasures available to retired priests and members of the Round Table.

'They're little bastards,' observed Father Dooley. 'Do they count as natural hazards or is my round buggered again?'

'Diggery diggery delvit, little old men in black velvet,' replied his playing partner, who had a small bet on the outcome and was not about to make concessions.

'Feck it,' said Father Dooley, moving his ball.

'You'll be taking a penalty, then, will you?'

'You'll be taking a punch in the mouth if you're not careful.'

Father Dooley had once been a boxing man before he discovered his calling and in truth had had a small stiffener before setting out, the morning being cool and a faint drizzle adding to his troubles. To be truthful he was much avoided in the confessional, as certain doctors are not consulted, having a manner not entirely suited to their professions.

'You little bastard,' he told one of his flock, a young man who confessed incautiously to a deed best kept quiet. 'If you're not careful I'll be taking you outside and smash your face in. Take ten Hail Marys, six Our Fathers and twenty push ups.'

'What's McIlroy been up to? Is he not paid to destroy the buggers?

'Will you not moderate your language. Sure this is a public place.'

'What's wrong with my language and where do you think we are, on O'Connell Street? There's no living being for a quarter of a mile, except these little bastards ruining the greens.'

It was a problem, McIlroy admitted. He had tried the usual, everything from traps, to milk bottles, to whirligigs bought at the post office where they were intended to amuse children, if there are any today amused by whirligigs and since he got them cheap it seemed not. He had tried smoke and arsenic, though the members objected to greens that seemed randomly on fire while the idea of poison failed to appeal when a number of them went down with a mysterious stomach bug, in truth more a consequence of eating what the club restaurant chose to call meat soup where the meat had been purchased from a man who had scraped green mould off discarded lamb intended for animals but offered, on the cheap, to retired priests. 'What's a little mould?' he had asked the inspector. 'Is that not what penicillin is?'

The moles were, indeed, a challenge, though he had caught one alive once and not known what to do. He could not bring himself to hit it over the head. 'It's like the bomber pilots,' he told himself, war films being a particular favourite of his. 'It's one thing doing it from a distance, another up close.' He thought to shoot it, but how would it stand still? He could hardly tie its paws and make it stand against a wall. In the end he took it to the grounds of a private hospital in a nearby town, being a socialist as well as a nationalist, and released it there to undermine capitalism and private health providers.

He tried walking around firing his shotgun into the ground at random in the chance of hitting one of them but members objected to explosions just as they were lining up a particularly difficult putt. In the end it was poisonous worms that did it, though now Father Dooley found a chip onto the green deflected by one of the many dead birds that suddenly began to add another frustration to his day. 'I'm not taking a feckin drop just because some feckin bird chooses to commit feckin hara kiri and bugger my handicap.' Since this time he was playing with the Monsignor it was not a well judged statement of principle. 'Father, golf is one thing, and I know the frustrations it brings' -- as indeed he did, having neither talent nor a willingness to admit its lack -- 'but we must restrain ourselves must we not,' a truth he would have done well to remember a minute later when his own shot veered off to the right into an undiscover'd country, from whose bourn no traveller returns. 'Feck it,' he explained.

The road John McIlroy lived in was called Michael Collins Way, or was until it became evident that the postman was returning all letters sent there marking them RETURN TO SENDER. ADDRESS UNKNOWN. He was happy, though, to deliver junk mail, in large amounts. Now Ulysses Street, it was just around the corner from Innisfree Drive. Sitting at the breakfast table he was known to say to his wife, 'I will arise and go now, and go to Innisfree'. Not being a Yeats scholar she had her doubts for there was a woman lived in Innisfree Drive who was known to be free with men who came to her door with deliveries or even canvassing for elections. Even Jehova's Witnesses, in their smart suits, were known to give a miss to her for however secure faith may be temptation always awaits the unwary.

**

There are people who pass by and tell themselves that this is where they must come when they retire at last for surely life here must be what life is about. Just man and nature, hand in hand, and with all the charm of forgotten places. But is there a cash machine, they ask themselves, and somewhere to go when they fancy culture or an evening at the films, and can you buy Mediterranean tomatoes in olive oil and the *Financial Times*? So they pass on by still glancing in their rear-view mirrors, except that you cannot do that for long, roads around here not being designed for steady glances, while a rear view is not always the best way to see the world.

From time to time other people come by. These men have close-cropped hair, like stubble after harvest time. The women are dressed in suits with their faces pulled back. They carry telephones, which are useless here. 'No reception,' their little screens say, and not without truth. They carry black leather folders and bend down looking at graves, searching for history long since eaten away, and when they retreat to the bar they order bourbon, never receiving such, settling for a Jameson instead. After a time, and a drink or two, they ask if anyone knows of certain families that left here a century or so ago for they are searching out the forebears of American presidents looking for roots, it not being sufficient, apparently, that they own the future but that they must own the past as well. 'We must be on a list,' said Patrick McDoogle, content that they should be since every four or eight years there were free drinks to be had in exchange for a story.

Once a Senator had come by, in a fleet of black cars and with men talking into their wrists. He had walked around for an hour, visiting the church and stuffing a ten dollar bill in the poor box, a box that had never received money in any currency since it was installed by a man whose faith exceeded his local knowledge. There was a man with a camera who kept flashing away, with the Senator smiling a mouth of teeth and his wife, blond and full of legs, stepping with care in her high-heeled shoes. They had taken him to the cemetery and he stood crying, before it began to rain and he stepped back into his limousine, looking out through the misted window before they moved off again, and not a drink did they buy for anyone. Nor did they visit the post office with its postcard view of Ballygoran taken one summer's day that sold no more than half a dozen a year for who would want one except those he stopped for a minute wanting the postmark to send back home to be stuck on fridge doors with magnets shaped like comic book characters?

Is it so unlikely that the Americans would be drawn back when so many had chosen the boats and Atlantic swell rather than stay to die. What with the English and the potatoes, it was a deal to bear when there was another place with more of your kind? All the same, it takes something to turn away from your dead and leave your living in the name of nothing more than survival and the rumour of relief. Had they not suffered before and still drawn their dark clothes about them until the storm had passed, and was

America not a godless place inhabited by Protestants who had gone there because even Cromwell was too soft for them? So they had turned their rosaries in callused hands, each bead a frozen tear, a pearl turning back into merest grit. 'Will you not come to us, Patrick?' 'How could you leave your ma who bore and raised you?' 'There's no future here.' 'There's no past there.' And so, a last tight grasp, a heaving sob or two, and the wind caught the sails. Three weeks or more it could take, lying on wooden racks down in steerage, eating salted herring and throwing them up, with nothing but white-tipped waves mocking them and not even birds after the first two weeks. Many arrived with scabs on their faces from the lack of fruit, or from scratching their heads at their misery, landing at Castle Garden where men chalked letters on them , teaching a new alphabet, and confidence men, with practiced smiles, put an arm around them the better to lead them astray.

Then they would be taken through arrow straight streets by their relatives who had gone on before, tilting their heads back and looking up at white buildings soaring above having never seen anything taller than the church at home or the trees that had been growing for a hundred years in the wood that fringed their town. What if they lived in tenements, with nine of them in two rooms and a key to the toilets that they shared with others in a back yard that fringed an alley where drunks would do what they do? This was where it started not where it ended for here everyone was climbing upwards and tomorrow not the same as today. They had travelled more than three thousand miles. What were a few miles more? They were in another world.

Sometimes news would come back. Sometimes it would not. 'We are doing fine here. There is plenty to eat and I have a job.' Some would rent suits from photographers and have their pictures taken, smiling brightly in their borrowed finery. Truth and lies. For who could admit to a mistake even if their gentle deceits might taunt those in misery. Others would disappear and that would be the end of it, forgetting being the price of entry, a way of purging guilt. Meanwhile those left behind would stare at the sea looking, perhaps, for answers they knew would never come, waiting for a sail to break the horizon, a son's return, a hope redeemed. There are paths still to be seen along the cliff edge where year on year women would walk in hope and return in despair. It is what makes a country. Its defeats. When at last they could no longer make the climb they would stare into the blue flames of a banked up fire, watching as jets of gas, released from the wood, flared for a second with a sudden roar, seeming to see something there, to hear in the sound a familiar sigh though what is firelight seen through a tear but a false rainbow? Kathleen, Kathleen, where are you, my fine daughter? Will you not see me once more before I die? And the fire will die down until a chill fills the room and there is nothing left but ash and a woman who has lived to know loneliness as deep as the sea that has taken the child she nursed and saw running free until all hope was gone.

There are days when the mist rises up over the cliffs and tumbles down into the town, a cold hand closing around it. On such days the fog horn would sound out like a wounded whale, its mournful low note a reproach to hope, less a warning than a doom, a sound that would cut to the heart and turn people inwards. No more. Some had decreed that it should be stifled, the hand of bureaucracy smothering its mouth, but those who had once heard it, heard it still while those at sea sailed blind, never knowing what might lie ahead.

There were other stories came back. One was of a peat digger who dug tunnels under New York, where it was hotter than in the tropics, and built a bridge over the East River in the brittle cold of winter, where Indians, it was said, would eat their lunch sitting cross-legged on girders a hundred feet in the air, cutting their food with slivers of ice and dreaming of Wounded Knee and those who died in the snow in penance for a fool. Had he not gone on to employ others until he was rich enough to buy votes and so become a politician. Perhaps he was one of those who became President and sent men from Notre Dame with sharp suits and cold stares to reconnect him to the sod.

Then there was a nun who, it was said, had repented of much when she first arrived in New York, though primarily of being a nun. She had travelled to St. Joseph, Missouri, and made a fortune in ways best not recorded by anyone but St. Peter and, she must have hoped, not even by him. She sailed the mighty Mississippi, so it was rumoured, doing trade of a sort until she married a Senator who did for his electorate what he had dedicated himself to doing to her. When he died, in circumstances not mentioned in his memorial service, she inherited everything, including a hundred square miles of land and the bitterness of her neighbours. She was there still, face tanned leather, arms more sinew than flesh, waiting to see if God would repine and gift her a life.

It was a great country, America, and built from the ground up by the Irish who became policemen and criminals, knowing the two not to be distant from each other. In New York they ran Tammany, which ran the city. In Boston, they ran the Church, which ran the city. In Ireland, those who had hesitated at the gangplank ran nothing but into debt. Can miles of ocean make such a difference?

***

Father Carrol had been on the telephone. He should have called the Monsignor, the Cardinal or, perhaps, the Vatican, but thought it better if he tried the *Irish Independent* and, as an afterthought, the *An Phoblacht Republican News.* How often, after all, was he going to have anything to tell the world? He had thought he might find himself in some more significant place than Ballygoran, for priests are not without ambition even if they prefer to think of it as a calling. Was it a sin, after all, to be ambitious when it meant no more than to serve as many as possible? Now here was a chance.

The Independent was a deal more sceptical than he would have hoped. Indeed the reporter seemed a little bored. The *Republican News* was more interested. Had the Virgin not chosen Ireland and would She have done so if She had not thought the island specially blessed and in need of re-uniting? Nonetheless, they asked if She had been seen only by the one girl and when they asked to know something of her he began to feel insecure saying he would telephone them later, for he had priestly duties to attend to, one, you would have supposed, being to confess to the lies he had come close to telling. He had better think a deal more about this, he realised, before venturing further. Perhaps he had best seek out Colleen and put her claims to the test himself before someone else did so to his inconvenience.

'Well, Colleen. Would you be telling me what happened.'

'I've told it all before, Father.'

'I know child, but not to me.'

He could see how she would not look him in the eye, twisting a lock of hair round her finger. You didn't have to be with the FBI, he told himself, to see that as a bad sign. He had often felt the lack of a lie-detector, thinking it would come in handy in the confessional, but God sees everything. If only he would let me in on it, he had told himself many a time. 'Is that the truth?' he would ask. 'Surely isn't this the confessional and didn't I come here to get it off my chest? Do you not have an Our Father or a Hail Mary, at all?' the smell of sweet alcohol drifting through the lattice.

'I was doing no more than get ready for the milking and there She was.'

'What did she look like?'

'Like in the pictures.'

'Pictures?'

'She was, like, standing there and was, like, shining with a kind of mist.'

'And did she address you?'

'Address?'

'Did she say anything at all to you?'

'Like, out loud?'

'Yes, Colleen. Out loud. As I'm speaking to you now.'

The hair was being twisted again as she looked not so much at him as past him.

'It seemed to me She did, though I didn't hear it exactly.'

'Not hear it? How could you not hear it if she was speaking?'

'I heard it inside. Inside my head.'

'And where else would you be hearing it?'

'You don't have to believe it if you don't want to. Tell the truth there are moments I doubt it myself since people won't believe a word I say.'

'Would you swear on the Bible?'

'That She spoke?'

'That She was there at all.'

'Of course She was there. Haven't I been telling you.'

Did he believe her? Not at all. He was used to children having a hard time sorting out fantasy from reality. Sometimes it was easier for them to bring the world into alignment with their imaginings than the other way around, if that wasn't a principle that applied to all. At the same time it would be derelict of him not to investigate and suddenly he had, he acknowledged to himself, something of a central role for hadn't he been approached by more than a few to seek his opinion, and who knows, it is a strange world, as he should know since it was his profession to tell people so. Which is why, early the next morning, in slanting rain, he stood on the hillside and checked his watch.

It hardly seemed likely to him that the Mother of God would choose to appear in the rain. Better, surely, a fine day with the wonder of creation on display. He himself was soaked through, having left his umbrella behind, believing, as he should not have done, the previous night's weather forecast. Rain later, it had said. Later than what? It was cold, too, the wind having shifted to the North. It was five o'clock. He had a mass at seven, so it was not the hour that bothered him so much as the sense that somewhere a young girl was laughing to herself at his foolishness.

Then the rain stopped and a thin mist rolled down, picked up in places by the wind and spun like grey cotton candy. The top of the hill had disappeared and glancing around he saw it had equally closed off the world below. He was isolated, able to see nothing but a few yards in any direction. He seemed to have been whisked up into the clouds, as he had dreamed more than once he might be when his time at last had come. It was then he saw her, or saw something. Certainly the mist seemed suddenly to assume a shape, a form.

'Is it you?' he called, 'Holy Mother of God.'

Did She beckon or was the mist merely set on a move by a sudden breeze? It seemed later that She had? Certainly struck through with a mixture of terror and awe he had taken a step forward but in doing so put his foot down the entrance to a rabbit hole and fell forward, hearing the crack of the bone and his own anguished cry. 'Holy Mother of God,' though this time not enquiring as to Her identity. The mist dissolved, the figure vanished, as well it might in the circumstances, and he was alone, in the rain, with no pain yet but himself soaked through alone, that is, with the exception of a cow which chose this moment to contribute to global warming.

He slipped and slithered his way back to his house, his mind a turmoil. After a few minutes the pain had caught up with him so that it was all he could do not to shout aloud, for he had no desire for anyone to see him. Had he witnessed a miracle and if so what was the nature of his relationship to a woman who had been greeted with blasphemy? Had She been there in truth? Or had he seen no more than a phantom conjured from water vapour and the wind? What was it Dr. Johnson had said about reality? It was something you can kick, he had said, an ignorant man, when you came to think of it, for could you kick love or faith or even Australia from where he sat? But who was he to speak of reality when he preached of the Holy Ghost.

He closed the door behind him and called the ambulance. Then he dialled the number of a fellow priest, awakening him from his slumbers for he had never held a seven o'clock mass, having a liking for sleep and a parish that shared his values. 'What were you doing out so early, father, and on a hillside, too?'

'I like a bracing walk,' he replied, suddenly glad that a lie detector was not a standard issue after all.

'You'll be a regular Long John Silver,' said the ambulance man, when eventually he came, the ambulance station being twenty miles away, as he had said the same to many a person before. 'Well, let's hop to it, father. Show a leg.'

***

Mrs. Hanratty lived in Primrose Cottage whose tangled Garden had not seen a primrose for the last several years. In their place were nettles and ground elder and every plant that betokens defeat. Inside her front room a large grey cat watched with studied indifference as a mouse made its way along the high gloss skirting board and around the trap set five years before by Mr Hanratty on the eve of his death, his shortness of breath finally becoming too short to sustain him. Ballygoran cats had developed a curious indifference to mice. It was not of course the same mouse that had sniffed briefly at the sliver of Irish cheddar pressed down by the sweaty hand of a man in a trap of his own before passing on. This one proceeded to the pantry that had better things on offer including a supply of Mars bars – 'I've a terrible passion for the Mars bars, there's no denying, though I went without for a whole Lent one time.' The cat's lack of interest was a result of being fed liver and steak by a woman whose love had switched seamlessly from man to animal.

Once a week she would be joined by other widows for a game of bridge, a glass of sweet sherry and an exchange of gossip – the Neighbourhood Pry they had been called by some. They had all lost their men in one way or another, men dying earlier than women to even things up. There were no more widows in Ballygoran, though, than any other town, the balancing of injustice being a general rule. In a small town, however, it can be more noticeable.

'What did you say trumps were?'

'Diamonds.'

'Diamonds, is it?'

'It is.'

''Well I've none of those.'

'You are not supposed to tell everyone. It will be the ruin of the game.'

'We're only playing for matches.'

'A game is a game. What would life be without rules?'

'Sure I'd not disagree with that but it is not much of a game when I've no diamonds at all.'

So the game would continue throughout the afternoon, Mrs. Heaney never quite grasping its principles though she and her partner won an occasional game for chance has a way of favouring even those to whom life consists of no more than mysteries large and small.

'Was it diamonds you said?'

'That was last time. Now it's clubs.'

'Only this time I've two of them and one of those an ace.'

They would break for tea from time to time, the kettle whistling away until they finished the hand. They took it in turns to bake a cake, Mrs Heaney, though, never quite mastering that art any more than she had the cards.

'Did you put treacle in it?

'Certainly I did, for I am a lover of treacle. Did you not have it on bread sprinkled with sugar?'

'And was it plain or self-raising you used?'

'Ah, there you have me. They are different, then? I thought they were no more than different brands. Didn't my mother say that if I learned to cook I should be doing it all my life? She wanted me to marry money.''

'And you did not.'

'He had money right enough, though it turned out it was not his own in its entirety. Trumps?'

'Trumps did you say? Did I not finish telling you it was clubs not diamonds.'

'Could we not make it diamonds for I have several of them?'

'Did you hear how young Seamus was done for speeding. It's the third time, they say, and we've only the one camera so you would think he would slow down just there.'

'There's nothing in the camera. Never has been. Garda Toibin times them, on his watch. It's Japanese.'

'I don't think it's fair to use Japanese.'

'They're all the same at that age. Wasn't Eamon a devil when he was twenty and today he's in the Round Table or whatever it's called where they meet up to drink for charity?'

'He's a credit to you, even if he failed his exams.'

'There's failure and failure. He was good at the woodwork. Made me a beautiful box with "mother" written on it, though he left the "h" out on account of his dyslexia.'

'That's fashionable these days. It's going around.'

'Why would you need exams when you've a talent for business and his looking so brave besides. He was a great sportsman. He could have played for Ireland if he'd had a mind but he went down with the glandular fever.'

'Is that not what they call the kissing disease?'

'Well, he was not married then. I think you'll find that trick was ours.'

'Is it? Well, if you say so. Should we not try poker? I've heard that's a fine game.'

'Do you know how to play?'

'I do not but you should never let a day go by without learning something.'

'Why not start, then, with the fact that clubs are trumps.'

'That would not be diamonds, then.'

'What kind of a cat is that? When it purrs the cups rattle on the dresser.'

'I was giving him a spot of liver earlier.'

'I'm partial to liver myself. It's a great life they lead is it not, nothing but eating and sleeping and a mouse or two.'

'He's not one for the mice to tell the truth, though he's caught a bird or two when they've been slow on their feet.'

'They're selling two tins of beans for the price of one at O'Reilly's.'

'I've no great liking for beans.'

'No, but they are two for one.'

'Or we could try pontoon.'

'Pontoon, is it? The Yanks call that Black Jack, or is that a kind of cheese.'

'Do you know how to play that?

'It couldn't be harder than trying to remember which is trumps when it keeps changing all the time.'

'I have them on bread and butter.'

It was a mark of their meetings that no one felt obliged to follow the logic of conversations which admittedly had none but these meetings were not about logic but the need to forget and filling the air with sound had the eternal advantage of inhibiting silence which is where all troubles are born.

***

Cats are one thing. Dogs, though, are something else. Mrs. Finnerty lived with her dog Lucky, though in truth that was a misnomer for he had just one eye (a dog's life in Ballygoran being a dog's life indeed) having been hit by a golf ball struck by Father Thomas whose remorse was touched with gratitude since it stopped him going out of bounds. Mrs. Finnerty lived, too, with her memories which she replayed every evening as she sat by the window, a cup of cocoa cooling in her hand. There comes a time when the past is more vivid than the present and the future a land best not visited.

As a young woman she had wanted to be a doctor and had begun to train as such in Dublin, a place that was a swirl of people where none looked up at the stars or quietly contemplated their lives. It had ended when she forgot that acts have consequences, abandoning her dream to raise a child who became the axle around which her life turned. The child grew into beauty such as can stop the heart but when she was just turned sixteen her own heart had stopped. Her young daughter. The beautiful Jeanine. She had been living on borrowed time Mrs. Finnerty was told in the hospital, though who had lent it to her she was by no means clear if he could take it away when she was in the fullness of her life.

So she was laid in the churchyard and Mrs. Finnerty, as she had taken to calling herself after the young man who had abandoned her when her passion was high, was not the only one to mourn her passing. For the town knew that a light had disappeared and would never shine again. Nor did it, except in her memory where Jeanine still ran towards her as bright as the day, still planted a soft kiss on her cheek, the cheek where her hand strayed as the evening drew on. At such moments she could still feel those lips, still embrace the warmth of her, though the cocoa was cold and the fire burned low.

How it came about she could not say, how other girls made their way to her cottage in fear and in hope having heard she could help them as they sought the kind of absolution no priest could offer. She had learned skills enough in her time in Dublin, understood what fear and pain could do. How, you will be asking, could a woman who has lost the one dearest to her bring herself to terminate life? Because she believed children are to be loved not abandoned and that young girls should be set free who otherwise might be imprisoned by necessity. But were those scraped out of life not other Jeanines in the making, with a right to run through the fields and learn love's pain? She knew that they were or why would her fingers even now be as restless, seeming to knit with invisible wool, and why one day did she shake her head and shut the door on another girl who wished to end what she had begun?

In a town such as Ballygoran, where everyone knew, or sought to know, everyone's business, how could she have plied her dubious trade? She could because it is places such as this which understand that we are more and less than we hope to be, that what is necessary takes precedence over what is desired, and that there are times when rules and prohibitions and religion's injunctions are to be laid aside in the face of distress. Nor had she responded to every request. She could look a girl in the eyes and read something there others could not, but those who we turn to in time of need may be those we ignore when need has passed. For all it was understood she was not to be betrayed she was not someone whose company was sought.

When she walked to the shops, her dog running almost sideways and banging into occasional trees, his remaining eye growing white as he aged, people would not stop to gossip or speak of the rain any more than they would with Mr. Murphy for they both had the feel of death about them and that is something we all deny or why would we climb from our beds to face another day.

What, though, of those children who might have been, those with no name and no baptism to save them from eternity's pain? Is there a shadow world, perhaps, where they run and play, freed from time's grasp? Do they look down on us with a certain pity who every day must live with a hopeless hope and a heart full of regret? Does each one recognise the mother they never saw in life and see the tears they shed at day's end even as the years pass and they tell themselves how right they had been and how their lives would have been destroyed if Mrs. Finnerty had not opened the door to their desperation and stilled their terror?

Was Mrs. Finnerty a good woman or a bad? How will she answer when at last she is summoned to account for her life? There are those who are certain for how could such as she be allowed a glimpse of Paradise except that if Jeanine is not there waiting for her with arms and heart open, ready to kiss her cheek and hold her close for ever, well what is the use of Paradise at all?

***

Every now and then the didicoys pass through or, rather, stop a while in any field whose gate has not been secured with a padlock large enough to defy bolt cutters. For a week or two they knock on doors with clothes pegs to sell, sprigs of lavender 'for luck' they say, threatening the reverse. There are those who believe that even if they can maybe read a palm or tea leaves, they are men and women with no loyalty but to themselves or their tribe. And if anyone mislays a spoon or has a pet die well, then, it is the didicoys in their painted wagons that have cast a spell or entered through a closed window.

'What a life,' said Mrs. Shaughnessy, looking at some corsets she has had her eye on. 'Will you be reducing those,' she asked of the proprietress who had decided to branch out now that she had a rival whose underwear was less protective than provocative.

'Reducing it? They are difficult to get your hands on, there's such a demand. They're made in France, if you know what I mean.'

Indeed she did, for it was the label that had first attracted her who had always worn her mother's pink ones, for which whales had given up their lives.

'I seen one of them by the bins. He was dark and had a pig tail.'

'Pig tail would it be. Well, there you go.'

'And he'd not washed in a fortnight by his looks.'

'They're against washing, I've heard. They find one another by smell.'

'Will you be reducing it in the sale?'

'The sale? I had one of those a year or two back and never saw the purpose to it. People expected me to cut all my prices.'

'Did you not?'

'I did not.'

'They have sales in Dublin.'

'I'm sure they do. They've money to burn while I have not.'

'And why would he have been by the bins?'

'He's hoping I've put my financial dealings there.'

'In the bin?''

'They want to go around pretending they're me.'

'But anyone could see they are not.''

'They sell your details. Perhaps I could give you a little on account,' she said, more out of habit than of any intention of doing so.

'That you could, but I see you've taken a liking to those corsets, jet black as they are with crimson buttons. So I'll tell you what I'll do. You can pay half down and the rest at the end of the month.'

'That would be this month?'

'There are others would like to give them a try. How long ago is it that Michael was taken?'

'That will be three years this Friday.'

'Time enough to think of corsets. You cannot mourn too long or you will be seen as strange.'

'He was a man.'

'He was a man. Up there on his horse.'

'We had to send him to the knackers.'

'The horse.'

'Certainly the horse. Mr. Jones said he would make a fine adhesive. The hooves I think. Have you thought to tell the polis?'

'About the…?'

'The didicoy. You don't want one of those in your bins. Who knows what you might have decided to dispose of.'

'Mostly peelings.'

'Do you suppose they paint their own wagons?'

'Certainly they do. It's in the blood. And those things mean something. It's how they communicate.'

'So it's not the smell.'

'That's ants.'

'Ants? But they don't have noses.'

'They leave signs.'

'Ants?'

'No, the didicoys. They puts signs outside your house.'

'My house?'

'Everybody's house. If you give them something they put a sign up saying 'Come and Get It.' Could we make it half now and half before Christmas because I'm having my drains done.'

'Did you read about the Dublin priests?'

'Terrible. Could you imagine they would do such things, and then you have to drink from the same cup they do.'

'Do you think they've always done this, right back to St. Patrick?'

'So we're settled about the corset, then? Was there anything else you fancied?'

'You can overdo it with men. I mean, corsets are one thing, don't you feel?'

'Certainly you can. Feed a cat too much and it'll be sick.'

'A bit of fish will spark its interest, though.'

'That it will. Cats. Men. What's the difference when it comes down to it?'

***

The doctor's surgery in Ballygoran was not so much a medical facility as a social club. There were the usual coughs and sneezes and the occasional tragic case but otherwise it was a place to meet up and discuss aspects of the human body more difficult to engage with in the greengrocers.

'It's between my toes.'

'Between your toes, is it?'

'Mind you, it comes and …'

'goes. That's the way with them right enough. My mother had verucas.

'It's not verucas. It's corns.'

'Are they not the same?'

'Not at all. Not at all.'

'And my father had gout. They were a pair. They would sit there at night with their feet in salt water and if they needed something from the kitchen there would be wet footprints all over the wood veneer.'

'Corns are quite different from verucas. Verucas come from putting your feet where you should not.'

'That would be athlete's foot, like young Michael had when he competed in the hurling.'

'The feet are the worst are they not.'

'This is true, though there are places I won't mention.'

'Did you go to the fish shop today?'

'That I did not. The last time I went there he left the bones in my kippers and Mr. Flynn had to hit me on the back or I would have choked.'

'I heard he had hit you.'

'It was the kippers. You tell others that.'

'Oh, I shall. I shall. I only mention the fish shop because he had this peculiar fish they caught. The last of its kind, he said.'

'What will they do about it?'

'I bought it for the cat but it sicked it up. I've been trying to entice him back from number 12 where she lured him with a piece of steak.'

'For a cat?'

'There's no loyalty with cats. A bit of steak and they're anybody's. Have you finished the magazine?'

'It's ten years old.'

'It's not the age that counts, is it Mrs. O'Brian? Are we not as young in heart as we ever were?'

'In heart maybe, but I don't remember having to go to the lav so often in those days.'

'It's the water. They're putting something in it. I heard men are growing breasts.'

'It's the homosexuals you are thinking of.'

'There's no call for that around here, is there.'

'There is not at all. God made us as we are.'

'Verucas as well?'

'I doubt he made those. It's the shoes. They come from China where it is fashionable to crush women's feet.'

'You are right certainly. I never find a pair that really fits. What was Mrs. Cairns here for, do you think? She's been in there a terrible long time.'

'Give him his due, he is not stingy with his time. I spent half an hour with him and I only came for another bottle of expectorant.'

'I'm glad you brought that up,' said Mrs. Flynn, who had been a fan of the music hall in her youth.

'It was my adenoids,' replied her companion, who had been inoculated against humour along with measles when she was six months old.

'I've been having hot flushes.'

'Enemas?'

'Enemas? What would I need with those?'

'With friends like those who needs enemas,' tried Mrs. Flynn, knowing it was useless but not able to stop herself.

There was a silence except for the grandfather clock beside the mantelpiece ticking away the seconds of everybody's life.

'It's my age,' she said.

'I don't see the point.'

'Of hot flushes.'

'Of hot flushes, yes.'

'I don't think they have a point.'

'I mean why should we have hot flushes just because we've got a bus pass.'

'It's hormones.'

'I thought that's what we had at fifteen.'

'Yes, well you get them again.'

'I read where the Americans inject them into cows.'

'So they'd get hot flushes?'

'It didn't say. Maybe it's cold on the prairies.'

'That's Canada.'

'The prairies?'

'Yes. And the cold.'

The virtue of their conversation, like so many others in Ballygoran, was that it had neither logical beginning nor end. It could thus be picked up, dropped, reclaimed over time and in different places, knitting their lives together, as perhaps they were. They sat now for a few minutes reading the notices on the wall that described diseases that made better reading than the magazines scattered on the table: 'FEEL FREE TO BREAST FEED,' said one, though someone had crossed it out. 'DO YOU HAVE BLOOD IN

YOUR POO?' asked another, impertinently as it seemed to Mrs. Flynn as she squinted her eyes to read a third. 'HAVING DIFFICULTY READING THIS NOTICE?'

'He was a fine man.'

'That he was. Who are you speaking of?'

'The shoulders on him.'

'Right. I have you there. And the eyes.'

'Blue.'

'Blue?'

'Like sapphires.'

'They were hazel with flecks of gold.'

'We are talking of the same man?'

'Maybe it was the light. Ah, the loss of him.'

'A fine man. Should we have a cup of tea when we're done?'

'That would be the thing.'

'And him a priest.'

'The waste of it.'

'There should be a rule. They should only take ugly men as priests.'

'Sure, there are enough of them in Ballygoran.'

'Ugly priests is a great idea.'

'Do you remember Father Blaine?

'Father Blaine. Now there's a man who could curdle milk. He would terrify the life from me, with his glass eye.'

'Taking it out and polishing it before the sacrament.'

'Remember when he dropped it in the cup.'

'Who can forget, and the blasphemy.'

'There's a real echo in that church.'

'We've been waiting here an age. Does the man not realise we have things to do?'

'Things to do, indeed. What are you doing this morning?'

'Not much, for I knew he'd keep us waiting. I would have brought my knitting but I've run out of the angora.'

'To tell the truth I've never fancied angora. I always look like I'm moulting. It's bad enough with the cat.'

So the morning drifted on, as mornings were prone to do in Dr. Michael's surgery, with people coming in from time to time to collect repeat prescriptions from the near-sighted receptionist who as a result was sometimes a little random in the prescriptions she handed out.

'Is yours for the piles, Mrs. Toibin, or would that be the flatulence? Oh, I have it here. Doctor said I was to tell you not to read about the side effects or it would bring the rash on again.'

***

He had been a doctor in Ballygoran for thirty years having abandoned his ambitions to be a surgeon. Over time, he had settled into this place as an armchair will accommodate itself to a backside. There were regulars who thought themselves dying and had done since he first saw them decades since. One week it would be a mole they thought changed. The next they could not move their bowels while the following week they could do nothing else. Every now and then, though, a patient would come through the door who filled him once again with the desire to cure the world, and if not that then this single needy person who looked to him for help.

As for those who sat in the waiting room, well they were probably doing his work in their own way, though he understood the bargain that required everyone should go away with a prescription as children must leave a party with a bag of delights. He was sure he cured some, though time was often on his side since they were on their way to being better when it occurred to them to seek him out. He recalled that his function was to do no harm, which had once seemed to him to set the hurdle on the low side, and had done his best to abide by the injunction, but harm inevitably will be done from time to time in that it would take a genius to recognise every condition. In general, though, it seemed to him that the odds were in his favour.

When people wanted a little help, a certificate signed that was not perhaps entirely accurate when it suggested that work was impossible, a passport photograph endorsed for a cousin he had never met and who looked like a man on the eve of a major bullion robbery, well, he was happy to assist. For what is the function of a doctor in any community but to have someone to respect, someone you can drop your knickers for without suspicioning any funny stuff, at least that was what one of the two ladies waiting in his surgery was observing to the other, while he sat in his surgery thumbing through the racing paper, giving himself five minutes or so respite from the human condition. At last he judged a sufficiency of time had flown by, life ticking down towards some unknown destination, and reached for the buzzer that would summon the next person asking him to cure them of what could be cured and reassure them over what could not, bending the truth from time to time as he judged only right when necessity required it. 'Tell me the truth, doctor,' they said, meaning, he knew, in many cases, 'lie to me doctor for I have troubles enough without being burdened with reality.'

***

The Monsignor was summoned from the golf course to take a telephone call. He was not pleased. For once he had not sent the ball flying off the fairway, indeed off the golf course, so would not have to kick it until he got a decent lie, God understanding such necessities. There it was, right in the middle. A golden eagle had laid an egg for everyone to admire.

'It is urgent,' so they said.

'It is always urgent. I'm sure it can wait.'

'They said it could not. It was a priest is calling.'

'It will not take a minute,' he called, who knew it would take ten for did he not have to make his way back on the electric cart that had been donated by the man with many sins but more money.

'Not another virgin,' he called into the telephone once he had reached the club house and been handed the phone, 'sure I've had three virgins already this year,' an announcement that served to draw the attention of half a dozen of his fellow priests who had settled down with a whisky apiece, their travails on the golf course being finished for the day.

'There was a time when virgins were rare,' he shouted, to accompanying nods from those sitting around a low table with its striped tablecloth, their black clothes making them look like so many vultures contemplating a zebra.

'Now they come along all at once. It is too much for a man to bear. What is the child's name? Is it the young hussy who wears French underwear?'

Six glasses of whisky were set down carefully on the table, this being time to listen rather than drink.

'Do you want me to examine her, is that what you are saying? Could you not do that yourself for I am mighty busy? My ball is well positioned and someone may interfere with it if I am not careful.'

A Monsignor is a man of some power and influence, he used to remind himself from time to time. He has a certain liberty of action if it seems wise, discretion with respect to erring priests ('and what other kind are there?' he asked his housekeeper, she being deaf beyond redemption) and to young couples seeking exemption from certain rules. He was, so to speak, on call, as a doctor may be required to climb in his Ford Cortina and lance a boil.

'When did she see this? ... Is she brainless? ... Is it mischief she is up to? We are not going to build another runway I can tell you that. You have no idea what we lost on that. Why do you not tell her to forget what she saw for I can be sure she saw no such thing. Would the Holy Mother appear to someone who wears French knickers? ... Well you may think so but I do not ... Very well, but not until I have finished. I have left my ball alone for long enough.'

He returned to see his fellow players smoking in a circle, their smoke rising up as if a new Pope had been elected which would not, he thought, be such a bad idea given that the present one spent so much of his time gaining frequent flyer miles instead of being infallible.

'You know,' said one of them, 'life is a lot like golf.'

'Save it for Sunday,' objected another.

'One moment we are on the fairway to heaven, the next in the rough. No one ever had a perfect score. It is just a case of picking the right club and you are on the green in one and putting for the hole, for heaven's gate.'

'If you were a Muslim there would be seventy virgins waiting for you, though why they should want seventy I have never been clear.'

'I heard tell it was a mistranslation and what is promised is really seventy raisins.'

'Seventy raisins? And what are they supposed to do with that, bake a cake?'

'I think it is symbolic.'

'Of what? Seventy virgins are one thing but seventy dried grapes are quite another.'

'And what is heaven to you?'

'A day with no rain, a new set of clubs and a magic ball.'

'Will we still be priests in heaven?'

'How come?'

'Will we have to abide by the same rules as now. For who knows, maybe the two heavens will get mixed up and we'll get the seventy virgins.'

'More likely the raisins you ask me.'

The Monsignor came towards them, gliding on a golf buggy perhaps practising to be Pope.

'We waited for you for it is not every day you end up on the fairway. It is human to err, Monsignor, but perhaps not to hook to the right quite so regularly'

To hell with them all, he thought. It was only on the golf course they would have the nerve to make fun of him. Did they not realise he could have them washing the feet of the poor if he wanted

'It's a hundred and twenty feet,' said one of them, reading his mind while stepping back to allow him to swing.

'A hundred and twenty feet, is it,' he said, who thought it was closer to eighty, though what the difference when his only tactic was to hit the ball as hard as he could. He looked at where the flag hung limply and settled himself before swinging like King Richard at the Crusades cutting down the Saracens. As he did so, however, the flag fluttered into life until it was like a pointer dog showing where the slaughtered quail had landed. He looked down at the ball and swung. When he looked up hoping to see it bounce on the green, like a flat stone skimming across the ocean, there was nothing in sight.

'Hooked to the right,' said the priests who had a small bet with him, knowing it was as secure as the rock on which the Church rested. 'They're Protestant balls. They have no faith to keep on the straight and narrow.'

'You need a new set of clubs, Monsignor. They're like everything else. The older they get the more they forget what they are for.'

'Was the phone call important, Monsignor? You look out of sorts.'

'Another virgin.'

'Another virgin is it. Sure we were just talking about them.'

'Some adolescent girl has seen something which she takes to be Our Lady and was probably a puff of smoke.'

'Sure we've been having a fair number of them of late. It is like 1976 when they were popping up like mole hills all over the place.'

'One of the girls at the convent.'

'Well what do you expect. They are kept away from the boys and we know what that can lead to.'

His meaning was doubtless innocent but it was an uneasy set of priests who now directed their steps towards the clubhouse, already tasting the peaty strength of a half cask whisky.

***

'Didn't he always keep two pennies in his pocket for his own dead eyes,' she said, 'in case whoever found him had no small change about them.'

'He was a careful man.'

'That he was, and always thinking about his death. 'You're to put your ear to my mouth and listen hard,' he would say, 'and fetch a mirror and see if it mists. For I've no desire to be buried alive.'

'It was a fear he had.'

'And wasn't it one of many. There was a time, do you remember, when the shoe shops had those machines, x-rays they were before anyone knew the harm they could do. And you'd put the children on them so they could see the bones of their feet, all glowing green. They would stay there happy as spinning tops for a half hour if need be. Well today, of course, the dentist flattens himself against the wall or goes half way down the corridor for fear it will burn him from the inside out, though they get you to hold your own finger there alright, not caring what would happen to it. Anyway, he was one of those who had watched his toes and now he expected them to drop off any time soon. The same with his hand. Didn't he have one of those glowing watches on his wrist. Radio active they were, like the one's they marched against at Aldermaston. So it was good bye to his hand. He had an alarm clock beside his bed at night, and when he found out the damage they caused, didn't he take it and put it on his wife's side instead. A careful man, indeed, at least when it came to himself.

'As are all men, as it seems to me.'

'Isn't that the truth. They think of nothing but themselves and where their next meal is coming from and the football and young women they think would be interested in them and they with hair growing out their ears and stomachs you could hear a street away.'

'Ah, but do you remember when we were young?'

'That I do. For we were a beautiful pair, you and I, and didn't the boys want to be with us, and weren't we chased after all day long.'

'That we were, whatever the nuns said.'

'Sister Agnes!'

'Oh, Sister Agnes, and she with a moustache on her that could have won a competition.'

'And then there was your David. There was a fella.'

'So he was, and he and I walking out together for three long years.'

'That was a terrible thing.'

'It was. It was, and we getting ready to be married.'

'A terrible thing.'

'So I married James.'

'Not David at all. Well, life's a strange thing, after all. Were you not happy, though?'

'Sure I was from time to time. There could have been worse. But David, there's something I never got over.'

'Him dead at nineteen and so beautiful, for he was as fine as any man I have seen.'

'That he was.'

'Even lying there in his coffin.'

'Don't go on about him for it is more than I can bear.'

'Even these years later? Don't bruises fade with time?'

'Bruises do, but not scars, not a scar such as this, and him only driving for a week.'

'They said if he had taken the bend only ten miles slower.'

'If apples were oranges they'd come from Spain.'

'Is that what they say?'

'Thirty-one years come September. I remember the leaves in the churchyard and the way they fell so light on the ground. I watched them fall so as not to cry. And the sycamores spinning down and the rain that started and wouldn't stop as though the angels in heaven couldn't hold back their tears.'

'That was a terrible time ago.'

'It was yesterday and I'm there in my dreams, even as the other lies beside me snoring away to remind me of what I have lost.'

'Do you not love him then?'

'Love him? There were times I thought I did but then the rain would come, or it would be autumn again and I would find myself looking up for the sycamores and seeing the leaves all stained rust so there would be no more room for love that had all been used up those years ago on poor David.'

'You have to go on.'

'That you do.'

'For the children if for nothing else.'

'Ah, sure, the children, and aren't they a blessing.'

'They've gone away, though.'

'And what else would they do? Would they be staying here where there is nothing to do? No, I've one in Australia and another in Spain who married the maid he met in a hotel when he was selling the vacuums. They've children of their own now, of course.'

'Do you see them often?'

'Australia is a powerful way away and we've not the money to be going. They've not been back in ten years. As for young David, we don't see eye to eye, I'm afraid.'

'Did you name him for the other.'

'That I did.'

'And did your husband not mind him being named for another?'

'He knows nothing of him. It is a secret I hold tight. You know of him because we were young together but I wouldn't want others to know, not at all.'

'You didn't want to hurt his feelings.'

'His feelings, is it? No, not that at all. It is that I want somewhere to go in my mind. It is what keeps me going when all else is lost, for I have memories I'd not let go, not until it is all over and I'm at St. Peter's door. When I am there at last I will have a question to ask: how could God have placed that tree where he did knowing that David would be coming that way for He knows everything they say but, sure, knowing everything is no good at all unless you're prepared to do something about it. Are you finished with those prunes for I have a terrible need for easing myself what with the suet puddings he is always demanding?'

***

The Monsignor looked at her with the air of a housewife inspecting a bruised peach, affronted that they could expect her to buy it.

'I'm told you have seen the Virgin, and you with one sock down and one sock up and a smear of chocolate on your face.'

No reply.

'Was it you who saw Her at all or should the two of us forget this nonsense and be on our way. I was once in Egypt and saw this lake out in the sand, bright and shining and inviting us all to slake our thirst for I wouldn't buy water from one of those fellows who went around with a tin cup on a chain and probably had us down as infidels worth killing off with the runs. And would you know it, it was not there at all. A trick of the light, do you see. And that is what you thought you saw no doubt. So, no blame to anyone and we're both home in time for tea.'

'It would be the heat?'

'I beg your pardon.'

'What you saw was a mirage from the heat. I saw it in Lawrence of Arabia, along with the sinking sands and him being beaten by the Turks and worse it is said.'

'You frequent the fil-ums?' he asked, as he might ask a nun if she was often in brothels.

'I was with my ma who has a thing for Peter O'Toole.'

'Irish is he?'

'It's the blue eyes, she says, and the white of his body.'

'I don't think the whiteness of his body is a fit subject for a young girl, do you, whether he's Irish or not?'

'It was my mother I was speaking of. She has a weakness for blue eyes, she said.'

'We were talking of this nonsense of yours.'

But for the word nonsense he might have got his way for she had been inclined to let the whole thing go being no longer clear what had happened or if it had.

'I saw Her right enough.'

'Did She speak to you?'

'She may have.'

'May have?'

'It was like the confessional. I am not to say.'

'Are you setting yourself up as a priest now,' he asked, glimpsing a sullen intelligence in the girl.

'I know what I know.'

Then he changed his tack for he had learned that if you cannot go one way then it is best to go another.

'Well, what may have been may have been and if it was it was a blessing. But it was meant for you and no other and you had best store it away as a comfort for I can find nothing that would provide the proof that I need.'

'And is that not what faith is, Monsignor. Is that not something you know is so but cannot prove?'

'Well, that's as maybe but let's call it a day. You are a girl of a certain age and fancies that may seem real enough one day may seem something else the next. Run along and say a Hail Mary for your soul.'

'You do not believe me, then.'

'It is not a question of belief. I am not going to raise money for another runway.'

***

What of Peg who they all thought mad? They pass her by thinking it a kindness, for what is to be done about someone as damaged as she. Does she not live with her mother who is scarcely less mad than her having been deserted at the altar by a man who ran the whole length of the church with her veil snagged in his shoe and he pursued by spirits, in part, no doubt, as a result of the spirits he had consumed? Maybe that was why spirits have been her refuge ever since though the reason he ran was perhaps Peg herself, for she was born within six months, a birth that lasted the best part of a day, her mother's screams echoing down the street so that everyone closed their windows despite the heat, screams and the kind of words that were seldom heard though sometimes to be seen written in the public toilet outside The Shamrock, along with drawings to educate those in need of such.

At first she would wheel a pram, given to her by Catholic Aid, brazening out her sin, for had she not been ready to marry in church who might have taken herself away. It was not long after, though, that she realised something was wrong, having been told as much on the day of the birth but choosing not to believe it, as who would not knowing it was for life and nothing to be done about it.

They had asked if she would be giving the damaged child away but there was a stubbornness about her, that was no doubt another reason for her desertion. So she withdrew into her house and into herself. None of the other children would have time for her daughter when at last she allowed her out, except they would call her names and throw the odd stick at her until she chased them away, biting one so hard that she would bear the scar for the rest of her life. Though the police knocked on their door they left without it opening, knowing she had been taunted, understanding the cruelty of children supposed to be innocent but all of them carrying the mark of the devil.

Thereafter, she was left alone as she walked the streets, head tilted down a little seeking an invisible path. What guided her feet none could say, for she chose a different way every day marking out her territory, perhaps, or in search of something lost, and something was clearly lost that could never be recovered. Nor would the rain stop her, neither the snow. She would wear a greatcoat when the ice rimed the trees silver black and great boots that left tracks like those of a creature from another time.

No da. He's off and gone. But he's waiting for me I know. I seen him in dreams. I dream and there are people there and I cry and he's coming. He's not at all, she says, and the bottle on the floor where she falls over it. She falls and I can see her lying there and there'll be no tea unless I reach the jam down and spread it with a spoon. No knife. Don't you touch the knife. No ma but I know where there's a knife. I must be going. Get a breath she says then snoring though the day. Wrap up, she says. Not asleep. And crying like me and it spilt on the floor. No jam at all. But it's cold. The coat is behind. I'll take a breath, though. Song. She sings a song. No it's me, for I hear it and the breath coming out, steam like the kettle. Let's have ourselves a cup shall we? We'll share as we've no money at all. In her purse she keeps it. Comes back empty but a jar of jam.

Walking this way. Been here before. No. Never. Boys throw sticks and stones. Little idjits! Pay no mind. Head down. He's here somewhere. I know. Said he would come back. Come back Jamie she says in the night. Crying, like me. Cold and the blanket gone until morning and the sky so bright. You were to be my hope, she says. My hope she says. Her eyes all water. Jam, I say but she turns away. Poor child. And who is that? No children here and the others throwing stones. Walk on. So I do. I am called Peg. I hear it shouted at me. Mad Peg. Alone. Want a cat to hold. Dirty, filthy things, she says. Seen a cat and bought it home. Home in my jumper and laid it down. It did nothing. She threw it out. And the sky bright. I seen white rain. My fingers cold, hurting. Not by the fire you idjit. That's the way to chilblains. Chilblains, she said. And when I've gone, she says. What'll you do? And can I leave you or should I do away with you? Do away. Like gone away. Like my da. And I put my boots on. Go look for him. A handsome man she says. You'll catch your death. And it's all bright in my eyes. No cat. I looked for it. No cat. Uphill today, my mouth a pain. Tooth wobbling. Fairy she said and I looked. A penny, she says. That's what it is. Can you say that? I can say that.

I go in the trees. Don't be wetting yourself. I go in the trees and there's little things. I can see them. Black little things. Pick one up. It's still. And it's white rain and I go back. In the road. Down the road. One of them looking. Head down. Say nothing.

Hello Mad Peg,' and I am going on. Path to the door. Take you boots off. Warm. 'What did I tell you?' Look down. Fire hot. Wipe your behind. Idjit, she says, and I lay down for the dark and to see my da. Idjit, she says and the dark comes.

***

Professor Thomas Percy O'Leary had retired from Trinity College, though he disliked the word containing, as it did, intimations of his being 'tired,' having simply run out of steam like an old boiler. He had been made Emeritus, which he translated as 'redundant,' and certainly at the ceremony conferring the title the orator had seemed to deliver his brief, and as it happened, inaccurate speech with evident satisfaction. He was given a paperweight and informed that his email account (not that he had ever really used it) would be taken away, along with his room and access to research funds, his research, admittedly, for many years having consisted of doing nothing more than attend the International Conference of Professors, an organisation that seemed to exist to arrange wine tasting in various foreign resorts.

Once, on a visit to Norwich Cathedral, being interested in Sir Thomas Brown's *Urn Burial,* he had noticed a plaque dedicated to a minister who had delivered his sermons 'entirely without enthusiasm,' which seemed to him an entirely correct position and which sentiment he embraced at a cost to generations of students who were numbed into semi-consciousness by a delivery that made the word monotone seem altogether too excited and varied. He regarded younger lecturers, with their flashy pieces of technology, who gave lectures apparently believing they were auditioning for some Hollywood film, as betraying the seriousness of their profession.

He had, admittedly, suffered from two unfortunate conditions, being a diabetic and subject to narcosis. The problem was that he was not good at monitoring his sugar intake and as a result was liable, when chairing meetings, to sudden, red-faced bouts of anger, once attacking the professor of French for the irregularities of his verbs, throwing a copy of his Anglo-Saxon primer the length of the table until someone found a Werther's Original to restore his sugar if not his mental balance. He was equally oblivious to the effects of his narcosis so that at international conferences he would introduce the speaker, return to his seat and immediately, and in full view of everyone but the speaker, fall asleep. He would be woken by the applause and had an all-purpose question ready which never failed: 'I wonder if you put sufficient emphasis on women?' Even radical feminists would be taken aback, afraid they had failed in their radicalism.

On another occasion he had been chairing a session at which a foreign lecturer went on well beyond his appointed time. Accordingly, he scrawled a note saying 'ONE MORE MINUTE,

PLEASE' and was about to pass it to the man whose accent was impenetrable and who placed his emphasis on the wrong syllable with such consistency that it did indeed seem a previously undiscovered language, when he realised that he could not remember whether the word 'minute,' meaning a period time, was spelt in the same way as 'minute' meaning very small much as Miss Heaney had worried over the word 'wind.' Since the man in question, besides being incomprehensible, was also on the short side he feared he might stop and ask 'minute what?' meaning small. As a result he covered the note with the sleeve of his leather-patched Harris Tweed jacket, in desperate need of re-lining, and the man went on strangling the English language for a further 30 minutes (unit of time).

Asked to teach American literature, a request he regarded as perverse, at the suggestion of his wife he offered a prize for the most phallic drawing of Florida, an act of generosity that, unaccountably to him, led to a delegation of young women to the Dean objecting to his anthropomorphising of geography, though as it happened he had received three entries, one from the girl who led the delegation for whom £10 was evidently worth having.

His personal habits were also somewhat strange. He was liable to summon the Estates Office if a light bulb failed in his room and if they did not respond then to call the local fire brigade who finally suggested they would be happy to see the building burn down if he was not restrained or if the college did not invest in better light bulbs.

Required to have a computer he was amazed when he opened his first e-mail to find someone offering treatment for erectile dysfunction, wondering how they knew. He was also moved by the young Nigerian prince who had been deposed and sought help in transferring his money abroad and was willing to pay generously for any assistance. There was also, apparently, a young woman in Russia who was anxious to make contact with him except that the university introduced a new programme that swept such requests away, showing a callous disregard for human need as it seemed to him. For someone bemused by technology, however, he found himself returning to his emails several times a day, not sending any but in hope that there might be something of interest beyond being copied into messages sent from one office to the neighbouring one asking if they fancied a cup of tea.

He had his triumphs, though, a note in *Notes and Queries* and attendance at the annual conference on the Anglo Saxon World, picketed on occasion by those who regarded Anglo Saxons as historic villains and a threat to Irish pride. He even joined a march protesting at an anomaly in university teachers pay, which was now out of line with that of another profession, chanting along with everyone else: 'RECTIFY THE ANOMALY. WHEN DO WE WANT TO RECTIFY THE ANOMALY. NOW! NOW! NOW!' Eventually he became head of department as age slowly removed those ahead of him, though in truth affairs were really run by his secretary Pauline, with her steely eyes and red-striped jumper. Under his name she would send out gnomic notices, remove words from the letters he dictated if she had not heard of them, substituting her own, or simply leave them out because they seemed to create a negative impression of the department to which she was devoted . Hence his reply to an Indian student that there would not be a summer school was made more positive by removing the word 'not' so that he turned up the following July.

Whether out of guilt or something else, she offered him a room and they were married a year later so that thereafter there was always a slight smell of curry in the department while her new husband enrolled as one of the professor's graduate students or, to be more accurate, his only graduate student. By tacit agreement his PhD turned into a marathon rather than a sprint so that after a while he seemed to have the permanency of a familiar pair of slippers whose utility was no longer questioned.

The Professor had taken early retirement, though not quite early enough for many of his colleagues who suffered from his ban on teaching any writer not as yet certified as being dead. 'Time will select the syllabus,' he had proclaimed, even rejecting the lecturer who asked if he could teach Graham Green on the grounds that at the time he was almost dead. It was a notion he had picked up at Cambridge where he attended Jesus College. Being England, of course, where New College, Oxford, was the oldest and public schools were private, that was not in fact its name. It was The College of the Blessed Virgin Mary, Saint John the Evangelist and the Glorious Virgin Saint Radegund, near Cambridge,' and though difficult to fit on the t-shirt he had a liking for those introducing him to list its full name. Radegund was a Frankish princess, a concubine of Clothar I, King of the Franks, who planned the murder of his brother's children and subsequently burned his son and family to death. Understandably, Radegund left in a hurry and founded a convent, not least because her uncle had already killed her father, and defeated another uncle. No wonder, the Professor might have thought, were he given to such random concerns, Radegund remained a virgin, unless that was a courtesy title given that she was, after all, a concubine, virginity, perhaps, being on sale or return.

He had an MA from the same university, discovering that he was not required to do any work in order to acquire one, a practice discontinued by Harvard in 1869 but still flourishing in countries where advancement required a small tip to those in authority and simply surviving for half a dozen years. And why should he not use it since outside every church across England, he had discovered, were notices bragging that the local vicar had bribed his way to an Oxford or Cambridge MA.

He had, however, picked up something else, or, rather, someone else while in Cambridge. He had married his bedder whose ancient title concealed a more modern truth. It was not for nothing that a 1635 edict had banned women under fifty years of age, knowing that the young men whose rooms they were obliged to enter would have mated with a hat stand if nothing or no one else were to hand. At the time he was there their role had been defined as 'looking out for the needs of young people who are far from home,' which is exactly what his wife-to-be had done though he himself had been somewhat confused by her advances until she took matters in hand.

Coming from rural Ireland, where he had passed his exams in the face of bullies who thought intelligence a sign of homosexuality, he was thrilled, if somewhat baffled, by Cambridge where the colleges were like so many castles guarded by men in bowler hats called porters who were never seen to be porting anything. Why was Latin necessary to study English, he wondered, as he read of Caesar drawing up his boats on the shores of Gaul and discovered how absolute an ablative could be from a man who wore a gown and a monocle? He read his essays aloud to another man, with hair growing out of every visible orifice who spent the entire hour trying to press a filter cigarette into a cigarette holder or, having eventually despaired, lighting the wrong end. He learned to punt though soaking his trousers so people thought he had wet himself. He adjusted his accent to the point that when he went home his parents could not understand him, though in truth they never had.

For his PhD he went to Aberystwyth where rain flew horizontally up Pier Street which would have to change its name soon, he thought, as one day he saw the end of the pier drop off. If Ballygoran had seemed remote, however, Aberystwyth seemed even more so. If you travelled for two-and-a-half hours on the single track railway you would reach Shrewsbury which he knew the Anglo Saxons called Scrobbesburh, the town of the bushes, which perhaps hinted that it had been a haven for homosexuals and was anyway hardly an incentive to stop off, this place in which they pronounced the name of the town as Shruwsbury on one side of a bridge and Shrowsbury on the other. So he decided to return to Ireland where they do not call their towns after shrubs, though in truth, as he discovered, Dublin means 'town of the hurdled ford,' or derived from 'black pool' which was hardly an association likely to be of benefit . He had a fascination with language which seemed to him a series of codes within codes.

There was a lectureship at Trinity College, whose real name was no more Trinity than Jesus was Jesus, being The College of the Holy and Undivided Trinity of Queen Elizabeth Near Dublin, the Queen Elizabeth being something of an embarrassment and the Irish meaning of 'near' not being too apparent given that it was located plum in the middle of the city. But then this was a country that boasted an airline whose destinations were seldom as advertised, passengers arriving at what they had taken to be major cities only to discover that they lay some way distant and that they would need to take another travel pill or so before finally arriving there on buses that lacked the glamour of air travel as it had once been before you were obliged to travel with someone's knees in your back and buy food from hostesses also required to clean the toilets, presumably washing hands between functions.

Once there he remained unnoticed, which is a sure way to progress one's career. He then published his major book – *The Great Vowel Shift: Why?* – which to everyone's surprise, though it carried the imprint of the East Alabama University of Christ's Second Coming Press, won him a chair, the appointment panel being radically divided over the two preferred candidates, he coming through on the rails, his relative invisibility proving a key to advancement.

Once he attained his chair his wife insisted on calling him professor even in the privacy of their own home – 'Professor, would you pass the salt,' 'Professor, the cat has been sick.' -- a title she used whenever they needed the car repaired, wrongly assuming that mechanics would share her respect for a man who could speak Anglo-Saxon, as, so it happened, could she, though only whispered urgently in his ear when otherwise he might seem to have forgotten his function.

He had hoped to retire in Dublin, having invested a small inheritance in an assurance company. His Anglophilia, however, was such that he put his trust in a British company, established in 1762 and triple-A rated, though evidently by those living in fairy land for the company was Equitable Life which duly betrayed him along with its history. He had been wise enough, however, not to put everything there. He also put money in technology shares and a little in a housing market that was booming and promised to go on doing so before failing to do so. Which is why he had retired to Ballygoran where he had been born, though his wife was far from pleased.

It was distant from Cambridge, with its rich people who said 'hice' for 'house' and had names that were not pronounced as spelt. His wife remembered, in particular, a Mr. Featherstonehugh, which apparently was to be pronounced Fanshaw, a man who would dress up in fancy clothes and destroy restaurants for the sake of tradition. To think, she had had her choice of young men into whose rooms she had had free entry and, indeed, had sampled from the free buffet of testosterone-charged blue bloods en route from Eton and

Winchester to the British cabinet. Why she chose him she could not now remember for surely it had been a strange decision since even then he had had his peculiar habits, wearing a deerstalker hat (he was an admirer of Sir Arthur Conan Doyle) and smoking a pipe whose tobacco had little to recommend it beyond the fact that it masked the smell of the rancid milk he kept on his window sill and forbad her to throw away. 'I'm making cheese,' he had explained and indeed it did eventually turn solid, that being its closest approximation to his intended product. But evidently she saw something in him that others did not. Certainly he had not ventured the usual random assault and indeed it was she, rather to his astonishment, who had crossed the line bedders were instructed not to cross.

It was far, too, from Dublin, with its buses and packed pavements and undergraduates who drank to become poets. There she had been included in public events, pockets full of Werther's Originals, and relishing her role as professorial wife, though she fitted in poorly with others who tended to look at her as someone who had been washed up on the beach. To be sure, every now and then a vision of Featherstonehugh would float before her eyes even if she had heard rumours of his imprisonment for embezzlement no doubt surprised that once you have left university what were once pranks are unaccountably regarded as crimes unless rewarded with high office.

In Ballygoran they lived in a cottage near the convent school where he watched the young girls in their navy blue knickers playing hockey as nuns with flying habits blew their whistles, or at least he did until his wife changed his study to the front of the house where he would not be tempted and could watch the postman arrive with unsolicited mail and the milkman run from house to house so as to be home in time for his wife who had heard about milkman and discovered it was true.

He was now at work on his second book -- to be called *The Great Vowel Shift: Why Not?* -- not being a believer in the reckless speed with which others published. Meanwhile, and after a time, he settled into the speed of life in Ballygoran or, rather, to his relief the lack of it, Dublin having always seemed a place where everyone was rushing somewhere even if it was never clear to him where that might be. At least they did outside the gates of Trinity for within he had always taken pleasure in a certain calmness that was the effect of stately grey stone buildings, though he had always been resentful that the public were allowed in believing that Samuel Beckett might be waiting for them or the Book of Kells some kind of book of magic such as Harry Potter might have owned, knowing of Harry Potter only because a young lecturer had proposed a course on the book until a brusque note from Pauline, under his name, had set things right.

Had he but known it he was held in some regard in Ballygoran for the Irish have always had an admiration for those of learning. 'There goes the professor,' they would say, as he wobbled by on his newly-acquired bicycle, behaving as they believed a professor should, namely seeming to notice nothing, not even the cats that wandered across the road in front of him until, recognising that he would not give way to them, as steam does to sail, they resentfully picked up speed before glaring back at him no doubt wishing they were still witches' familiars as, who knows, perhaps they were. He still wore his deerstalker hat and scarf in all weather and in truth what more could any man want than a functional bicycle, a task to go to every day, and a well-made bed, for his wife had not lost the skill that had once brought them together, nor the desire that she thought might be reciprocated if only she blew hard enough on the embers.

And who knows, one day when *The Great Vowel Shift: Why Not?* is published, there might be those who will make their way to this outpost of Anglo-Saxon scholarship to be shown around the house where it had been written by a woman from the Fens. 'There's the desk at which he wrote,' she would say, having pocketed the entry fee, for she would be getting by on only half of his university pension. 'And there's the bicycle on which he did his thinking.'

'Now there was a well-made bed,' they would perhaps comment as they left, noticing a number of black cats on the opposite pavement with what appeared to be grins of satisfaction on their faces.

The academic career is not for everyone. After all, there are doubtless those for whom six hours of teaching a week might seem excessive, for whom twenty-two weeks of vacation might appear a challenge, but someone, he reassured himself, has to educate the young in need of scholarship alongside the drinking and copulation to which they otherwise seemed to dedicate themselves. Did no one notice his going except He who unaccountably keeps a tally of sparrows dropping out of the sky? Of course there was his wife who now had to take the right coloured bin out for those who took the rubbish away in yellow vehicles which kept repeating that it was reversing in a voice that reminded her of Mr. Featherstonehugh.

***

Once a year the citizens of Ballygoran gathered together for a music festival. Strenuous efforts were made to prevent Sister Hilda from taking part but she was a force difficult to resist. The truth was that anyone who could play an instrument, or believed they could, was invited. It is said that animals can sense an impending disaster. Birds take to the air, deer dart into the forest before the tornado strikes, the tsunami sweeps in, the ground heaves with an earthquake. So it proved once a year in Ballygoran as, with the first light of dawn on the appointed day, dogs and cats took themselves under chairs, hedgehogs rolled themselves into prickly balls, cows farted in apprehension.

People who never spoke to one another on any other day exchanged the odd word. They would climb into their lofts and recover instruments that only emerged once every twelve months. Year old spit was shaken from flutes. Violins and double bases were tuned, though not necessarily to the same notes. Thousands of miles away whales doubtless swam perplexed as low frequency versions of Clair de Lune reached their defenceless ears. Another millennium of evolution would be needed before they had hands to put over them.

The piece they would play was agreed at a vote and everyone was required to rehearse on their own until the moment they would come together. This year it was to be 'What are we going to do about Maria?' the nuns having rigged the ballot, requiring their pupils to fill in their forms in class. They were also asked to master 'Climb Every Mountain,' this having edged out 'My Way' on the grounds, Sister Hilda explained to her charges, that it was sung by Mr. Sinatra who while, like many Popes, being Italian otherwise shared little with the pontiff. The task of conducting fell to Mr. Baines, who taught music and woodwork and undertook the task because he believed he was a sinner who must purge his guilt and that such purging required suffering.

As a gesture, the Indian couple from the post office offered to perform something from a Bollywood film but Bollywood had yet to penetrate as far as Ballygoran so that the sight of two people with bangles on their wrists twitching their heads from side to side like a scene from *The Exorcism*, which some had attended under the illusion that it might be theologically stimulating, left their audience bemused even as it set a dog, no doubt waiting for Sister Hilda, to chasing its tail in an image of infinity. Mrs. Ryan could not watch, having had a disastrous affair with an osteopath.

'They're all right with the stamps, though,' observed Kathleen Flynn, with a boy friend in Germany who a geographically challenged school had sent on an exchange to the nearby state school.

In case of an emergency, Mr. Murphy and his hearse were ready, not in expectation of their normal trade, though Mrs Murphy always lived in hope, but because the doctor had thought it best to be elsewhere and Mr. Murphy was as close as they could get to someone trained to deal with the human body, though admittedly somewhat too late to deploy the kind of first aid that might be called for. His hearse, for all its measured pace, would also be quicker than an ambulance that would have to come from twenty miles away and whose crew were still resentful following their last call out which turned out to be about rescuing a cat that had trapped itself in a tree. 'I asked for the fire brigade,' insisted Mrs. McBride, 'could I be blamed if they send the likes of you with no interest in cats.'

There was a sign outside a tent which read: 'Catch the Greased Pig,' though this had proved more hopeful than accurate, the organisers having failed to catch it in the first place since they had chosen to use pig fat on it. This had offered it a glimpse of its own future so that it was last seen on the Dublin road where it showed a surprising turn of speed, like all of us imagining it could outrun its fate.

The priest had already been to the harbour to bless the fishing boats, sprinkling with water craft already having a surplus of such. Now he wandered around doing his best to look interested and aware of the sins those he passed had committed, one or two of which had struck him as particularly innovative. In common with others he was surprised at the lack of rain, though clouds were gathering to the east so that perhaps it might be in the tradition of other such celebrations after all.

When young he had not been without ambition, seeing himself in Rome, perhaps, or maybe on the radio seeking to find some moral in daily events – 'sure, I see where the currency is down this week, and isn't that the way. One day we are up, the next down.

And God is a little like that – up in the sky yet down here on earth.' But the telephone never rang and his own career had had few ups nor could he persuade himself that Ballygoran was anything but down. Here comes Mrs. Michael, he thought, with her moustache and breath like drains. 'Hello, Mrs. Michael.' 'Hello, father, let me give you a kiss for I have won on the tombola.' Instinctively he took a step backwards and raised his hand as if Dracula himself had spied him and had a thirst on him.'

'And what did you win?'

'A tin of sardines, though the key is missing.'

'Ah,' he might have thought, and is the key not missing from all our lives unless we embrace the faith.' But there was no radio producer to hand even had he spoken out loud as he was half convinced he might have done.

'Sardines are just the thing.'

'So they are, father,' replied Mrs. Michael, who was genetically disposed to believe anything said by a priest. Had he realised as much he might have had a deal of fun but having just been introduced to the somewhat baffling traditions of Bollywood and already catching something of the aroma given off by Mrs Michael he was anxious to be off.

'I must be going to the bookstall for I suspect they will have some bargains on offer.' Once you have committed yourself to faith, he acknowledged to himself, there is no going back for the books would surely consist of the usual stained paperbacks along with hard-backs about the ten greatest miracles or histories of the

Boer War. They were not great readers in Ballygoran and if they were then the visiting library could satisfy their needs as, he had heard, it satisfied the needs of one of his parishioners, though she had made no mention of it in the confessional, but that was the way with the best sins. People kept them to themselves not thinking how boring his life could be given the pettiness of the transgressions he was obliged to punish. 'I had the last piece of chocolate,' 'I put the wrong bin out and said I had forgot.' Heaven, they presumably assumed, must have shuddered at the evidence of such wickedness. Give me adultery any day, he thought, as he by-passed the book stall in favour of the hand-made cakes and pickles.

'Hello, father. Would you like a little sample of my lemon curd?'

'Not at all,' interjected Seamus O'Grady, 'you'll be wanting a little of my home-made wine.'

'Wine? Do you have grapes, then?'

'Did I say wine? What I meant is a little something I prepare like my father before me.'

'The one who…'

'He was not as drunk as they said. Anyway, the brakes had never been any good.'

'But I thought …

'Nor the steering either.'

The day had begun with the sky aflame, a warning, as it turned out, not only for shepherds. It is true that many awoke with a sense of expectation, even if that did not extend to their cowering pets. Chairs borrowed from Murphy's funeral parlour would be set out on what they all agreed to call the village green, which was certainly green even if theirs was not strictly a village. There was a stage of sorts, erected by boy scouts watched over with suspicious zeal by some of the Christian Brothers. An awning hung over it in expectation of the rain which invariably came this, seemingly, being a ceremony expressly designed to provoke it. The previous year it had been made of red flannel whose dye had bled onto those below as tough they were attempting a synchronised nose bleed.

'I'm off home for a wee while,' Mr Baines explained to himself, there being no others around once the Christian Brothers had driven their flock back to school. 'And a wee drink.' It was not tea of which he spoke but even when in converse with no one but himself he was inclined to a certain discretion. It was a hopeless hope, however, for he was bound to fulfil his function no matter how much he might resent it.

As it happened it did not rain, which some found disconcerting having equipped themselves with Wellington boots and rain hats that did nothing for their looks. In fact the problem was rather the opposite. By eleven the temperature was such that ice creams, made locally by Mary O'Rourke (in competition with the Almanses and their repertoire of jingling Italian operas) from the unpasturised milk of her unvaccinated cows, melted before they could be licked away and young Kirsty McBride fainted at the coconut shy, for the festival was accompanied by a fair of sorts.

'Pregnant,' observed Mrs FitzPatrick, who thought the worst of everyone, though admittedly not always without cause.

There were gypsies in town to run the Ferris wheel and the shooting stall. They were there, too, to sell their usual twists of lavender, read fortunes and steal the odd bicycle or two.

'There's a fine young man you will be meeting in a wee while,' a woman with rings through her ears and a scarf bound round her head said to the lesbian Kathleen O'Flynne, who kept her inclinations to herself and Maureen McDowell who worked in the un-co-operative co-op.

'You'll be coming into money.'

'It's a pity I have none at the moment, then,' Kathleen replied and left the tent without paying, thus incurring a gypsy's curse, and there are those who believe in such for there has to be something to account for Irish history.

The first event was for the under elevens who had been set to learn the violin and for whom this was the first chance to express their resentment. Their parents looked on with a mixture of pride and dismay for the lessons had cost good money and the results were hardly commensurate. Mr. Baines waved his baton like a man signalling for help. The piece, though, was short and most can stand pain provided it is not prolonged.

'Ah, the darlings,' observed Mrs. Fingle, the greengrocer's wife, 'what was that they were playing?'

It was a question that had occurred to others but a certain latitude must be granted to the young. The same logic, however, was less justifiable when it came to those for whom music was supposedly a pleasure rather than an imposition, but the saving grace was that nearly a quarter of the town came together for the communal singing and so fiercely concerned was each individual with his or her own performance that the inadequacy of others blessedly escaped them. It was those mistakenly gathered in front of the stage who bore the brunt, though most took care to stand on the far side of the green where the river flowed like liquid crystal over the flat-topped stones where fairies were said to cross on a midsummer's eve.

There were a few assorted musicians who accompanied what was charitably called the choir and several of these had a skill and professionalism that made their involvement something of a mystery. It was, then, a communal event designed to express the solidarity of a community which seldom came together except to mark the death of one of their number. It was communal except that by tradition there was a soloist and there had been no denying Sister Hilda her role, a fact which had led some to doubt the power of prayer.

Richard Rogers and Oscar Hammerstein can surely be absolved of any guilt for what followed. Nor can Miss Julie Andrews bear any blame. There are doubtless those whose teeth are set on edge by 'I'm just sixteen going on seventeen' and the enumeration of a series of favourite things that would embarrass the manufacturer of teeth-dissolving sweets, but 'Climb Every

Mountain' has become an anthem for football teams, on a par, understandably in the case of many lower division clubs, with 'Always look on the bright side of life.' In almost all circumstances it is an anthem of hope and endeavour. In Ballygoran, in the heat of a summer's day, with wasps clustering around the home-made jam and red ants pioneering the upper slopes of sweating thighs, hope was about to be extinguished.

The choir were arranged on stage, with some seated on the funeral parlour chairs and others on two rows of benches, one set higher than the other, the topmost requiring those standing on it to bend their heads lest they should touch the awning which this year was yellow and which, interestingly, and perhaps as a consequence, had attracted a number of bees doubtless under the misapprehension that this was a lake of pollen. Mr. Baines stood with his back to the audience whose apprehension was tangible. Being fair skinned, he did not take to the heat. Also, having bought an ice cream an hour before he was discovering that while unpasturised milk may have a distinctive flavour it may also have other qualities.

For the moment, though, he prepared himself as a soldier might before a battle as the enemy, in the person of Sister Hilda, mounted the stage, beaming at the audience even as they edged further back towards the river. A refreshing wind suddenly sprang up causing the awning to flap gently and the confused bees to fret across it. On the local food stall a young violinist was stung as he pushed a scone thick with coagulating raspberry jam, made by a medium temporarily unaccompanied by a long dead but still loquacious Native American, into his mouth. His cry seemed to act like a prompt to Mr. Baines who raised his baton high and then moved it swiftly down as a signal to all to begin. The musicians obeyed. The choir were evidently taken by surprise, each member in turn beginning the first line as they realised that the ship was launched. 'Climb, climb, climb, climb, climb, climb, climb, every, every, every, every, every, every, every, every, mountain, mountain,' they separately intoned. A whole mountain range was evidently being climbed by a team of climbers roped together by nothing more substantial than musicians who were trying to adjust their speed to match that of the choir. Since they were all climbing at a different rate, however, this proved difficult.

Mr. Baines rapped on his music stand as a sign they should stop and begin again but such musical etiquette was not one with which the singers were familiar. The musicians, though, obeyed to a man and woman, except a freckle-faced young man who was serving in the orchestra as an alternative to a custodial sentence. The choir continued, though making an effort now to adjust to one another. Mr. Baines rapped again and this time finally did secure obedience, though the singers ceased one by one, so many green bottles sitting on a wall. The problem was that as they stopped so Sister Hilda took this as an instruction that she should begin, except that she launched not into 'Climb Every Mountain' but 'what are we going to do about Maria?'

The wind chose this moment to intensify as Mr. Baines's stomach chose this moment to suggest a solution to the problem of having ingested ice cream from a dubious bovine source. The awning suddenly pealed away like the top of a can of sardines leaving the bewildered bees nothing to land on but the members of the choir, also, as it happened, dressed in yellow. At such a moment a school bench placed on planks balanced on two trestles put in place by resentful boy scouts is not the most secure of places to find oneself, the more especially if you wish to swat bees that have decided you are the unlikely source of pollen.

It was now that Mr. Baines bolted from the stage, heading for the one portable toilet, desperately hoping it was unoccupied. The young violinist had now begun to scream, holding the note longer and more precisely than he had when playing the violin earlier. Sister Hilda, it seems, realised that something was wrong but rather than recognising the plight of the choir, which was, of course, behind her, finally understood that she had indeed been singing the wrong song, and switched effortlessly to what some of a less than musical bent might have recognised as 'Climb Every Mountain' even as those on the top bench began to fall onto those below, their personal mountain proving anything but secure and expressive of true endeavour.

Those at the rear of the crowd instinctively stepped backwards, several of them falling into the shallow river, not at all like fairies bringing with them three wishes though by now there were a number of people who were fervently wishing they had chosen to pass the day in some other fashion. Mr. Baines, however, was safely in the portable toilet, though the same could not be said of several others who had frequented the ice cream stall and were now clustered around the same toilet as wasps gathered in ever greater numbers around the jars of jam.

In the end things were not as bad as they might have seemed. There was only one broken bone and a somewhat bent trombone. Colm Barry's bicycle was rescued from the gypsy clairvoyant, whose arrest she had not foreseen. The bees came to their collective senses and set off in search of something more likely to transmute into honey than the yellow canvas which blew across the road and up into the air, wrapping itself around the church steeple. The wasps, drunk with raspberries laced with pectin, dropped to the ground to sleep it off, dreaming, no doubt, of future picnics they could ruin by stinging people in unlikely places. The problem of what to do about Maria was settled when Sister Hilda was asked to tend to Kirsty McBride who had recovered from her fainting fit and been given a free coconut if she would distract the unremittingly enthusiastic nun for ten minutes. A few of the women in their yellow dresses gathered together like the petals of a daisy to try another assault on one of the greatest musical partnerships in history while others were drawn to The Shamrock where a few chairs had been set outside in the belief, perhaps, that a café culture might be encouraged even in the absence of resident existentialists.

By and large the occasion was thought a great success, if largely by those who had opted for The Shamrock and then only after a Guinness or two, or three, had begun to put things in their proper perspective. That night, though, it was rumoured, a number of fairies might have been seen crossing the flat stones in a river now black with night anxious to put some distance between themselves and Ballygoran, for fairies surely have ears and, who knows, perhaps, a liking for American musicals of the golden age.

***

Michael O'Donnell had the fortune to live a mere hundred yards from The Shamrock, in so far as he had only a small distance to manoeuvre should he have had a drink too many, itself not a concept understood by those in a town in which alcohol was like the oil on a bicycle chain, necessary to the proper functioning of the machine. However, as many have discovered in their lives, there is a down side to propinquity. His thatched cottage was set back a little from the road down a short path. It was what estate agents might call picturesque, which is to say in some state of dereliction. It was, though, home. The problem was that it had a prevailing smell of urine, this not a product of his own kidneys' transmutation of black velvet Guinness into yellow green piss but that of passing drunks for whom this was the first discrete place in which they could unbutton and unburden.

'Better out than in,' they would cry. 'Ah, thanks be.' 'Sure I could do with another.' 'A wee wee is a great thing.'

It was not great, though, should you happen to lie abed listening to the plish plash, the hissing stream, the intermittent torrent. Such things have a way of infiltrating one's dreams which begin to have a watery theme and necessitate noctural visits to the toilet that might have been avoided but for this auditory prompt. It was so bad that he felt he could identify each of the micturaters by their particular rhythms, volumes, durations. Every now and then they would vary his night by projectile vomiting, though given the limited range of food available in The Shamrock a similar differentiation was not possible when he emerged the next day.

There came a time when he realised he could take this no more and determined to do something about it. He erected a small gate but they simply opened it. He padlocked it only to find himself excluded when he lost the key and to realise that he had now offered them a handy target. He erected a sign which said, 'Private Property. Trespassers will be Prosecuted,' though he had wished to write something more directly descriptive of the offence he was anxious to discourage, but who reads such signs at night time and when necessity rules? He might as well have instructed dogs not to foul the footpath, which they are born to do and which they did do outside his cottage, evidently to challenge the marking of their territory by those humans who proclaimed it theirs by a little quasi-judicial spraying of Guinness-smelling urine.

Finally, he concluded that a more radical approach was necessary. Though he was not a practiced electrician, he strung three rows of wire along the side of his house where the night time pissers were prone to direct their pee and linked the wire to the mains electricity. The effect was impressive. It threw Brian Conroy ten feet backwards into the bushes and required him to visit his doctor to whom he tried to explain how he came to burn parts of himself that are not usually thought combustible. Michael Murphy plainly had a natural insulation for he remained standing but noted a disturbing St. Elmo's fire around his exposed member like the blue flame of brandy poured over a Christmas pudding or the Northern Lights which flow across the cold sky as you near the pole. All would have been well except that the local representative of the Garda (guardians of the peace of Ireland) himself liked a drink or two and was not immune to the sudden call of nature. Accordingly, he turned down the short path into Michael O'Donnell's cottage, unbuttoned, and found himself thrown into a holly bush, feeling a mixture of pain and pleasure he could neither disentangle nor understand.

Of course it was impossible for him to confess what had happened when he visited that same cottage the next day. Instead, he explained that complaints had been received and that electrocuting Irish citizens was not something that could be approved, though he could not for the moment cite the particular law which proscribed sending 240 volts through their private parts. He granted there was a problem, as he could scarcely do otherwise having had to negotiate pizza-based vomit as he entered and aware, as he was, of a prevailing smell. In the end they agreed that a light would be the thing, a light that would come on when anyone entered the short lane. 'Proximity lights, they are called, Michael. They would be the thing.'

Certainly proximity was what he objected to, the proximity of urine to his house, and so he installed one at the top of the wall, just below the thatched roof, and awaited his first victim who duly stood fully illuminated, like an actor caught by a surprise rise of the curtain. Within a week the problem was solved and he would have been free at last to sleep the night through without interruption were it not for the fact that his lack of skill as an electrician led to a spark, which led to a fire in the thatched roof, which led to smouldering ruins on which, obligingly, a number of habitués of The Shamrock duly urinated, now doubtless feeling it their civic duty. Did Gulliver, after all, not once put out a fire in similar fashion they might have asked had they been well read in Irish literature this being a country constructed out of words and Swift read as a realist.

***

After a time the God who presided over Ballygoran – for surely He did, or why would so many utter his name when they got up each morning, opened the curtains and saw the rain – relented. Instead of rain it was snow drifting down like a quiet blessing.

'It'll turn to slush,' observed Mrs. O'Connell, who saw a cloud in every silver lining and was one of the reasons so many swallowed anti-depressants along with their All-Bran each morning in an attempt to keep their spirits up and themselves regular. 'It's the bowels,' she had once told those waiting for their piece of steak and a pound or two of sausages. 'That's always what starts it. There's bacteria in meat.'

'And me without my galoshes,' said Miss Fencham, who slept with her poodle and let it lick her plate.

'They say plastic bags are just as good.' They were believers in plastic bags in Ballygoran and to hell with the planet.

'I've got tripe in mine.

'Do you cook yours in milk.'

'Mind how you go. The doctor's in Dublin for the funeral so there will be no one to help.'

'And she only went in for her finger.'

'I don't think you can blame the finger for was she not hit by a car.'

'Perhaps she was thinking of her finger and did not look as she should.'

'She was also drunk.'

'Yes, well that may have been part of it. She had a fondness for the drink.'

'Fondness, was it. She had it delivered to her door so as not to waste good drinking time going to the store.'

'Well she's gone now. She was seen with an American.'

'An American was it. Sure they're a strange lot are they not? Always wishing you a nice day when it is clear it is not.'

'And the chewing gum.'

'And the voices. You can hear them a mile away.'

'It's maybe because they live so far apart.'

The conversation stalled for a moment as those in the butchers paused a moment, having missed the drift.

'And what has the American to do with her dying?'

'You may well ask. Will you be clearing the pavement Mr. O'Donnell, for I'd hate to slip with the doctor at a funeral?'

Mr. O'Donnell was at that moment skinning a rabbit and wondering who had won the three thirty having placed a small wager or, rather, a somewhat large wager on a horse for no better a reason than its name – Butcher's Friend. The rabbit had been unlucky enough to intercept a bullet fired by Matthew Pierce who wanted to join the army and meanwhile was practicing by firing at a glass bottle, a young man whose principle skill to date, like so many of his age, had been driving second hand cars into trees.

'It's worse if you do,' said Mrs. O'Connell, 'for there's ice underneath. On the other hand you'll slip just the same if you don't.' Over the years she had developed logic to her pessimism which made it impossible to escape. Some thought she was a manic depressive who was still awaiting the manic phase.

Mr. O'Donnell, having his fingers inside a rabbit and his mind on horseflesh, made no reply.

'It's pretty, though,' said Mrs Pierce, wondering which might be the worse fate – to be trapped any longer with Mrs. O'Connell or to fall flat on her back so that everybody could see what she had on underneath, which was nothing since it was not good drying weather. 'The whole place looks better for being buried under snow.'

'It would look better for being buried altogether. I'll have a piece of the rabbit if you've taken all the shot out of it for I broke my teeth once on a pheasant and can't chew as I used to.'

Many years before Mrs. Pierce had been Miss Ballygoran (not that there was much competition that year, the Foot and Mouth having kept many on the farm or else smelling of disinfectant which was not likely to impress the judges). Since then, though, various parts of her had dropped or shifted in ways not easy to predict when she had been seventeen and thought the world created especially for her delight.

***

There was not much crime in Ballygoran, if you except the occasional public drunkenness and Mavis Ward's tendency to speed on her mobility scooter. The licensing laws were to be obeyed, but a certain flexibility was allowed for. There had been murders in the past when people chose to kill one another to demonstrate the holiness of their causes, but that was in the past. For Garda Toibin it was a relaxed place to be working if not one that would guarantee promotion for there was no one to judge how he might be doing. Yet there was a man who had not left the past behind him knowing, like a William Faulkner character, that in Ireland the past is not dead, it is not even the past.

The border was a fair way away but Michael Sligo was determined to cross it once he had perfected the bombs on which he had been working for some time, albeit in secret and with no more advice than he could glean from websites which mostly had to do with blowing people up while facing Mecca and even these he viewed imperfectly given the internet whose speed resembled three fifths of a quickstep – slow, slow, quick, quick, slow. He was, of course, working at a disadvantage in that it seemed he required industrial quantities of hydrogen peroxide and though Miss James cut people's hair in her back room, and had been known to dye them a variety of colours – though mostly black -- it was unlikely he could persuade her that a few thousand people were in need of turning blond, though he had made several visits in case that should prove his only source. Fertiliser was another matter, as any one passing through on certain days could have affirmed when he had not yet realised that it should be solid rather than liquid. Once he understood, however, if he failed in his primary endeavour he could probably have cornered the market and made a fortune.

The mechanism for firing was another matter. He would have tried a mobile phone but reception was so poor to non-existent that he could hardly practice with it and besides he had never quite understood how to turn the one he had on and when he did failed to understand the need to use it on a regular basis so that it had a tendency to die on him. He bought an alarm clock but it was digital and he could not work out how it could trigger the explosion of which he dreamed. Next he tried a clockwork train with a face on the front of it apparently much loved by children.

Why did he wish to make a bomb and who did he wish to direct it against? The first was easy. Ireland was not free, nor was he only thinking of the Protestants who had acquired the six counties by acts of appropriation and betrayal. The fact was that people from other countries were coming in and taking the jobs he had no intention of doing, though that did not include bomb making in which his fellow countrymen were acknowledged masters. There were the two at the post office who kept telling him he had got his postage wrong and who worshipped elephants. Who knew who might follow them? There had even been a professor who had got his degree at Cambridge where the spies were so that he had watched him cycling uncertainly past doubtless intent to penetrate his one-person cell. His subsequent death he regarded as deeply suspicious, though at 93 many would have thought he deserved his rest.

Michael Sligo worked on his own knowing that the secret service and Garda would be monitoring him. If he saw a woman under forty he suspected a honey trap. Then one day, seemingly confirming his suspicions, Garda Toibin knocked on his door. In truth he was seeking information about a dead dog but to Sligo he was there because he had been discovered and so attempted to strike out at him with the cucumber he happened to be holding in his hands, having a liking for cucumber sandwiches despite what he suspected were overtones of English Protestantism. The Garda swung back, never previously having been assaulted by a member of the gourd family. 'Hang on, Michael, I'm only here about the dead dog.'

'Dead dog? I have an alibi.'

'Michael, what's that?'

Only then did the would-be bomber realise he had left his garage open to reveal floor to ceiling bags of fertiliser. Still holding the cucumber like a gun, he ran through a number of possible explanations mentally crossing each one out as unlikely to convince.

'They're for friends.'

'For friends? A birthday present?'

'It's out of the rain. The soil needs replenishing you know.'

Now Garda Toibin may have found himself in a place scarcely at the centre of terrorist activities, and have spent most of his days thumbing through the *Police Gazette* with its advertisements for part time work as security guards, but he knew, as did everyone in Ballygoran, that Sligo was a republican who regarded all other republicans as soft on Protestants and the Pope a backslider. He had also watched as he had driven a car full of fertiliser through the town on a regular basis. Happily, though, he also knew that when it came to technical capacity he was some way short of capable having been hit on the head by a hurling stick in his teens, which may also have accounted for his dedication to planning mass slaughter, a fact widely known in the town and tolerated as people will tolerate much as long as they are informed, a fact that would benefit those making announcements in train stations and airports who dedicate themselves to concealing the truth from those they mean to inconvenience.

'It would be best if you gave it to them, then. For there are rules you know. And by the way, are you planning to go blond? I'll drop by in a day or two.'

And so, as Garda Toibin reached for his bicycle – this being all he had in case there should be need for high speed pursuits – the lives of many were perhaps saved, although already the clockwork train was proving difficult to adapt to the task of setting off a ton of explosives.

'Free Ireland,' he shouted after the dwindling figure.'

'Not free,' he shouted over his shoulder, 'but a bit cheaper maybe.'

***

There is, it is said, nothing worse than a convert. Those raised in the faith permit themselves a little leeway. 'That is not so much a sin,' observed Brion in The Shamrock one evening, 'as an inclination.'

'I would agree' remarked Seamus, drink, as was their way, being what they had in mind.

They were having this conversation because Mrs. Connelly, having cowed her husband with her righteousness, had launched herself on a crusade to do the same with others. The priest had explained that she had been sinning for most of her life so she had set herself to purge her guilt by transferring it to others.

'I think she is more of a Baptist than a Catholic,' said Brion, 'for they are terrible down on drink.'

'Is that not the Salvation Army?'

'They are equally misguided, though they're good with the second hand clothes. Her trouble is she has no sense of proportion.'

'Proportion is it.'

'Am I not a Catholic?'

'That you are.'

'But do I go to mass every day and sometimes twice?'

'It would be difficult to fit it in, what with the peat digging and the necessary relaxation.'

'That woman is on her knees more than is healthy.'

'More than is healthy.'

'And her husband.'

'A broken man. He used to be here most days, now if she sniffs a little on him he's to the coal shed. She has the key.'

'Is that what you heard?'

'It is what I was told by someone, though I can't remember who before you ask.'

'She's as bad with the fish.'

'The fish is it?'

'Not content with the one day she serves it every day, believing it to be holy or some such. You can smell it on them. They're followed by cats.'

'Religion is a fine thing in its place.'

'Fine thing.'

'Too much of anything, though.'

'Too much. You are right. My wife used to cook turnips every day. Someone told her they cured cancer, or was it piles. I put my foot down. Now it's broccoli, so I have developed a detestation for that vegetable. Do you want cancer, she asks? I'm beginning to think the answer is not as straightforward as you might imagine.'

'She's got to be stopped.'

'My wife?'

'Mrs. Connelly. She has written to the licensing authority.'

'Is this driving we are talking about?'

'Driving? Why would it be about driving? She has written to say Michael opens after hours and that pubs should not open during the day.'

'Is she mad entirely?'

'This would be the evidence.'

'Could the priest not have a word?'

'The priest has problems of his own with her. Often she's the only one in the church, so he could have a lie in if she weren't there. She is always on at him to preach about sin and such which is not what you want to hear when you go to church.'

'She thinks the nuns are not hard enough in the school. She heard they let them run around in their knickers.'

'The nuns?'

'Have you ever seen nuns run around in their knickers?'

They both paused for a moment as their imaginations stirred into activity.

'No,' Seamus admitted, not sure whether it was a matter for regret or relief.

'That would be terrible,' replied his companion, who had plainly been thinking of a different nun.

'And are the licensing authorities likely to respond?'

'Not unless they're Baptists and I don't recall ever seeing one of those.'

'How can you tell them?'

'They have this disapproving look I'm told. Or was that Quakers?'

'Quakers. I've heard of them. What is it they do?'

'Not a lot. They used to make breakfast cereals and chocolate, I think.'

'Now that's a strange religion.'

'Practical, though, for what did we Catholics ever make but more Catholics?'

'Did you hear about the health inspector?'

'Is this still Mrs Connelly we're talking about?'

'It is not, though it would not surprise me if she didn't want everyone inspected to see if they are having a good time so she could stop it. No, I am talking about the food inspector who went into the Co-op.'

'Why would he do that?'

'There had maybe been complaints.'

'About the food?'

'Given his title I would imagine it was not about their views on politics.'

'And what did he do?'

'I heard how he was taken ill.'

'He had their corned beef then, did he?'

'No, he did not. I think it was the sight of the whole thing. They don't train them for places such as that.'

'Sure what's wrong with the co-op, except you never know what they're going to charge.'

'I had some salad cream that had a picture of de Valera on it. I haven't seen one of those for forty years.'

'No good was it.'

'It was fine. They don't make salad cream like it anymore. It's all e this and e that and lists of chemicals. I don't think they have chemicals at the co-op.'

'How is the poor man?'

'It is not known. They sent a car for him all the way from Dublin.'

'How much was that salad cream for it sounds just the thing.'

'I could tell you what it cost two weeks ago but that would hardly be a guide as you know.'

'I heard talk there was a supermarket tried to buy them out.'

'That would be the company that is destroying shops across the whole of Ireland.'

'That would be the thing. They're owned by the English as I heard, which is why a number have a tendency to go on fire.'

'And with all the rain we've been having. So they've changed their mind, have they?'

'Who can tell, but why would we need such? I went into one once in Dublin. It was filled with everything you would never want. They have foreign things that kill the bacteria if you drink them.'

'Are you sure you are not confusing that with disinfectant.'

'And if you are after cheese they have fifty kinds instead of the two at the co-op. You can have too many things'

'Not at the co-op.'

'Cheese is cheese is it not.'

'That it is. It is indisputable.'

There was a pause while both stared into space, in thought too deep for words.

'What were we talking of?' said Brion, pushing a match between his teeth where a piece of chicken had been lodged in case of later hunger.

'Baptists, I think.'

And so the evening drifted on. 'They should have been in the music hall,' observed Michael to no one in particular, and not without a certain admiration, as he swabbed the counter with a rag that would have caused the food inspector a relapse if he had been incautious enough to return.

***

Every day Jerome took the tablets to keep death away wondering whether death might not be preferable. He lay them out in a line on the breakfast table. This was a ceremony and these the host he was to consume. A glass of orange juice, a coffee freshly made, a sliver of toast and these. Every day the same.

Now he sat in the dark writing, he told himself, though how could he being in the dark. He wrote in his head, who had not written on paper for three years, or was it four. There was a painting on the wall. He was dead, the boy who painted it. There were no tablets then. You just died. You just became thinner until you could see through the skin and all the beauty disappeared. Nor was this some romantic poet drifting away. There were the lesions and the sickness and eyes like coal sinking into snow.

He turned the lamp on, a circle of light making the dark darker still. He was alone now, who feared nothing so much as loneliness, abandonment, desolation. He had come back because this is where he was from. It was not home, simply where he had been born and raised. Like a salmon coming back, except not to spawn, just to die.

They did not know him here, except as the boy who left when his mother died, his mother who had been the centre of his life and still was if no longer there. She had been a light in the darkness, a consolation, a retreat, a love who had left no room for others, nor did it for all the others were passing shadows, all of them save one. So what had it all been for, that drift of men and boys, faces scarcely seen, strangers before, strangers afterwards? One day after another, one night segueing into another.

Then his editor across the table explaining why it would be impossible to publish his book, the trade being what it was, readers being as they were, critics being as obtuse as they had ever been, and all the while trying to catch the eye of the waiter and already reaching for his wallet. Rejection, well he knew about that.

Outside the window snow floated down with a slow relentlessness in the orange glow of a street lamp, each flake transmuted into gold, God, apparently, being an alchemist as well as an ironist. He turned and watched. Time itself was surely slowing, so long did each flake take to descend. Then a figure passed by, leaning forward. It stopped briefly, responding no doubt to the light in his room, though he could surely not be seen. Then she disappeared immediately in a swirl of gold. And it was a she for he recognised her. In the darkness he smiled. 'Mad Peg,' he thought, acknowledging in another what he could not see in himself, someone hurrying on towards nothing. Time is shedding its skin, he thought, sitting there looking out into the night though there was nothing to see but snow falling amber bright.

The snow was still on the ground when they buried him. It was a small funeral. The exhaust from Murphy's hearse hung in the air. The few gathered there stamped their feet, urging the priest on for there were warm fires to go to, banked up against their return.

There was no wake, but in Ballygoran no one's death passed without notice.

'Was he not one of those?'

'It's said he was.'

'Well, it takes all sorts does it not.'

'That it does.'

'He loved his mother, though.'

'That he did.'

'And her not what she might have been.'

'He looked terrible, though.'

'Well he had … you know.'

'But he loved his mother.'

'Certainly he loved his mother. It makes up for a lot. You can't say it of everybody. A fine hat you are wearing.'

'I think sometimes I should have chosen the green.'

'But for a funeral. Just the thing I would say. Is it mauve it would be?'

'No, purple. It's the royal colour.'

'Royal is it? Well, just right for a funeral, though I wish I'd worn my other shoes. I can't feel my toes and I lost my ears before we went into the church.'

The priest reminded them that they had come from dust and would return to such and they tried to gather some earth to scatter on the coffin but it was frozen hard, and when they did find a clump it hammered down on the coffin so that it seemed he was knocking and asking to return. Had anyone thought to put a mirror to his nose, Mrs. O'Connell thought. Then she was walking back, trying not to turn her ankle for this was not the weather to be out and about and, truth to tell, she had hardly known him at all, though she had known his mother, poor woman. And how had she felt when he told her, always assuming he did for people like that kept their secrets, as well they might for it is not natural, she told herself, not natural at all, though in truth sex had always been something of a mystery to her and not at all connected to what the priest said about sacraments.

And did he know all this when he turned towards the window and saw time coming to its end? Did he understand that, pills or not, he would end in that same snow with only those who knew nothing of him but what they chose to believe drawn to the graveside? Why else, though, did he turn around if he did not already feel something close to hand, if the sight of mad Peg alone in the night had not reminded him of himself. In the bleak mid-winter, they sang. Well, it had been bleak mid-winter in his heart since the boy who painted the picture still hanging on his wall had turned his eyes upwards and sank down into himself with a sigh he could hear still and that was the same as that which sounded out in the early hours as he, too, gave up what he had long felt had never really been his.

***

Back at the golf course, the priests continued their competitive stories. 'That's nothing,' said Father Desmond, holding the whisky decanter like a baby ready for baptism. 'Did I not have dealings with a young girl who was known for her friendliness and had been arrested twice for it. And she came click clacking into St. Stephens five minutes before I should have been off in the bus to catch the cheap airline to watch the golf at St. Andrews. She had a skirt on her that should have got her arrested a third time. She goes into the confessional, her legs sticking out for everyone to admire. So I went in and she says she has sinned by saying a bad word, so I asked which word was that? And she said, 'How the fuck should I know. This is last week we're talking of.'

Well, I was in this hurry but I made the mistake of asking if she had any other sins to confess and she said, 'how long have we got?' And I knew, of course, that they don't let you on those planes if you are late so I said, 'Say five Hail Marys and we'll call it quits,' and she said, 'don't you want to hear? I've got some good ones.' So the truth is I stayed and ended up having to say twenty Hail Marys myself and missing the plane'

'You think that's something,' said Father Connerty, the oldest in a group in which age had suddenly become a matter of pride again as it had once in primary school. 'I'm ninety-two next birthday,' he had been telling everyone for nearly a year. 'I was a priest for a while to a group of theatricals in the army, so they began with a starter of three Hail Marys, but that was just their opening bid. They had sins I had never heard of. Believe me, when you've been stuck in a field for six months you look forward to confession. They would tell jokes and dress up as women. The jokes were disgusting but one or two made passable women.'

He was interrupted in his story, however, for they all knew his proclivities, the younger among them – now in his 60s – taking care to lock his door each night.

'Sure that's nothing,' said Father James, looking at them through his whisky, as he looked at much of the rest of the world on most days of the year. 'I was going to the sacristy having run a little low of the necessary and there having just been a delivery of communion wine, when I came across these gypos and had they not been stripping lead from off the roof. They'd done it before which I only realised when rain came through when I was baptising a bastard for a favour. This time, though, I caught one of them in the act. I held hold of him, for he was a thin man, though I feared he might have a knife about him somewhere. 'I'm calling the police,' I said. 'I understand the necessity,' he said. The necessity was it, I thought. 'But first,' he said, 'would you hear my confession?' 'I'll hear your confession when I know the law is on its way,' says I. So I take him to the house and hand him over to Mrs Callaghan, who has muscles on her would scare an elephant, and I made a call. 'We'll be right there, father,' said young O'Donnell whose father dug the graves for many years. 'Just you hold onto him and if he struggles hand him over to Mrs. Callaghan.'

I took him in the parlour while Mrs Callaghan guarded the door. 'Sure I can't say anything with her in earshot,' says he, 'for I've my reputation to consider.' 'Your reputation,' I said, 'man you are known as a thieving, gambling, riotous kind of man. What reputation do you have to lose?' 'That's the reputation I mean,' he says. 'If it were known a woman got the better of me where would I be in this life.' So I asked her to move off a little for there was no risk of his escaping, the windows have been painted shut these many years since we all made the mistake of employing George Finian to do our odd jobs. Then I sit him down beside me and what do you think he said? He said, 'Forgive me Father for I have just stolen the lead from off your roof.' 'I know that,' I said, 'did I not catch you at it.' 'That you did but I would get it off my chest for is that not what confession is for?' So I gave him half a dozen Hail Marys and an Our Father or two, thinking he would be punished hard enough when it came to it anyway. But as soon as I finished did he not stand up and say, 'well, Father, I'll be off now.' 'Off,' I said, 'you'll not be off for I have the police coming and I've a tale to tell them.' 'That you would surely not,' says he, 'for have I not just confessed it and are you not bound to silence over anything I said.' And I could think of nothing for to say except 'get out you bastard, get out.' And what does he say but, 'you'll have no need to confess the language,' he says, 'for it is no more than the truth. My mother was not a one for marrying, nor my father either. So I'll be saying goodbye.' Then he has a kind of afterthought. 'That woman there,' he says, 'she's not available in any way is she for we've need for women who can do the heavy lifting and smack a head or two if need be.' And out he went, except a moment later I heard a thump and him cry out. 'Would you like some tea,' said Mrs. Callaghan a moment or so later, rubbing her knuckles as she did so. And he never came by again though it took us a score of jumble sales before we could replace the lead.

'I was to Italy, once,' remarked Father Connerty.'

'Weren't we all?'

'I was to Italy,' he continued, turning off his hearing aid, preferring a not hearing aid at times. 'And I was staying at this small hotel near St. Peter's which struck me as very busy when I first arrived. There would be people at all hours and a deal of crying out.'

'I know what you're going to say,' interjected Father Matthew, interjections, however, meaning little to a stone deaf man.

''Will you be paying by the week, the day, or the hour,' I was asked when I first arrived, thinking that people could maybe afford only the briefest stay. Then, one afternoon, I was going down the corridor to the bathroom, having nothing but a basin in my room, when this woman came out and do you know she had not a stitch of clothes about her person. And the corridor was so narrow I had to turn sideways when she squeezed past.

'Padre,' she said, and I could tell right away she was Irish.

'No,' I said, thinking maybe the hotel had its own priest.

'Your clothes,' she said. And I thought maybe she was saying she had need of them to cover her up. So I was starting to unbutton when she shrieked. 'And you a feckin priest! If I'd have wanted that there was plenty back in Donegal.' Would you believe such a thing, and her Irish, too. 'Would you like to confess?' I asked, for in truth I could think of nothing else to say. 'Confess is it,' she says, 'I'm not the one talking to a naked woman.' Then she sort of looked at me a moment, myself not knowing where to look for there was sin in every direction, and after a moment said, 'but I could maybe offer you a special rate for are we all not from the old country.'

'Special rate,' said Father O'Donnell, who had retired three years early on account of unfounded rumours. 'It's amazing what you can buy now the currency is strong again.''

'Sure that's nothing,' said Father Geraghty, holding his glass up hoping, perhaps, that a single malt would descend from the heavens with divine accuracy. 'I was in Africa once at a school for those in need of care and protection. I was there as a result of a misunderstanding about something similar, and you know what I mean.' And how could they not who had read the papers, after all. 'It was terrible hot and for some reason God had decided to create things that took a liking to biting and stinging and burrowing down into you and giving you a season ticket to the latrines.'

'It was a penance, father.'

'It was a pain in the arse. But once you've signed up to the army of God you have to accept a wound or two, do you not. Anyway, there was this witch doctor with a degree in philosophy from Trinity, and we would have a drink or two most nights, which made me think he was maybe telling the truth for he had a special liking for a Jameson which I had taken the precaution of shipping out ahead of me in a box marked 'Religious Items' which in my case was a kind of truth.' They all nodded, being converts to the same faith. 'As I understood it my job was to tell the natives they shouldn't use the contraceptives and it was his job to cure them of the sickness they got as a result. Anyway, there was this young boy.'

'I say we should call it a day,' said Father Connerty who understood the value of silence not least because the battery on his hearing aid was giving out. 'We've a big day tomorrow, being booked on the links at 7.30.'

'That's an unholy hour.'

'All hours are holy when it comes to golf.'

'I'll drink to that, or I would if there were anything in my glass. Does no one have bottle?'

'I've nothing but some expectorant, though I think it has alcohol in it.'

'I wouldn't come within spitting distance of that,' said Father Matthew, but by then the battery was dead and his companions were already easing themselves out of leather armchairs whose arms were pitted with cigarette burns and which smelt faintly of decades of priestly farts.

***

A teacher at the Protestant school had disappeared with one of his pupils, having taught her things not on the curriculum. They had been seen hand in hand catching a bus to Dublin where sin was normal and then had come a postcard to her mother from England which surprised no one. 'Having a wonderful time,' it said, and her only fifteen and hence not qualifying for such. There was an investigation with a man coming from Dublin which was like the Devil sending his deputy in the view of some. Had anyone noticed anything in chemistry lessons when the Bunsen burners were roaring away and chemicals were mixed promiscuously so that fumes came off you could light. Maybe it was that, some said, that had turned her head. Of course she had no religion, unless you counted Protestantism which few were inclined to do. The father was sent after them, a burly man who had played hurley in his youth and could surely cause damage if he had a mind. But he came back empty handed except for the Duty Free so that not everything was lost.

'She was doing so well in biology,' her mother had told the other mothers at the school gate not, perhaps, something to boast about in the circumstances. 'She was planning to go to the secretarial where they teach them to write things quickly,' she added, thinking that evidence she would have had no time for debauchery if only she had not been entrapped by a man who all were inclined to agree was not unattractive. After all, he had dark hair and bright eyes and a body that suited his clothes so well, not disguising his muscles, he being a teacher of physical education even if he had chosen to educate a young girl into the physical who should have kept his distance when they were jumping the vaulting horse for there were plenty of young women who might have chosen to go with him if only to convert him to the true faith. For some, indeed, indignation at his betrayal was mixed with regret that he had turned his back on opportunities which might have been so much more rewarding to all concerned.

'It'll be abortion' said Cathleen O'Dowd, who herself remained unmarried despite a willingness to submit to the indignities she assumed necessary as a prelude to that holy state, the gap between those indignities and the promised sanctioned bliss nevertheless leaving her more than a little bewildered.

'They do that there. There are chemists shops that will do it, so I'm told. They are a strange people who care nothing for what is right and wrong having discovered that they have a preference for the wrong and no one to tell them otherwise. Where would we be without priests to remind us that we are doomed to suffer the fires of hell?'

'Dublin,' suggested Mrs Haughty, and who would not agree with her who had travelled there only to see young women with skirts up to their waists, even in January.

Later, she had the gall to send a piece of her wedding cake home who had married in a Protestant church and had not therefore qualified for baked goods of such a kind. There were other postcards from Paris, Berlin and other godless places, he evidently being determined to take her on a grand tour of Sodom and Gomorrah.'

'And what will he do? And what of her education who has been denied the classes in chastity that might have been the making of her?'

But mothers are mothers and know the pains they were born to bear. Thinking themselves safe at last, their children up and betray them with the first man who speaks to them of love while meaning something other, men having a way of making words mean what they wish. 'From the moment they wake to when they say their prayers as fast as they can so they can get to dream their favourite dreams it is nothing but sex. Even at church you can see them looking around in search of sin.'

'All school teachers should be castrated. It's the only safe way,' suggested Mary McCaffery who herself did not have a perfect record of safety.

'Along with priests for they can be worse than teachers.'

'The priests, is it. Well there's certainly an argument for it.'

'The Italians used to do that to improve their singing.'

'There are easier ways to go up an octave.'

'Our Eileen has brought home a note. They are thinking of going to Lourdes.'

'Why would they want to go there? There's not a cripple among them, though Margaret has a stutter.'

'It's a holy place.'

'You can be holy in Ballygoran. And it's in France.'

The last was thought to be a powerful argument.'

'If you have a cold over there they cure it with a tablet up the bottom.'

'I had a cousin went there. Broke his leg. Out came the suppository.'

'Rome would be different, though.'

'You are talking of suppositories?'

'No, for holiness, though they don't speak English.'

'Neither do the French.'

'It's closer, though. They speak Latin.'

'She'll be back.'

'Who would this be?'

'The girl who ran off.'

Nor was she wrong for a school teacher at the front of the room with a piece of chalk like a cigarette in his fingers and all the girls yearning for him is not the same thing at all as a man in a cheap hotel in St. John's Wood pouring himself a miniature vodka as his socks steam on the radiator.

He did not accompany her back for it would not have been the headmaster who greeted him but the Garda. She stepped off the bus having told no one of her coming. There were those, however, who thought a school master sufficient of a catch to ignore the inconvenience of age since even corrupted by sin and Protestantism, the two naturally allied, he was one up on an undertaker's assistant. Once she would have been regarded as soiled goods. Now, to the young men of Ballygoran, she was like a library book that shows signs of having been read but is still worth flicking through the pages.

***

It had never been a good idea, perhaps predictably coming from Sister Benedicta whose judgement had never been the best beginning with her purchase of the people carrier that had so far carried none, its cylinder head being cracked open like the Red Sea. Now she had suggested 'a little trip before Christmas,' to replace the Nativity play for which they had been preparing since September until the Virgin Mary had suddenly confessed to being pregnant which, while wholly appropriate for the role, was, illogically, judged a disqualification. 'What have you been up to, Celia Callaghan?' she had asked, somewhat redundantly. 'And how could you play the Mother of God with you in that condition? You had a 'B' in chastity,' she reminded her tearful pupil, which was true enough though there had evidently been some grade inflation. They had thought to recast the role but several of the most likely choices had not even managed a 'B'.

Strangely, in all the years they had staged a Nativity play, with tea towels on the heads of the female shepherds, held on with elastic bands, and gold milk bottle tops stuck onto cardboard for the kings' crowns, they had never thought to suggest that the Virgin Mary, hours away from delivering, might give some intimation of being such. One shameless girl, no doubt wedded to Stanislavskian theories of realism, suggested a cushion only to be looked on as a Jezebel who had no business knowing even the role a cushion might be made to play

'We will go to Dublin, for there are some wonderful churches there you will wish to see,' Sister Benedicta announced, having secured the agreement of the Mother Superior who anyway had wished to visit her bookmakers and had never liked the nativity play with its overtones of theatre and hence of immorality. One of their girls had gone on to become an actress, which was shame enough, but was then rumoured to have appeared in a film with nothing on and in full colour. Personally, she had a liking for pasty white in her charges that suggested innocence if perhaps also a poor diet.

Sister Benedicta was supported by Sister Wendy, who thought ill of no one, finding good even in the ultimately degenerate. 'There's a little bit of good in everyone,' she would say with that disturbing smile that betokens those untroubled by doubt or evidence. So, genocidal dictators could, to her mind, be redeemed if they once collected foreign stamps to raise money for charity.

'What of Stalin, Sister?' asked Denise Riley whose transfer to the state school had been delayed, her reputation, perhaps, going ahead of her. 'Was he not a godless man and a terrible persecutor of people?'

'Well, Denise, it is hard to say. I had an uncle like him.'

'Like Stalin, Sister? Was he godless, then, and a persecutor of people.'

'He was not. But he had a moustache very like his. His weakness was toffees.'

''Stalin's, Sister?'

'Certainly not Stalin's, child. There were no toffees in Russia. It was all cabbages.'

The people carrier had been repaired, or so they were assured by the man at the Ballygoran garage, except that it now developed a disease that might prove fatal and that at the least would require the kind of expenditure that could only be met by a month or more of fund-raising teas or the kind of threats to possible donors in which Sister Agatha was so proficient being converted while still a prison warder and hence having developed transferable skills. That left the priest's Morris Minor (Morris Minors being the vehicle of choice of the clergy despite having been discontinued decades earlier) -- he having refused to come if they intended to use the charabanc -- and Mr. Murphy's hearse, provided, he explained, no one should choose that moment to die, there being no guarantee, however, for, as he noted, they often chose the most inconvenient moment, like a rugby match.

So they assembled outside the school for a photograph even as the drizzle began.

'Denise Riley, stop pulling Mary's plaits. God sees everything you know.'

Denise Riley rather hoped He did not.

'Smile everyone. Colleen, do not do that. It's not nice. And Mary, were you picking your nose? Did the disciples do that do you imagine? Maeve, could you not look so miserable.'

'Please Sister, I brought a note.'

'That you did and you could no more spell in that than you do in divinity. Now, smile, for its digital. Very nice, except we will have to do it again for was not Denise Riley putting Devil's horns on Mary. You were indeed for is the proof not here on the digital? Think good thoughts everyone. Mary, you are not thinking good thoughts.'

'I was Sister?'

'What were you thinking of?'

'I was thinking how it would likely be warmer in the car.'

'That is not a good thought. You should be thinking of the lepers who are missing pieces of themselves but still paint those lovely Christmas cards with their feet.'

'With their feet, Sister? Will I catch something from it, do you think, for feet carry diseases?'

One of Sister Benedicta's better traits was that she recognised a lost cause when she saw one and so, offering up a prayer to St. Anthony, who was her resort at such moments – finding lost things and such like – asked brightly, 'Now, who is going in the father's car?'

No one raised her hand, having seen him vomit too recently to volunteer.

'Well, I'll chose for myself.'

'Sister, I have forgotten my you know what.'

'I do not know and you had best go and get it for the upholstery is nearly new,' nearly new in her reckoning being anything manufactured since the war. 'Denise Reilly, what did I tell you. You will make the saints in heaven cry.'

'How long will it take,' asked Maeve, eying the hearse which was quite the best looking of their caravan though not a car, as she had explained loudly, to be seen dead in.

'How long is a piece of string?'

'String, Sister?'

'It will take as long as it takes,' she replied which, in retrospect, was a wise remark since those in the people carrier learned a little something about the Ballygoran garage while those in the hearse, which was normally only required to move at walking pace, found there was a reason for that beyond the decencies required of being laid in the ground to await the trumpet call though how, Denise had asked Sister Wendy, were they to hear it when they were buried six feet deep.

'They are not in the earth child, but in heaven.'

'Why would they need to come down again only to be dug up?' she asked, not of course in search of knowledge.

'They will not be dug up. They will rise.'

'Rise, Sister. Like float?'

Even Sister Benedicta understood that whatever Denise was she was not a seeker after knowledge.

'We shall only know when the trumpet sounds.'

'What about the deaf, Sister? For it seems unfair they should miss out through being hard of hearing.'

Sister Innocence, who suffered from Tourette's Syndrome, told her to 'shut up you little gobshite.'

They had had meetings about Sister Innocence who for the most part was docile enough but every now and then would recall her infirmity and display a vocabulary as rich and varied as it was obscene, an effect that was the more startling in the cathedral given the care that had evidently been taken to ensure perfect acoustics long before Tourette's became the threat it is. They had suggested she should be posted to a silent order but the Monsignor pointed out the logical flaw. Sister Wendy had proposed Africa, probably on the assumption that it was so far away that it would be impossible to hear her from Ballygoran. So Africa it would be, just as soon as she could have the injections.

If it had just been a matter of language it might perhaps have not been so bad but she had a tendency towards what can best be called inappropriate laughter. As a body was being lowered into the ground and the priest was reminding all gathered there that from ashes we come and to ashes we go so she would be liable to burst into cackles of laughter. When on a more joyous occasion the same priest asked whether anyone knew of any just cause why the couple concerned should not be joined in holy matrimony, her sudden burst of laughter was misinterpreted by the bride's mother who struck her putative son-in-law across the face for the sins which in truth she should not have been able to imagine but was.

Meanwhile, she was like an unexploded mine awaiting the unwary. 'God in Heaven, what feckin weather,' she now opined.

For all their natural resistance to authority, to rules about the length of their skirts, the distance they must keep between themselves and those who even now were conspiring against their supposed innocence, a trip to Dublin was not without its appeal. They felt as doubtless prisoners do when granted bail. They had not wholly escaped but were for the moment released from bondage as the Jews (not to be mentioned in front of the Sisters) had escaped from Egypt, an incident somewhat glossed over in divinity classes, though plagues of boils and locusts were invoked as a warning less to the ancient Egyptians than themselves should they stray from a path that was alternately narrow and steep and not usually extending as far as Dublin.

In the end the hearse was not available. Mr. Kenny, who lived in a cottage somewhat implausibly named Shangri-la, while not actually dead was apparently showing every sign of considering such.

'We're on call,' explained Mr. Murphy, like a midwife, as in many ways he was except that he delivered people from this world into the next.

'Has he had the Last Rights?' enquired Sister Mary.

'The penultimate, I think,' Mr. Murphy replied, not himself being a practicing Catholic having developed doubts about people rising from the dead since he had spent his life ensuring they did not by burying them six feet deep.

'Can he not wait, for it is not often we go to Dublin?'

'He's not up to taking requests, though I understand he is an accommodating man,' the evidence for which being the fact that he had tolerated his wife conducting an affair with the man who drove the visiting library van which would arrive once a month so that people could borrow their Agatha Christie or practical books about gardening in wet soil. It was in the van, indeed, that she had been seduced between the Romance section and Embroidery, dropping more than a stitch, an affront, he privately acknowledged, to the duodecimal system which he had otherwise treated with the proper respect. She had been seen entering the van and then leaving looking flushed and clutching more than the regulation number of books. Yet Mr. Kenny, it seemed, understood the need for a little vehicular passion and anyway she was always sure to bring him books on Irish heroes through the ages, one of whom, in his deepest soul, he would wish to have counted himself among.

As a result of his decision not yet to go gentle into that dark night, however, those who might have travelled in style, if somewhat slowly and with the grooves where the coffin slid pressing against their dimpled thighs, had to be transferred to the charabanc, hastily summoned, even though it still smelled of disinfectant.

'Have you all gone?' asked Sister Mary once they were all on board, 'for there are no toilets on the way and we will only stop for the sandwiches and lemonade.'

'Sister?'

'Processed cheese, Catherine Anne O'Rourke.'

'Sister, I'm allergic.'

'Mary McAllister, it has been processed so all the germs have been removed.'

'Get a feckin move on,' suggested Sister Innocence.

It was a long way to Dublin in almost every sense and though the exhaust was plainly living on borrowed time, so that the charabanc sounded a little like a Formula One racing car while providing evidence to the contrary, it was a journey almost without incident if we leave aside the fact that the sandwiches had, unaccountably, not made it on board (Sister Mary suspecting Mary McAllistair) while the lemonade was in an advanced state of fermentation which resulted in its tasting like the TCP with which cuts and bruises were liberally bathed in the infirmary and having a certain alcoholic content.

'Sister Benedicta has a tube of Polos so we will not go hungry. There's one between two.'

'Is it all right to drink this, Sister?'

'It's been passed by Father Connelly,' Sister James was tempted to say, sharing with Mrs Flynn a fondness for the days of vaudeville.

'If you hold your nose it's not so bad at all, Sister. Are the bits really lemon?'

It was a question well worth asking for there was certainly something floating in the bottle.

'It's Rosalie McCafferty's spit, please Sister,' offered Veronica. 'I saw her drinking from it.'

'Will you hold your tongue, child. You'll be spoiling everyone's enjoyment,' though in truth there was not much evidence for that as they debated how much of a Polo you could suck before it was someone else's turn.

What did they make of Dublin which had always been held up to them as a kind of Sodom with Guinness, in which men wrote dirty books in pubs? The Sisters may have had it in mind to take them to the General Post office and the cathedral but for their part the girls were more drawn to the long-haired boys who stood in groups at street corners, cigarettes in their mouths and acne, like a field of poppies, on their faces, but what is a little acne when the sight of boys is like a glimpse of a gazelle to a lion.

'Stick together,' cried Sister Benedicta, 'for there's a terrible mass of people who'll be stealing your handkerchiefs,' her worry for handkerchiefs being primarily because they were usually stuffed into knickers. And so they crockodiled along O'Connell Street which pulsed with life as Ballygoran did not, aware, suddenly, that there was a world beyond hockey and praying and bodies that, alarmingly, were transmuting into the very thing that evidently caused such consternation in those who had decided that it was wrong for others to enjoy what they had sworn to abjure. But that is cities for you. It is there that possibility becomes manifest, that difference may be celebrated rather than distrusted, that seeds germinate and passions are born. Yes, there was passion in Ballygoran but it was to be driven down or translated into romantic regret, loss generating its own language. And what of religion? It was about sin and confession even as secrets became the more necessary. It was about punishment and denial, even if denial cannot be sustained and, you might be tempted to think, to the greater good of the human spirit. Cities may not be about those who know one another's business, about those who cling to history believing it alone to hold a key to the cipher of life, but they offer something in their place. They throb with energy and in amongst the noise and dirt new things are born, existence preceding essence. This is where the world seeps in, where rivers are tidal moving in and out, a regular pulse which itself generates new life.

Did the girls think anything of this? How could they when they were bathing in the rosy light of acne which like everything else will one day pass away. 'You wouldn't,' whispered Colleen to Denise.

'I would,' said Denise.

And she would.

Nonetheless, they were all rounded up, as a dog will sheep, and swept into Bewley's on Grafton Street for a sticky bun and cup of tea, a place where Brendan Behan had once come to sober up or regret having done so. Sister Mary made the mistake of asking for tea to be put into a polystyrene cup with a picture of a former Pope she had bought and in which she had a preference for drinking. 'Could I have it with a slice of lemon. It always makes it seem fresher.' So it did, but it was a mistake nonetheless for five minutes later, when she had nearly finished, she glanced down and noticed that most of the polystyrene had dissolved away. Sure that liquid polystyrene was likely to be fatal, she disappeared to the toilet to make herself sick by putting a finger down her throat. Though this may have saved her from imminent death it caused her another problem for, looking at herself in the mirror, she was shocked to discover that the strain of being sick had caused two large swellings to appear under her eyes making her appear a direct descendant of the elephant man crossed with Quasimodo.

'Holly Mother of God,' observed Sister Benedicta on seeing her emerge from the toilet. 'Was it the sticky bun?'

A mother tugged her young daughter to her, startled to see a swelling nun.

'Cool,' remarked Bridget O'Reilly, having herself something of a gothic turn of mind and hence being impressed to see Sister Mary transform herself into a Halloween grotesque.

'Cover yourself,' said Sister Agnes urgently, 'for you are scaring the children. Have you been stung by two bees? Are you allergic to raisins, for there were many in my bun? Is it Legionnaire's disease, do you think, for I have heard tell they travel the world infecting people?'

'You look like a feckin clown,' offered Sister Innocence.

It would take two days for the swellings to go down. Meanwhile, she covered her face looking like someone on her way to court for some disreputable crime, but first she was taken to hospital, thus releasing their wards into a godless city where sin was rife with magazines on sale that were Satan's own publications and there were likely to be Protestants you could not detect, them being skilled at looking like normal people.

Despite the fact that Christmas was approaching, it began to snow raising hopes that would doubtless be dashed. Sister Benedicta had taken Sister Mary to the infirmary to see if they could deflate her eyes. That left the remaining nuns outnumbered, a fact not lost on their charges though there were other nuns, in a Catholic city, scurrying around doubtless on holy business so that possible reinforcements were maybe available in case of need. Music was seeping out of shops as they passed and ahead was a Salvation Army band playing Silent Night so that people were covering their ears. They walked to the Liffey, whose tributaries, unaccountably, are called the Dodder and the Poddle, rising from the Liffey Head Bog (ah, the music of Irish place names) which to their eyes was no more than a stretch of grey water which might flow through the veins of Irish men and women who had been driven abroad by need or ambition, but to them simply flowed between two undistinguished roads of little interest and this in a country where one bridge is named for Sean O'Casey and another for Samuel Beckett, the latter with no waiting signs.

'Can we not go in the shops,' asked Veronica McCafferty who seemed so innocent but quietly lived up to a surname which recalled T.S. Eliot's criminal cat.

'Which shops might you be considering?' asked Sister Kathleeen, who had taken elocution as a child.

'One of the big ones that sell everything.'

'We'll not keep together in there,' she replied, as might the commander of a destroyer shepherding a convoy in the North Atlantic.

'Sure, I'll only be a while and Bridget will be with me,' urged Veronica, which was a little like Burke assuring people he would be accompanied by Hare and, indeed, there was less reassurance than provocation in her reply but already Sister Kathleen was finding it impossible to control such a parcel of girls along a street full of strange people with coloured hair and pieces of metal stuck through their noses.

'Very well. We'll meet here in ten minutes,' she declared, surely knowing in her soul that she was putting that soul at risk but if nuns cannot have faith who will, though even nuns should surely temper faith if not with reason then a certain scepticism which, after all, must also come from God.

'How can twenty-one girls come into trouble,' the constable asked, having never been to Ballygoran, taught in a convent or apparently having any understanding of human kind.

However, while the Garda may have had some difficulty with their compatriots, whose interpretation of patriotism extends in the direction of murdering as many of them of their kin as possible, they had little difficulty in locating a clutch of schoolgirls, not least because they had already received a telephone call from the owner of a tattoo parlour uncertain of the wisdom of complying with the requests of young girls who had such particular tastes. So, Sister Kathleen's faith was rewarded after all.

There was no singing on the charabanc going back to Ballygoran. Sister Mary held a pack of frozen peas to her face. Veronica clutched a plastic carrier bag on which was inscribed 'THIS BAG IS BIODEGRADABLE,' which was accurate enough in that it contained an item of underwear that might have scandalised even Madonna (the film star and not the other Madonna, though Sister Benedicta's 'good heavens!' might have led one to think otherwise).

On the whole, had there been a vote the girls would have decided the trip a success but the Catholic Church is not much in favour of democracy, tending to favour infallible dictats.

'Feckin disaster,' observed Sister Innocence whose injections were beginning to make her feverish. 'feckin, feckin, feckin disaster.'

For the nuns, all was not lost. A bet had been placed for the Mother Superior that had come in at ten to one and aside from the incident with the polystyrene and the near miss at the tattoo parlour, it was felt it was better than an over-literal nativity play in which the Virgin Mary might at any moment give birth in the presence of shepherds and wise men for whom birth and its cause was best kept a mystery.

***

It was Christmas Eve. A few days earlier the snow had been deep and crisp and uneven. Now it had disappeared to be replaced by grey slush and sufficient black ice to ensure a broken bone or two to enliven the season. In homes across Ballygoran families were re-assembling for the festivities, bracing themselves to renew annual arguments whose origins were often forgotten but which were none the less virulent for that. In the O'Brien house, Christmas tree lights, brought down from the loft, were laid out on a newly vacuumed floor while Michael O'Brien searched for the one dead bulb preventing their operation. In the kitchen mince pies were burning, one small sherry not having proved sufficient to a cook whose hands were still cold from being thrust into a frozen turkey. Along the mantelpiece were cards from those not seen for thirty years and whose return addresses had long since been lost. Some had contained round robins designed to humiliate listing, as they did, the achievements of children, grandchildren, pets, vegetables, along with details of Mediterranean cruises, salary rises, fertility treatments, diseases triumphantly defeated. 'Should we maybe send one out ourselves,' asked Michael, having just located the faulty bulb so that the carpet was suddenly lit by a spotted rainbow of colours, 'saying that our Mary has become a prostitute and that we are writing from prison?' 'Did you say Protestant?' his wife called from the kitchen, alarmed, raising another sherry amidst the blue smoke of incinerated mincemeat.

There was a day to go but the starting pistol on alcohol consumption had already been fired so that in houses around the town corkscrews were twisted, bottles tilted, glasses clasped even as brussels sprouts, parsnips and potatoes were prepared in the knowledge that such would be impossible a day later when no one could reasonably be expected to be in full possession of their wits.

There was a tradition of the local shop keepers sending cards, though quite why was never clear since they had no competitors and hence no need to encourage loyalty. There was a card from the co-op with a picture of Ballygoran as it had been in 1948, with a crossed out message saying 'Loose Talk Costs Lives.' The butchers showed a turkey hanging from a hook alongside a pig's head with the slogan PEACE ON EARTH emblazoned across it. The fish shop settled for a conventional scene of the good shepherds, though the faint smell of kippers was advertisement enough. The owner had tried to introduce the German tradition of serving carp at Christmas (carpe diem, had joked Father Connelly when travelling in Lutheran Germany, Latin jokes not being easily shared in a country short both on Latin and jokes), but knew he had little chance in a town dedicated to tradition or at least resistant to change.

That night they would all make their way to the church for midnight mass, Mrs O'Hagan embarrassing herself, as she did every year, by pulling at the priests hands so that a deal more of the sacramental wine poured into her mouth than was strictly necessary to effect trans-substantiation. She required, as she explained to a neighbour, a little fortifying and fortified wine provided the necessary component though in truth she, and many of the others who made their way unsteadily back to their seats, had already taken the precaution of topping up a tank that might otherwise be at risk of running dry. 'Christmas,' explained the priest, 'is not just a time for eating, drinking and giving presents,' a sentiment with which his congregation evidently agreed since they were nodding their heads even as they were thinking of the need for a little something once they got back, Mr. O'Brien meanwhile wondering where he had put the receipt for the underclothes he had brought his wife since she always returned anything he bought her, especially underclothes which made her suspect he had something in his mind that must not be encouraged.

'Go in peace,' the priest finally said, releasing them from their necessary act of piety, though in truth peace was not likely to be the primary condition on the following today when a cousin tried to introduce obscenities into a game of scrabble and long-established resentments were unwrapped along with presents which themselves were liable to be taken as implied insults. 'Would this not be the same set of grapefruit knives we gave you two years since?' 'Very like, for I knew you favoured them. Not many people use them these days, especially me who has always been allergic to grapefruit so that my neck swells up if I come near them, but, then, you knew that of course from the time I nearly died when I was a child.'

'It's for the kiddies, really,' observed Shelagh Callaghan who had had the good fortune never to have had them and hence knew nothing of their tantrums, sulks, tendency to be sick on furniture bought on hire purchase. 'I love to see their little faces light up.' There were, in truth, faces lit up but it was less the children than their elders once the Jameson's, dandelion or ruby red rich port type wine had been opened before the men took themselves to The Shamrock 'for a Christmas taste,' as they explained, escaping from familial captivity as Steve McQueen was even then escaping from Stalag Luft III on television, had reception been good enough to distinguish precisely who it was on the motor cycle and why he had one in a prison camp.

The Shamrock came into its own on Christmas morning. At first there was not a woman in the place, as seemed right to those bound to celebrate good cheer to all men, not women, as Seamus remarked having saved up for a glass of Paddy's which he had momentarily decided might be better than Jameson's, though he was ready to make a comparison a little later. He had unaccountably been given a banknote by a wife who should have known better or was willing to pay to relieve herself of his company while she decided whether to turn two-week-old bread into bread sauce the mould having come off surprisingly easily.

Christmas has ever been a season for celebration and depression in equal measure. Any anniversary is liable to be a reminder of passing time, of lost loves and opportunities, of those who once gathered around a roaring fire but did so no more, unless it be that to which they had been consigned following a far from virtuous life. For those with children Christmas day began with a rustle of paper in the early hours when carefully wrapped presents were torn open as wolves descend on lambs. 'Will you go back to bed. It is five in the morning.' At about the same time Mr Andrews was rising for the third time to empty his bladder having been dreaming of waterfalls and spraying his garden until he awoke just in time wondering why he could not relieve himself in a single go but must turn it into an unending saga.

Eamon, the town's other postman, found himself getting out of bed before he realised that for once he could sleep in except that 'once you are up, you up,' so that he went down stairs in his striped pyjamas to make himself a cup of tea. 'Darjeeling,' he said to himself, then added 'happy Christmas,' having lived alone since his wife had died at her best friend's funeral choking on a pilchard sandwich so that for these many years there had been no one with whom to share his thoughts or even a Christmas cup of tea nor had he ever again been able to contemplate pilchards. His room was full of cards, though all but one had been addressed to someone else who would surely not miss them. That one he had sent himself, though it was signed with his wife's name and the word 'love,' which is what had left him on the day the pilchards did their work. Later, he, too, would go to the Shamrock where he would be greeted by all for everyone loves a postman even if he has, unbeknown to them, been helping himself to the odd card and who could begrudge him that.

It is six now, and the early risers are stirring, opening the bedroom curtains to see what the weather might be doing.

'They said it would snow,' observed Kelley Grammar from her lover's bed.

'Liars all,' replied the schoolmaster from the state school for whom illicit sex doubtless came naturally.

'Come back to bed,' said Kelley, who taught the infants, though what you might well ask who was setting such a poor example, 'for I have a Christmas present for you.'

She had given him such presents a few times the previous night, however, so that he no longer felt quite up to receiving another of the same kind. For someone who taught the three times table she evidently had ambitions to increase the level of difficulty.

Finally, with an air of resignation she said, 'did you take the giblets out?' thus giving him a glimpse of what married life might be like if either of them felt inclined to chance it as they did not, reserving the right to keep hope alive.

'Should we maybe take a trip on Ryanair to Venice or whatever they are calling Venice?'

'That would be fine,' she replied, pulling the duvet so that it covered her leg whose varicose veins were like an atlas of minor roads. 'It would be good to see it before it sinks entirely.'

'Are you sure that's what you would like?'

'What I would really like is for the fifth form to be put up against a wall and shot, the little bastards. I don't know why we don't arrange for them to go straight from the fourth into prison. It would save a deal of time.'

Teaching had never been her desired profession who had seen herself as a veterinarian until a spell pushing thermometers up dog's bottoms had turned her in the direction of state education. For his part, having been educated to a higher level (she being a product of a suspect teacher's training college, now converted into a home for girls in need of care and protection, though largely from those who ran it), he recalled a quotation from Chekhov: 'Only in social purpose novels do people teach and tend peasants, and how am I, out of the blue, supposed to tend or teach them.' Indeed, this was pinned on the wall above the computer in his solitary flat, though a computer, of course, was somewhat redundant when the download speed was a deliberate lie told to him by his provider who, it turned out, provided little and certainly not easy access to the darker reaches of the internet which was to have been his stimulus when Kelley was not available often being crushed by a load of marking as witches once were by stones.

'Well, we've a break for a while at least. Did I wish you a happy Christmas?'

She looked at him suspiciously, suspecting this might be code for she was reaching an age when she was afraid she might lose her taste for sex and so was determined to bank what she could and perhaps live off the interest.

'How did we end up in Ballygoran?' she asked, speaking aloud what was so often in her mind having kept her eye open for opportunities elsewhere in towns less inclined to see state schools as dumping grounds for those resentful of being beaten into salvation.

'There's worse places,' he replied, trying to slide out of bed without her seeing his backside which he suspected had more hair on it than was usual.

'Name one,' she challenged.

There was a silence during which each, no doubt, scrolled through possibilities.

'I thought you were doing the giblets,' he remarked, there being limits as to how long one can stare into the abyss.

'I'll do the breakfast,' she said, not rising to the bait. 'And I'm going to have everything I shouldn't for, sure, what else is Christmas for. Shall we have the full Irish?'

This time it was he who suspected it might be code.

'The butcher's bacon is terrible fatty, though,' she added, oblivious to the fact that he might be doing a Bletchley Park. 'And I wouldn't touch his blood pudding.'

So they separately slid out of bed, concealing what was not conducive to love on a Christmas day and made their way downstairs fondly imagining that no one knew of their liaison when in fact there was no one who did not, expecting nothing less of a state school where evil was endemic and where beasts, 'two-backed' or not, as he had described their passion, were surely the common currency, though unlike the headmaster they would not have recognised a quotation from *Othello*, he having studied English at University College Dublin before deceiving himself into thinking he should devote himself to educating the young.

***

In the post office Mr. Bannerji dreamed of the monsoon as beside him his wife rattled the windows with her snores and herself dreamed of cows wandering down streets which shimmered with heat. In the daylight hours they filled their time with work never quite understanding what had made them leave their home except a belief that movement and progress were somehow allied, a common enough delusion. At night, however, they travelled back to a place before postal orders and parcels covered with sticky tape and insufficient postage. Later they would have vegetable curry for lunch as those around them celebrated by eating a bird whose sole reason for existence seemed to be to be served up to people who wore paper hats then slept in front of television sets on which images would come and go. When you live in a foreign country, though, it is necessary to follow local traditions so that later they would eat their curry wearing hats while tuning in their radio to hear the English Queen who their neighbours despised but who to them brought back memories of a lost world. What it is to be an exile except that everyone is such in one way or another, sometimes from their own lives.

Across town, in the convent, all was serenity. The nuns, of course, had attended the midnight mass and now dutifully rose early to prepare themselves for the seven o'clock mass, a kind of sandwich of holiness. Sister Hilda was practising her scales while outside a cock was crowing. 'Feckin bird,' observed Sister Innocence, a sentiment shared but not articulated by her fellow nuns who had arranged for the bird's predecessor to be shot only to discover that, as with terrorists, there was apparently a second in command. There was nothing to be done about Sister Hilda, however, though there were those who fantasised a similar fate for her.

This, though, was their day of days when they were allowed a certain freedom that on other days they would regard as licence. There would be a glass of sherry at lunch and then again in the evening. Presents were frowned upon as perhaps encouraging the kind of relationships that could also not be articulated, but presents were nonetheless exchanged. Not that it was easy to come up with anything original once crosses and rosaries were ruled out. Cosmetics were impossible, though a deodorant was once unkindly given to Sister Marie. Mostly it was embroidered handkerchiefs with a Sister's initials picked out in needlepoint as Hawthorne's Hester Prynne had worn an embroidered scarlet A, though since that was supposed to stand for adulteress that model was not invoked even if Sister Agnes kept a copy hidden in her cupboard (with a cover entitled *Lourdes: A Mystery*) for was Hester's secret lover not a priest and did she not, deep in her heart, too deep for words and certainly too deep for confession, herself feel drawn to a man who could never reciprocate?

Ten days since Sister Mary had fallen while trying to fit an angel on the top of a Christmas tree whose pagan origins were conveniently ignored. At first it seemed that serious damage had been done though no one would volunteer mouth to mouth resuscitation this being more than can be expected even of the holy. By and by, however, she had recovered to be greeted by an obscenity from Sister Innocence which seemed to perk her up so that once more she climbed on a wobbly stool with her hands up the angel's skirt.

'Should we not have the baby Jesus on the top there,' asked Sister Agnes, who at times lamented she could have no child of her own.

'And what if he should fall,' replied Sister Mary. 'Sure an angel can fly.'

Not one made of a toilet roll and aluminium turkey wrapper, thought Agnes, but held her peace.

'Should we not have more balls do you think?'

They looked at her strangely.

'There's only a half a dozen coloured balls and what's happened to the chocolate coins for we had them last year.'

'Feckin ate them,' offered Sister Innocence who had, indeed, eaten her way through the confectionary currency and been sick as a consequence.

'Shall we put the carols on the record player?' asked Sister Marie, the convent's technology being as behind the times as themselves. 'Or is it Harry Belafonte you are wanting?' she having a soft spot for her youth rather than a West Indian who had once sung 'There's a hole in My Bucket' though 'Scarlet Ribbons' stirred feelings for did she not wear such before she had given up on the world to wear black and white and live with others who perhaps treasured their own Harry Belafontes more than was decent.

'It's Cliff Richard for me,' replied Sister Agnes. 'For he's a Christian even if he does make a show of himself,' and what a show, she was thinking. He was her Christmas number one as they all knew for she played him whenever she could though 'Devil Woman' had been banned by the Mother Superior whose own secret taste ran to the early Rolling Stones whose lack of satisfaction she understood only too well given her commitment to the betting shops where she could concentrate on horses, though the fact that young girls went through a period of equine fixation suggested that a degree of sublimation started early.

***

At the Seaview Hotel Mrs. McCann and Miss Prynne were joined for breakfast by a commercial traveller who had had the misfortune to break down on his way through the town and the greater misfortune to entrust repairs to the local garage. He wore trousers with a sharp crease and a cravat that should have been a warning in itself. He sold non-prescription spectacles, he explained, as eyes which once saw the world with clarity slowly gave up by stages. Out of nothing more than habit he had made a desultory attempt to sell his landlady a pair but even he could see clearly enough to know that she was not someone enamoured of sharp creases and cravats. She put him in the back room next to the toilet not wanting him wandering around at night with who knows what on his mind, salesmen, to her mind, being people who would sell their mothers if need be and probably had already. She had given a room to one once and heard noises from his room that made her think he was maybe dismembering the corpse of a young virgin, had he been able to find one, when in fact he had been trying to mend the bed onto which he had fallen in a state of drunkenness.

They made an unlikely trio as she served them porridge, her menu not allowing for alternatives nor even, judging by her glare, abandonment, though Miss Prynne left hers as she had every day she had lived there. There followed a boiled egg prepared some time earlier, along with a piece of toast (likewise) and margarine. If there were those who thought breakfast the most important meal of the day they had best avoid the Seaview Hotel in Ballygoran which boasts no stars from motoring organisations nor from a tourist board which, after all, has its standards. It should not be thought, though, that Mrs. McCann was unmindful of the season. Alongside the egg and toast she had placed a sprig of holly. Admittedly, it was plastic but these days what is not. Even in fancy restaurants guests reach out a hand to feel the flowers on the table even as real flowers have long since had any scent bred out of them having been flown from Kenya or raised to bloom all year round in a Holland where people eat cheese with no flavour at all and which itself seems made of plastic.

For lunch, her guests would, she explained, have to make do on their own since she was going to visit her sister who herself ran an un-starred hotel ignored by the Automobile Association (Ireland) and featuring on no website. 'There are no baths,' she explained to her guests. 'I've turned off the immersion.' The salesman glanced across at Miss Prynne who stared implacably back at him. 'I have perfect eyesight,' she replied, in case he might have designs upon her.

***

'I'll not be having mistletoe in my house,' announced Mrs Gaherty, 'for we know what that leads to.'

Her husband rather hoped he did for a second cousin was among the relatives who had gathered to torment each other and she was so beautiful he could not believe her to be connected to a family that on his wife's side aspired to an ugliness of quite remarkable proportions.

'Shall I stuff the turkey,' he asked his wife, who looked at him suspiciously.

'You'll keep your hands out of my bird,' she replied with the finality of a judge pronouncing the death penalty. 'You can prick the sausages.'

She was not, though, a woman for sub-texts so he obediently took up a fork and was holding it, poised, when the cousin came in.

'Can I help at all,' she asked, her dark hair glistening in the light of the low wattage bulb. 'Here, let me, 'she said, closing her hand on his so that for the moment they stood together, hands clasped and upraised like the Marines who raised the flag on Iwo Jima.

'You can do the stuffing,' Mrs. Gaherty instructed even as her husband felt weak around the knees.

She released his hand. 'Mistletoe,' she said, glancing up to where Mr. Gaherty had manfully, if forlornly, hung it.

'It's coming down,' pronounced Mrs. Gaherty. 'The stuffing's stage and onion.'

'Do you have any rubber gloves?' asked the young woman whose violet eyes had rendered Mr. Gaherty immobile as though he had swallowed a vial of curare.

'Rubber gloves?' exclaimed his wife, recognising perversion when she encountered it.

The Beautiful One shrugged and smiled. 'Is there somewhere I can put my ring?'

Ring? She was engaged, married?

'It was my mother's.'

'Mothers,' thought Mr. Gaherty. 'Everyone should have one.'

'I'll keep it for you,' he managed to say though in a low voice that he seemed to assume would not be heard by his wife only six feet away.

'The button jar,' instructed his wife. 'You can go to The Shamrock.'

This was not a sentence he had heard his wife utter before which is why he did not move with the alacrity she evidently expected. 'Now,' she added.

'Can I go with you?' asked the Beautiful One.

There followed a silence which she could never hope to understand not being privy to Mrs. Gaherty's thought processes? How should she know that he had never been given such licence before, how know that the Shamrock did not welcome women, beautiful or otherwise, on Christmas morning?

'I need you to do the pricking,' said Mrs Gaherty with a finality that was not an invitation to discussion.

And so off he goes sans a beautiful young woman and sans his teeth which he had inadvertently left on the bathroom sink having polished them to a gleaming white, or as near to gleaming white as was possible after years of standing in the rain to smoke cigarettes his wife would not allow in the house.

***

Bridget O'Reilly's parents had declared a Christmas truce much as did the Germans and British on the Somme. Lacking a football, however, they were inclined to use Bridget since there had to be someone through whom to earth the static electricity they generated when in close proximity. Why had they not long since parted? Because like the earth itself they were liable to switch polarity, sometimes repelling, sometimes attracting. Now, with 'The Holly and the Ivy' echoing from the single speaker of their hi fi, the other having been damaged when Cathleen O'Reilly discovered that her husband was short on fidelity, whether high or low, they looked at Bridget seemingly working out a strategy.

'What?' she asked, herself calculating from which direction the attack might come.

'Would you like a peppermint?' asked her father, himself needing time out, it seemed, from hostilities though she had also recognised them as coming from the co-op which was never a guarantee of satisfaction despite the sign saying so which had been in the window so long it had faded. 'They've a funny taste but they grow on you.'

'They'll spoil her lunch,' said her mother, nonetheless taking one herself having a sweet tooth if not disposition.

'Could we not have a television that works?' asked Bridget for whom a day required to do nothing but watch would be preferable to talking to two people who might have beamed down from another planet. She treasured the idea that she might be an orphan or adopted, afraid that otherwise she might transmute into one of them.

'I'd buy one if I thought we'd ever get to see a whole football match,' and indeed ninety uninterrupted minutes was something of a miracle for anyone's television viewing in Ballygoran. They had been going to erect a mast on the hillside above the town but there were those who opposed it believing it would beam pornography in along with the programmes on cooking and selling your house for a profit even in a falling market.

'We could play a game,' her father suggested, who fancied himself a poker player as real poker players fancied him playing with them given the consistency with which he lost. That, indeed, was often the cause of the arguments that had ricocheted around the head of a young girl thus schooled in human relationships.

'Is that the turkey I smell?' her mother asked rather than break the truce.

'Did you cook the giblets inside it with its plastic bag as you did last year?' he replied recklessly, plainly feeling the lack of a decent argument.

'That was better than when you put it in still frozen through so that you were drinking for three hours before we ate it, the vegetables all burned or soggy.'

'Can we open our presents?' Bridget asked.

'After lunch,' they said in unison having got up the necessary momentum, as they judged, to carry them through the day.

'I can smell the plastic,' her father observed.

'I am amazed you can smell anything what with the Guinness you have been putting away.'

And so with 'The Holly and the Ivy' jumping back because of the smear of peppermint on the disk they warmed to a Christmas day to remember or forget.

***

Of course there was many a house in which Christmas was what Christmas has always been. There was excitement and love and laughter. Not everyone in Ballygoran was strange or over-concerned with alcohol, unless it was a small sherry before lunch and a sherry trifle for tea. Presents were as hoped and the mince pie and carrot missing from the plate by the fire, collected by who else but Father Christmas on his journey through the imagination and out into the world. There were those who thrilled again to the story of Scrooge and the regrettably insipid Bob Cratchit, believing in the redemption of all, except possibly Father Donnelly of whom the less said the better. But where's the fun in that? They were merely the cyclorama against which the others played out their tragi-comic dramas. Happiness and normality have their appeal, as does Marmite, but they are, perhaps, a matter of taste and, it has to be said, just a little boring, which is why children prefer their stories to be grim or Grimm, to consist of wicked witches or comic donkeys and bears with very little brain. So we must accept the fact that in houses throughout Ballygoran, as the lights went on and frying pans were set on stoves, there was sufficient laughter and affection to place in the scales and balance out the lives of those others who are perhaps happy in their way even if their way can seem a little strange. Human beings, though, are not to be measured as a metre length is by a platinum and iridium bar in Paris or some fraction of the speed of light. What is normal in one place is not in another, what seems odd or eccentric depends on where one chooses to locate the centre and Ballygoran was anywhere but in the centre.

***

For those without a family to torment them, and no Christmas meal unless they made it themselves, there was The Shamrock. Some came mid morning to brace themselves for what lay ahead. Others arrived for the lunch, prepared not by the barman, who dispensed nothing more than bags of crisps, pickled eggs, pork scratchings and pizzas, but by the daughters of the brewer who lived at the brewery a mile away on the Dublin Road, a place where they drew in water from the stream and sent out such as could induce dreams.

At eight in the morning the three sisters would arrive on the back of the horse-drawn dray, along with two large turkeys nearly as big as one of them who was the runt of the litter, though compensated for by another who could have wrestled for Ireland. They leapt down carrying the turkeys, entered the pub as the Goths once arrived at the gates of Rome, then swept round the end of the bar as the Germans had round the Maginot Line and into a kitchen the inspectors forbore to inspect.

For an hour one of them brushed and scraped until the worst of the grime had gone while her sisters slid the turkeys into two large ovens used only once a year. The order of attack was clear. At half past eight the ovens were lit. By ten all the vegetables were prepared while three Christmas puddings were set to boil and then simmer. By eleven they began to drink, being raised to it from babyhood when screams for food or clean nappies had been met by fingers dipped in whisky or something more potent manufactured not at the brewery but in the hills where stills were a natural part of the rural economy if not supported by the European Union that was usually generous to a fault when it came to farmers.

The thing with Christmas lunch is that there is not much to spoil. Admittedly the sausages can be burnt, and were, and turkeys can be either under or overdone, and they were. Burnt bread sauce also has a certain flavour it is hard to forget while the previous year the Christmas puddings had been prepared in plastic bowls which had then melted so that helpings came with a generous portion of organic polymers of high molecular mass. But the other thing about Christmas lunch at the Shamrock is that those who eat it have themselves been drinking for some time, though not as much, perhaps, as the three sisters (who had no longing to go to Moscow but might have settled for Dublin if three young men with cars had come along, which seemed unlikely given that they were blessed with looks more suited to rugby players than a beauty parade) so that theirs is not a discriminating palate or, indeed, a palate at all when it comes down to it.

This year, unusually, one of the sisters – the one bulked up by dumplings and her father's ale – succumbed entirely and was now slumped against the wall under a sign inviting her to wash her hands after going to the toilet, which struck the other two as unnecessarily fastidious. The meal was already late but on Christmas Day who is there that cares? The barman was serving a kind of hot punch into which he had emptied all those bottles that were never usually taken down from the shelf, so that the result was blue and green and red like spilled petrol in a puddle. He upended a bottle of lemonade, 'for the kids' he remarked, though there were none which was just as well for Christmas is not a time to be blighting the next generation. It was not the look, though, that attracted the drinkers, nor yet the taste, which was itself somewhat difficult to place, being somewhere on the spectrum from disinfectant to cough mixture, but the effect that made it so popular.

'What are you calling this, Michael?'

'85% proof, or some such,' he replied, having an in-built sense of specific gravity.

'Is that not a little short of the target?'

In the kitchen the smallest sister stepped over the largest and swung the door of the oven open. Out came a cloud of steam and not a little smoke. Though small, she had muscles that would be the envy of a caber tosser and managed to slide the turkey tray out and swing it onto the pitted table. With a flourish she removed a pin from her hair, bright orange thanks to the contents of a package she had bought in the co-op, and plunged it into the bird as Brutus did his knife into Caesar though lacking Latin or, indeed, life, it made no accusing reply.

'Is it done?' asked her surviving sister.

'Is it done?' she replied, seemingly believing this an adequate response to what others might consider a not unreasonable question. 'Give her a kick,' she added.

This last was an injunction to encourage the third sister, still slumped against the wall, with a smile on her face, to join in the final stages of preparation. There was a dull thud (but, then, perhaps all thuds are dull) followed by a scream, and the team of three was once more complete.

'Is it done?' asked the newly conscious sister, a little behind the curve, only to receive a slap from the smallest who though small was as strong as she was vindictive.

The second turkey emerged, satisfyingly burnt, thus obviating a further risky question. The sausages followed, looking like a row of carbonised effigies caught in the pyroclastic surge at Pompei

'I like them well done,' observed the middle sister, who had learned the arts of survival.

The sisters' mother had been pious to such a degree that she had called all of her children Mary. It is true that their second names differed but they had always been known to others as Mary

1, Mary 2 and Mary 3, an enumeration based on their birth dates rather than their girth or the numbers would have been reversed. To themselves, however, they were Mary, a simple inflexion sufficient to distinguish one from another.

'Mary, would you spoon out the roast potatoes. There's one on the floor behind you.'

'Mary, you've stuffing on your shoes.'

'Mary, you forgot the sprouts.'

In the bar the meal was an hour later than advertised but all were passing their time profitably, at least so far as the pub's owner was concerned, a man who seldom visited his tenant except when he fancied it might be worth checking that free drinks were not handed out from a misguided sense of human charity.

Several of those who seldom ventured out to socialise did so for this occasion. At a corner table Miss Prynne sat with the closest approximation to a Tom Collins that Michael could manage. Miss Heaney sat at another, with a pencil and pad deep inside a voluminous handbag in case she should wish to write a note or two. Indeed, there was already one which now lay crumpled in front of her with 'DRINK' written on it in a bright pink. You might think that two lonely women might have found common cause but in truth their cause was not common, though loss did indeed link the two of them. If they sat with their own thoughts, however, there were many others who compensated so that it was difficult for anyone to hear what others said.

The travelling salesman sat a little stunned, not having seen anything quite like The Shamrock at Christmas. He had offered to sit with Miss Prynne but her stare was sufficient to send him to a seat by the fire where sparks were flying onto his polished shoes as he drank the first of the two gins he had fetched from the bar, the one for himself the other, as he had imagined, for Miss Prynne. For all his trade, he plainly had some difficulty seeing the world for what it was. No one offered to speak to him for strangers seldom boded well. After all, Chekhov's characters suspected they might be playing host to an Inspector General even if Chekhov was not on the shelves of the library van there being little call for Russian writers even if they had trained as doctors.

Seamus and O'Grady as ever sat with half pints in front of them, though they were not the first. They spoke as though no time had interrupted the conversation that had flowed between them over the years, never reaching any destination but filling a silence which otherwise might have threatened their equanimity.

'The finger.'

'The finger is it?'

'I was thinking.'

'That much is clear,' replied Seamus, though doubting the premise. 'And of the finger.'

'As you say, the finger. Is it still there do you think?'

'Do you imagine it is still there?'

'Unless someone has taken it into their head to move it.'

'Not likely on the whole, don't you think?'

'It's just that he has been lying there for centuries maybe with his finger in the air.'

'Trying to attract the attention of a waiter perhaps.'

'A waiter?'

Even after many years Seamus still forgot the slowness with which thoughts set out on the journey across O'Grady's brain getting lost on the way more often than not and despairing of arriving at their destination.

'Are there any crackers do you think?'

'Is that for the cheese we haven't got?'

'No, for pulling. There's sometimes a joke or two worth reading.'

'If you are relying on crackers for a laugh you'd be better off in the bog with the finger.'

'Well, it's another Christmas.'

'That it is.' O'Grady was always better so long as he restricted himself to the obvious.

'We've seen a few of those.'

'That we have.'

'Sure I don't remember a one of them.'

'It is better that way. Sometimes forgetting is a blessing.'

'What was that you said.' Seamus looked to see if this might be a joke but since it had not come out of a cracker rather doubted if that was so.

'Do you think they've finished cooking the turkey yet? Should I maybe go in the kitchen and ask?'

'Have you seen those three. I wouldn't go back there if I were the heavyweight champion of the world.'

'Not likely though. I wish I had brought the finger along for it would have been good to shake someone's hand and leave it with them.'

'Good?'

'It being Christmas.'

'And Christmas being a time for leaving a dead man's finger in someone's hand?'

'Or on a plate, maybe,' he added, having just had a sight of the row of burned sausages put down with a bang on the table by the fire and thinking how like the finger they were, after all. 'You see the sausages,' he added.

'They're not at all like a finger,' responded Seamus who hardly needed a degree in stupidity to follow his colleagues thought processes. 'And I would not go on about the finger if I were you. It may not be centuries old at all but off some poor man you-know-who took against.'

'Who would that be?'

'Have your brains maybe gone on a stroll? There are times you raise ignorance to an Olympic sport.'

Far from being offended, O'Grady seemed to consider the idea.

'You know what they say?' said Father Daniel who sat at the priests' table by the door with a bottle or two they had brought in with them, corkage not being charged in the Shamrock even if Michael had known what it was. 'Give me a child before he is seven, but look out for Father Donnelly.'

They raised their glasses to the absent Father Donnelly then celebrating Christmas in a correctional facility.

'Do you know, I was thinking? What are we to make of original sin for surely there's not much point in getting out of bed if that be true, and is a death sentence for having a bite of an apple not a bit on the heavy side? Then there's women bringing forth in pain.'

'Ah, but they have the epidural.'

'I've never been sure that's a holy thing. It seems a kind of cheating if you ask me.'

'Why are we talking about religion when it's Christmas?'

They raised their glasses again seeing the logic of that. After all, they were all retired and had come down from the priests' home because the kitchen was infested with rats and they were not on active service even if they dressed as priests which was liable to win them a free drink every now and then. Indeed they had spent the morning dropping in on families to offer them blessings, families not quick enough to see them coming and put the whisky away. As a result they were already feeling relaxed and ready for the coming meal.

'Did you see those sisters,' said Father Michael, 'the middle one …'

'That would be Mary.'

'Mary, indeed, though not like our blessed Mother of God.'

'Not unless the Mother of God had been built like a brick shit house,' remarked Father Daniel who had once served in the military and had somehow never quite got it out of his system.'

'Anyway, the middle one was up for grievous bodily harm.'

'She hit someone?'

'Hit would hardly do it justice. She heard a little something about Father Donnelly and kicked him in the sacristy. It took him a day to recover.'

'Did he not go to the police?'

'He couldn't go to the toilet for the first day so the police were out of the question. Besides, it is Father Donnelly we are talking about. He would not have been anxious to have them come to call.'

'What happened to her?'

'He tried to get her to say six Hail Marys but she was not a Mary he could persuade to do anything after the rumours got out. Are we out of this bottle? Sure we only just arrived.'

'Which is why we have a second.'

'Do the Protestants believe in original sin do you suppose?'

'I don't think they believe in anything. That's the attraction.'

'Take contraceptives,' said Father O'Rourke, who until then had been chain drinking as he had once been a chain smoker, speaking a little too loudly so that those on the closest table turned round trying, no doubt, to discover whether this was an infallible instruction.

Closer to the door Miss Heaney sat, blue pencil poised, oblivious, as it seemed, to the noise around her. She chose this moment to reach down into her handbag and apparently absent-mindedly pulled out a cat. For a moment she seemed to express a certain surprise that it should be there and not at home ignoring mice. She looked around thinking, maybe, that there mightbe a servant she could hand it to before, after a moment, putting it back again. It made no obvious objection. HOME, she wrote in her notebook and tore the sheet off before putting it into her bag, an instruction, perhaps, to the cat should it choose to take any notice. She drew out a small purse and counted money onto the table before holding her glass above her head until it should be noticed and re-filled. It is hard to say whether or not she was having a good time but compared to her average day this must have seemed a reckless adventure.

The three sisters had now assembled the lunch on a trestle table and Mary 3 had begun carving with fierce attention, her sisters standing well away knowing that Mary 3 and a knife were not ideal companions. There was a pile of assorted plates, purchased at the summer fair and stored away against the occasion, and after a while the service began. Mary 1 took the money while Mary 2 stood to one side with a plate held above her in a way that in other circumstances would have seemed menacing and that in truth did so even on this day of peace and goodwill to all men. It had more the air of a protection racket than a silver service, not that there was any silver to be seen.

All but Miss Heaney paid their money and set to with enthusiasm and thankfully without any real sense of culinary discrimination. Burnt sausages, after all, are best thought of as crispy and there was a deal of crispy of one kind or another on their plates. Miss Heaney reached into her bag and pulled out a banana which she pealed with some delicacy before dropping the peel on top of the hapless cat who she pestered with correspondence.

The butcher had pride of place because he had donated one of the two birds, though he was evidently not pleased by the fate to which he had consigned it at the hands of the three Marys. 'I'll have a piece that's underdone,' he said to Mary 3 who looked at him as if he were a lunatic. 'And some stuffing.'

She was restrained by Mary 1 who recognised that expression and what it might presage.

'Forget the stuffing,' he added quickly, having once been caught in a field with a bull and remembering the look on its face as it measured him up, a look that he fancied he saw again now in a woman whose face was streaming with sweat which dropped with remarkable accuracy onto the burnt offering she had just presented to him.

'Sprouts,' she said, as once people challenged one another to a duel.

He nodded.

She scooped some up and dumped them onto his plate.

'Roast potatoes.'

He looked to her sister, seeking guidance.

He nodded again.

'There are none.'

'Right,' he said, though he could see a tray piled high with them on the serving table.

'I'll give them a miss then,' he managed, wincing as she smiled at him, gap-toothed, anointing him with a spray of sweat, and this a man who had fired humane bolts into cows' heads.

The truth was that he had once given her short weight on some heart and kidneys, she having a fondness for offal of any kind, even parts of animals of which others were blissfully ignorant, his scales being faulty for a week. She had returned with her sisters and though he was the one with a sharp knife in his hand, having just eviscerated a lamb, he had recognised a moment of destiny, pushing some sweetbreads towards her as propitiation. Only when he had added liver and some testicles did they leave, as silently as they had come, but in his soul he had known it was not the end. Now, in The Shamrock, he watched as she upended a spoonful of what by intent at least had been bread sauce but which clung to the spoon as a child does to the mother who has decided to send it away to boarding school. Time seemed to have stopped as the two sisters and he watched to see if it would come unstuck.

'Maybe I'll give it a miss,' he offered, only to receive a stare from both of them that made him remember having read a newspaper story about how the Americans could stare goats to death.

Before the appearance of the Christmas dinner The Shamrock had been abuzz with chatter but with the meal now served everyone was dedicating themselves to eating, separating the more burned from the less burned, savouring the unsalted sogginess of the sprouts and taking care not to damage teeth on potatoes whose surface resembled the Kevlar that so efficiently protected Irish troops on peace keeping operations around the world. The Christmas spirit, though, or perhaps simply spirits, meant that no one complained, not that they were likely to do so with the three Marys patrolling the room ready to respond to dissent. These were those with no one to go home to or who were seeking to escape the washing up that would stay in the sink as a reproach until Boxing Day.

After a while the plates were collected and anything left scraped into a bucket to give the pigs a Christmas treat. The plates were then piled into the sink in the back room before the Christmas puddings, which had been bubbling away, were lifted from the stove and upended onto plates. As ever they refused to leave their basins until encouraged to do so by Mary 3 who could intimidate everything, alive or dead. Eventually they surrendered to her hammering, though they did not come out whole. The water had got into one or two which as a result had an albino look to them but once a sprig of holly had been stuck in them and they had been set alight with brandy, or something brandy like, they would be acceptable, or else, thought the largest Mary.

Mary 1's hair briefly flamed before being beaten out enthusiastically and remorselessly by her sisters. But who does not like Christmas pudding, except Americans who regarded it, along with Christmas cake and mince pies, as a mystery never to be solved. And, indeed, everyone picked up their spoons and forks with an enthusiasm not dimmed by the bleached look.

'There's coins in it,' said Mrs Connell, who was wearing the purple hat that had gone down so well at the funeral.

'I had a brother nearly choked to death on one when he was six,' replied Mrs. Burke who had always been doubtful about people enjoying themselves too much.

'They bring good luck,' insisted Mrs. Connell.

'Not to him,' said Mrs. Burke.

And so Ballygoran's Christmas lunch continued, ending with a cup of decaffeinated coffee which, Father Michael objected, was like low alcohol beer or purgatory without hell, followed by a wafer thin peppermint chocolate which had fused to its paper sleeve but by then a little paper seemed to balance things out as cardboard put in a compost bin encourages the breakdown of garden refuse. The three sisters, who were wise enough not to eat their own food, had opened a plastic box of sandwiches (roast pancreas) to be eased down with bottles of their father's beer on which they had been weaned and to which they were addicted, though in the most benign way.

It was one of those moments in which the town came together. People smiled at one another as on another day they would not, or at least they did until someone suggested they should have a little entertainment. It is true that Sister Hilda was safely in the convent but when one or two began singing 'What are we going to do about Maria,' this being a song they recalled from their summer fair, the three Marys rose in indignation, a situation saved when Mrs O'Connell stood up seemingly in a trance and, back straight as the way to God, eyes staring straight ahead, began to kick her legs out and click her heels perhaps imagining herself to be auditioning for River Dance.

'Holy God,' said Father Daniel, as might have been appropriate in other circumstances.

Miss Prynne let out a small fart in memory of a past romance.

'Bar's closing,' said Michael having no chance of doing so.

'The toilet's blocked,' said Mrs Burke who had never liked Mrs. O'Connell and who had once been dismissed from her school concert for tying her shoes together and spoiling her solo.

It was finally resolved, however, when Mrs O'Connell discovered that what she could do at sixteen she could not do, at least for long, at sixty, a principle that extends beyond attempting Irish dance, once derided but now applauded around the world so that people imagine Ireland to be a place where people spend their time bouncing up and down in mock battles. She sank to her seat to desultory applause less from those appreciative of the art of dance than from a sense of relief on the part of those who would rather be left to drink in peace or at least without the distraction of anything that might generously be described as art.

***

Outside The Shamrock snow had begun to fall lazily. Away from the tangled words and the rush of chatter by those with a glass in their hands and unanswered questions in their souls, all was silent while, in the middle of the street, Mad Peg stood, arms outstretched, palms uppermost, her face tilted back so the flakes could kiss her face, a face full of joy and wonder. Then there was silence no more for she began to laugh and turn gently around rejoicing in a mystery, in a world transformed and for her alone. And as the snow melted on her face so it seemed that tears began to edge down her face, tears of purest gold. There was no division between her and the magic of all creation.

***

So, a year was nearly done, a year not in any essential way different from the years that had preceded it. To be sure, everyone was a year older though in truth not a whit wiser as how would they be when there was little to learn beyond the constant inconstancy of human nature. Some hopes had been realised, others mocked. Some had died as some had been born, a balance of sorts being maintained. If not happy, most were content or if not that then content not to be such. There were neither heroes nor villains. A Chekhov character may remark (and this, too, was pinned above his computer by the headmaster of the godless school) 'I've only had a walk-on part' but in truth so do we all in the lives of others. Ballygoran was an ensemble in which no movie star would care to play unless his character could be built up a deal.

View the town from the folded hills, even now clutching a grey cloak about them as the cloud presses down, and it seems no more than a scatter of houses, lights glowing even at midday. Yet we know otherwise. If you listen carefully you may hear 'Oh Little Town of Bethlehem' being tortured by a nun in the convent, competing with what is surely the wicked Cliff Richard singing 'Devil Woman.' Towards the harbour a door swings open and a slice of light pierces the gloom but since that is the door of The Shamrock the gloom can itself be nothing but an illusion.

In their separate houses people are playing out their lives like fishermen's lines seeking to land something of significance one day and if they do not then there is a satisfaction of sorts in the trying. Over the years people have left this place, and not without reason there being little to offer the young and little for the old beyond memories. Yet they will never forget a town unlike all others, except that all places, in truth, are unique. Life is a tragedy, or why did this country engender Yeats. Life is an absurdity or why did it harbour Samuel Beckett. But life is equally a comedy or why Jonathan Swift and Bernard Shaw. In truth, life is all these things or why did Leopold Bloom cook Molly a pig's kidney for breakfast on the 16 June, 1904, the Molly Bloom with the dirty mind who wrote letters to herself as does Miss Heaney in Ballygoran, the 16th of June marking the date of Joyce's first date with his future wife whose name was Norah Barnacle. You couldn't make it up, but he did, of course, and there is the redemption.

Bloom was a man for a glass or two, and where's the harm. Today, people come from round the world to eat kidneys for breakfast and visit the pubs where he drank, recognising that pubs may be sacred places even to the profane. 'Yes I said yes I will Yes,' said Molly, thus closing a book as all books should conclude for what can we say to life in all its kaleidoscope of patterns, its cascade of misunderstandings, its fecund admixture of all of which we are capable, all for which we should feel ashamed, all in which we glory, than Yes I said yes I will Yes.

298

Printed in Great Britain
by Amazon.co.uk, Ltd.,
Marston Gate.